ANATOMY OF AN INFIDELITY

By Sharon Jensen

If we forget the past we are condemned to repeat it.

George Santayana

Or more to the point, the past is always with us, ready to pounce and lead us astray once again. We cannot escape what is written.

Chapter One

1999

In the month we'd been using the new study lab, I'd never noticed that the clock over the door was made by the Chicago Lighthouse for the Blind. Was this a cryptic message to me, love is always blind? I heard each tick of the second hand as if a surgeon were passing a needle through my skin. Where was Raj?

We'd agreed to meet at the end of the day so I could pass along my notes and copies of the handouts from the presentation he'd missed. Dr. Aysha Quidwai, the author of "A Planet at Risk," was a visiting professor from The John Radcliffe Hospital in Oxford, England, the university's teaching hospital. Her research on environmental endocrine disrupters, a highly controversial subject, was disputed by many mainstream scientists. The Hoffman Auditorium where she spoke had been packed; house staff, students, and faculty were all eager to hear what the world's premier expert on the subject had to say.

Then Raj appeared, standing in the doorway as he ended a conversation with Dr. Jaworski, one of the residents. Without looking at me, he walked quickly past, heading to the bookcases against the back wall. They held review books for all the rotations available to medical students and he often picked one at random and browsed through it, wondering aloud which area to specialize in.

Intensely aware of his presence, searching for something to say that would break the strained silence between us, I pushed my chair back, about to get up. My cell phone lay on the conference table in front of me. Its sudden chirping startled me then I reached out for it, flipping it open.

In a quiet, intimate tone Raj asked, "Is something wrong,

Sophie?"

"No. Nothing's wrong." My voice trembled, the lie was not convincing.

Raj came right to the point, "Have you ever been unfaithful to your husband?"

"No." I gripped the cell phone mercilessly. My body felt as if it were made of fragile, just-blown glass, one wrong move and I'd shatter into a million pieces.

"Would you consider it?" The tremor in his voice betrayed how nervous he was, how much was at stake.

He was less than ten feet away. The low murmur of his voice echoed thinly in back of me.

I longed to say yes, my whole body straining toward him. Wasn't this exactly what I wanted? In the past week the sexual tension between us had mounted unbearably. So here was the moment of truth. Would I consider it?

Say yes now, and then you can back out later if you get cold feet. Not hardly. Not when I felt like one of those poor trapped souls caught on an unearthly plane between heaven and hell, powerless to do anything but watch as cataclysmic events unfold all around you.

"Yes."

The tension eased out of his voice, "Good. Tuesday night, okay? We'll meet at the mall in the parking lot by Macy's. Will you have trouble getting away?"

Not trusting my voice, I shook my head, then managed to speak stiffly, "No, it won't be a problem." Nick trusted me completely, the trust of a man who didn't want to know the truth.

Raj closed his cell phone and walked over to where I was sitting. His eyes were a liquid black, radiating magical warmth that drew me effortlessly under his spell.

"I've got to go. I'll see you Monday."

After gathering my things, I walked through the entrance into Jameson's office, turning sideways to bypass the stacks of yellowing journals and Xeroxed articles. Dr. Ronald Jameson, professor emeritus in psychiatry Texas Memorial Hospital, was spending the academic year at the Karolinska Institute in Stockholm, Sweden. In his absence, his conference room did double duty as a study lab; crammed into the remaining space were PCs with CAD instruction of clinical procedures, interactive tutorials and access to the National Library of Medicine MEDLAB databases.

Stunned by what I'd agree to with Raj, it nevertheless felt like I'd just mainlined the most powerful drug in the world, a potpourri of psychopharmacology's best: oxytocin, dopamine, and serotonin. My elation and sense of relief seemed to illuminate the whole office, lifting the burden of facing more hellish days of uncertainty.

I raised the blinds and levered open one of the windows; with shaky hands I lit a cigarette, inhaling deeply, blowing the smoke as far out into the air as it would go. Smoking was frowned upon in the medical center, but not that uncommon, even among the doctors. One curmudgeonly cardiology faculty member routinely got busted for smoking his pipe in his office.

In the distance the sun began its slow descent; a few billowy clouds were impaled on rays of sunshine. The hazy, saffron glow suffused the buildings and woods beyond, lightly gilding everything.

Three stories below, Raj paced the sidewalk in his nervous way, biting a fingernail. Chris must be late. Then I saw their white Toyota pull into the circular drive, the twins in the backseat, snug in their car seats. Chris hopped out and ran around to the passenger side,

Raj got in and took the wheel.

***

Traffic was still heavy as I worked my way down Lavoisier Boulevard, heading home. Most of the streets in the medical center were named after famous men of science. Priestley, Koch, Pasteur, Walter Reed, Fleming, there was even a Watson-Crick Boulevard named after the two men who worked out the secrets of DNA.

San Antonio's Bexar County Medical Center sat atop twenty-eight acres of grassy, tree-lined rolling hills due north of the city. The Hardin School of Medicine where I was a student was affiliated with the center's four leading hospitals. The majority of the staff and administrative offices were located at Texas Memorial; the other three hospitals were Rayburn General Hospital, North San Antonio Cancer Center, and the Luis B. Cisneros Trauma Center. The trauma center was named after a state representative who'd died in a plane crash en route to San Salvador, El Salvador.

Housed in the hospitals and buildings spread out along the flowered pathways were research facilities for Rheumatology, Infectious Diseases, Psychiatry and Neurology to name only a few. Everything was connected by underground passages which over time had become commercially desirable property. By the late eighties the brightly lit tunnels included kiosks, cafes, a few upscale boutiques, sushi and Chinese takeout, even an art gallery.

North of the loop, I took Highway 87 toward Boerne, Texas. Just east of Highway 87 the southward sprawl from Austin along Highway 281 and the northward sprawl from San Antonio along the same route led you through some of the prettiest parts of the Texas Hill Country. Gated communities with lavish homes had sprung up as well as more moderately priced suburban areas, like the one where I lived.

My commute was short, fewer than eight miles, then I turned past the curved river rock sign for Wooded Canyon Acres. Another turn and I shifted into lower gear as the road wound up the hill leading to a *cul de sac* with five houses arranged in a semi-circle on a bluff overlooking as yet undeveloped land. Our house was a pretty grey rancher with glossy black trim located at the furthest reach of the bluff; the large juniper trees and pyrocantha bushes gave it a measure of privacy.

Nick would already have picked up Liz at Nancy Metcalf's house, a family friend who watched our nearly four-year-old daughter during the day. I could see pale smoke drifting from the side of the house where he must be firing up the grill for Friday steak night.

Chapter Two

After a tumultuous welcome from Liz, and mad barking from Susie, our golden retriever, I followed them through the open patio door to the deck and the backyard beyond. The sun had disappeared beneath the horizon and all that remained of the day was a narrow strip painted blood orange.

Nick, backlit by the patio floodlights, leaned down and gave me a kiss on the mouth; I reached my arms around him and held him tight. Liz and Susie chased each other around the Chinese umbrella tree until they tumbled down in a heap on the grass. For an instant I felt like an interloper in someone else's family.

There were few things in my life that had ever caught me so off guard as being cast in the role of unfaithful wife. No, this was no one else's family but my own; until now we'd been settled in for the long haul. I had not been looking for love in all the wrong places. No foreshadowing events occurred. Analytical to a fault, I'd never been one to deny the truth of a situation that stared me right in the face. Unable to bear people who were not in touch with reality, I thought I knew myself too well, could control whatever life threw my way.

But the errant buzz of a tower of Babel of just plain wrong or silly notions about life seemed now to drown out everything else. I might have always clamored for the truth, but the actual journey to that lofty point was fraught with so many twists and turns, who could say they finally knew what was true?

What stunned me most of all was having blundered headlong through my life without knowing that there were forces so far beyond my control that free will would appear to be a joke of mythic proportions?

Nick gave me another quick squeeze, "After you get changed

come back and keep me company while I finish up here. There's cold Sancerre in the fridge."

The wine was perfectly chilled but I always liked to add a few cubes of ice just to hear the tinkling sound against the glass. Half way out of the kitchen after two gulps to settle my nerves, I turned back to the fridge and filled my glass again.

My thoughts were in turmoil as I changed into a cotton dress, shapeless from so many cycles through the wash. Unclipping my hair, I shook it out and brushed it. Staring into the mirror I noticed again the changes in my face from having given birth to Liz, then nursing her. My cheekbones were more noticeable but the oval shape of my face was softer, more womanly.

Looking inward, remembering the look of love on Raj's face, my thoughts were intermingled with both joy and terror. God, what had I gotten myself into? My life was already more hectic than I could handle; an affair would be madness. Unable to stop trembling, I gulped more wine.

Nick was just finishing up with the steaks while I set the table. We never used the formal dining room, preferring to eat in the kitchen at the heavy round oak table. When we moved in four years ago, I was pregnant with Liz and in a fever to build a warm, cozy nest. I'd painted the walls a soft pale yellow and put up crisply starched white valences across the windows; pots of bright red geraniums sat on the ledges. At an estate sale I'd found six blue and white Delft plates of scenes from Holland and hung them on the backsplash beyond the counters.

Liz babbled happily while we ate, excited about a new girl she'd met at Nancy's named Michelle. After dinner, I brought out the Limoncello I'd made last summer and filled two tiny liqueur glasses. A cluster of candles with the slightest hint of plumeria flowers burned brightly on the table, their scent mingling with the smoky aroma of grilled steak. The kitchen door leading to the side of the house was open and a light breeze rustled through the trees.

Nick scooted his chair back, slipping a small piece of leftover steak to Susie. Not wanting to be left out of the game, Liz tossed down another piece.

"Enough Miss Lizzie."

"Yes daddy."

Nick raked his hands through his hair then self-consciously patted it back into shape. Tossing back the rest of his drink, he let out a semi-mournful sigh. "What am I going to do about Linda? Christ, she is the worst secretary I've ever had. She is so unbelievably conceited, arrogant and impossibly obsessive."

I'd moved over to the outside door, liqueur glass in one hand, a cigarette in the other. "Does she still swab down the office every morning with disinfectant wipes?"

"Worse. She threw everything in my little refrigerator away, including my lunch. When I hung up after taking a call at her desk this afternoon, she brought out a can of Lysol and sprayed the phone."

"What a whack job." I'd only met her a few times. Linda, of the lank, greasy hair, and very large pores; her face was oddly narrow and beneath a hatchet nose her mouth was always compressed in a tight, mean line.

Her cold blue eyes telegraphed just how angry she was at the world. Very quickly she let me know that being a secretary was only temporary. An Orthodox Jew, she was married to a second year medical student. "Mark will probably do his surgical residency at one of the top schools, Johns Hopkins, or UCLA."

Nick got up and grabbed a beer from the fridge. "Maybe I can get Human Resources to transfer her to one of the labs in the basement."

"Good luck with that."

Beer in hand he wandered off to the den. I put my cigarette out, shut the door and sat back down at the table listening to Liz's further comments on her day. Susie hopped up on one of the chairs, a pert expression on her face as if waiting for a break in the conversation to tell us about her day.

Then while I quickly stacked the dishes in the dishwasher, Liz toddled off to where Nick sat in the den, climbing up on her daddy's lap and leaning into him, thumb in her mouth. He rested with his eyes closed and his feet propped on the ottoman; the pulsating bass of heavy metal that leaked out the sides of his headphones was so loud and tinny I could hear it across the room.

Dr. Nicholas Trudeau, my so handsome husband with his blonde hair and blue eyes, he was truly an Adonis of perfect proportions. Nearly six-foot-two-inches tall he was surprisingly brawny and strong. A good, sweet man he also had a searing intelligence and a passion for science and history.

Freshman year in medical school one of the women in my class asked me how I'd managed to catch such a gorgeous man. What do you say to a question like that, bite me bitch? I didn't feel too bad when she flunked out.

Watching him now with Liz, paranoia raised its ugly head, making my pulse race. That same sizzling in my brain I'd felt in the past after too many NoDoz tabs and no sleep: don't crawl too close to that edge it might suck you into a Stygian abyss.

Had I given myself away? Was there any reason for Nick to lose faith in me? Not yet. But how long could I keep up this pretense?

My secret burned inside, felt huge in my mind, I half expected outward tangible stigmata on my body. No scarlet letter needed here.

How was it that Nick didn't spot my agitation? Why didn't he suspect my radiant, glowing face? This husband of mine, this jailer, the one I must connive to escape from, what makes him so unaware? Locked away from his own emotions, he wasn't all that interested in mine.

Suddenly aware of my scrutiny, he opened his eyes, smiling drowsily. With a quick, wifely kiss--reassurance that all was right in his world--I scooped Liz into my arms.

"Time for a bath."

As I walked past him, he gave me a soft pat on the butt, "Do you want me to wait on the video? Are you going to watch it with me?"

"Bruce Willis? It was good the first time we saw it, I'll skip it now."

When Liz was squeaky clean and dressed in a pink nightie, I grabbed a beer and collapsed with her in the leather recliner in our bedroom. She sucked her thumb and stared intently at me as I read "Kate and Caleb" by William Steig. A laissez-faire sort of mother, I was indulgent with her thumb sucking. Indulgent and not always the best housekeeper either--glancing down the lower inside panel of the recliner, my heart was oddly pierced by the sight of a few fading streaks of breast milk from when I nursed her.

By nine Liz was asleep in my arms. The sound of raucous gunfire and screeching tires drifted down the hall; Nick had probably fallen asleep too.

Buoyed by all I'd had to drink, I felt steady, almost sane again as I watched Liz sleep, captivated by her perfect little button nose, the long eyelashes casting delicate filigree shadows on her cheeks. Her weight was like an anchor, keeping me safely moored.

I switched off the lamp and stretched to open the French doors wider. Venus was framed beguilingly by the moon's crescent shape. With the arrival of fall the Chinese umbrella tree had lost most of its leaves, piles of them drifted against the wire fence. The wind picked up, blowing still more leaves from the row of crepe myrtle trees.

My mind wandered, only for a moment, and then I was obsessing about Raj. It was like having JFK's eternal flame set up where the four corners of your mind meet. You couldn't go anywhere without running into it. To be alone with Raj, to make love to him, I wore the knowledge of him the way some women wear a mink, a second skin I reveled in.

It hadn't escaped my attention that history was repeating itself. My life was a page taken from Nabokov's "Lolita." With my head full of the ragged insecurities of being fifteen and hormones spilling across neurons like a mad accelerant, I had spun wildly out of control and soon was drawn into a secret, abusive relationship with Charlie Thompson, a man twice my age. And what flawed perversity of character kept me in that relationship for three years?

Like Mick Kelly, the young girl in "The Heart is a Lonely Hunter" by Carson McCullers, I believed devoutly that I was destined to do something special. And like her mother, mine told me the same thing.

"Everyone thinks they're special at your age. I was going to be a singer, dancing across the stage." My slender, so pretty mother twirled away from me singing a tune with her smoky voice as she thrust the feather duster along the shelves of the bookcase.

And still I believed.

***

I recognized later that Charlie was a pedophile, and almost certainly a sociopath. But hey, early exposure to sociopaths is not without its positive side. It leaves you hyper vigilant, and shows you the marked distinction between so-called "normal" and deviant behavior. Our violent physical fights honed my survival skills; Charlie was a force I had to constantly second guess for my own safety. Sex would always be linked in my mind with violence. Now if I wore high heels, if I stepped down too hard on my right foot, I could still feel the fiery pain from when I fell down the steps in his garage, severely spraining my ankle. In a jealous rage over an imagined lover of mine, he had shoved me out the door.

No wonder Nick and I were mismatched; his normal behavior and simple needs paled by comparison. Deep emotional attachment was alien to him. Trying to establish intimacy with him was like trying to rappel down the slick facade of a glacier.

***

I awoke with a crick in my neck to find I'd fallen asleep with Liz in the recliner. The clock on the nightstand showed that it was nearly three a.m. Nick was in bed; his steady, even breathing and the peace of mind that allowed him to sleep so easily always made me envious.

After settling Liz in her bed, I poured the last of the Sancerre in a glass, grabbed my cigarettes and slipped outside with Susie. She ran through the grass, disappearing into shadows down the sloping lawn. Moonlight transformed the Italian cypresses into eerie sentinels, flanked by fruit trees. The peach and plum, their skinny branches palely outlined, were not indigenous to this climate and always needed such careful attention. The blue-ivory light of the moon was benign, tempting me further outdoors and into the woods beyond, a mystic nymphet curled in dreamless sleep, free. No, I was definitely not free.

Seated on the cushioned redwood chaise, I drew my knees up, snug in my robe. I lit a cigarette and when the nicotine hit my brain something shifted inside; the full impact of adultery hit me like a blow to the chest. Could I really go through with it? What was wrong with my life that I would even consider something as destructive as adultery?

It wasn't even the seven-year-itch, Nick and I had only been married for five years. After graduating from the University of Texas at Austin with a double major in art and chemistry, I went to work at Texas Memorial as a medical illustrator. I met Nick there and in short order we were married.

From the start he nagged me about going back to school. "You're too smart to do medical illustrations for the rest of your life. I struggled to get a low A in organic chemistry and you made the second highest grade in your class. You should go to medical school."

He signed me up to take the Medical College Admission Test (MCAT) and I'd done surprisingly well. As a professor of physiology at the medical school Nick was very highly regarded; I'm sure his influence had a lot to do with my being accepted. Your typical first year med student is twenty-three, twenty-four years old when he or she starts; I was well into my thirty-first year with a six month old baby.

Nick was right on the money. From the start medical school was a magical place for me. I loved once again being caught up in the whirlwind of school, the nitty-gritty of chronic studying: cigarettes and coffee, a nasty ashtray full of butts, signaling an all-night cram session for my two hardest courses that semester, "Medical Pharmacology" and "Systemic Pathology and Laboratory Medicine".

I'd get a second wind, my fingers tripping the light fantastic on the keyboard, neurons firing as I typed up my notes. My mind ran on parallel streams of thought intertwined like a puzzle ring. One was tuned to the notes in front of me; another might be tuned to scenes of vivid, lewd and lascivious bodice-ripping encounters with the anonymous faces seen in the hallowed halls of the medical school.

It was impossible not to remain in a steady state of arousal when surrounded by so much testosterone and such prodigiously large egos. We'd all heard the same mantra: you are masters and mistresses of the universe, hand-picked with the goal of endowing you with the God-like powers to heal.

Someone less trusting than Nick would have seen right way that this hotbed of excess libidinal energy was not the best place for your questing, emotionally vulnerable wife. A Carmelite nunnery would have been preferable.

I'd come home absolutely wired most nights, mega doses of adrenalin pumping out like those women who lift cars off their injured children. You'd think my life was all about chasing Mastodons in the Arctic Circle.

Time to tackle the second job. Bathe the baby, feed the dog and then serve the Chinese takeout Nick had picked up on his way home. Drink another glass of wine, cuddle up with Liz and Nick in front of the TV, until bedtime.

Too wired for sleep, so I hit the hard stuff. A half glass of Southern Comfort put me out but I always woke up later, tense with longing, sleep evaporating like steam from a bathroom mirror. It was no good trying to hide from the bright spotlight of my mind.

A deep sadness, the very ache of existence would steal into me. I'd wake up before my soul had returned to its mooring in my heart, only to catch it wandering around the barren cosmos, listlessly looking for what? Afraid my restlessness would ruin Nick's sleep, I usually slipped from bed and headed to the den to study or read.

One night, having read just about everything in the house, I wandered into Nick's study. On the top shelf of his bookcase, nestled importantly against the rich dark wood, was a complete set of the works of Hans Selye. Selye pioneered the study of stress-related illnesses.

As if led by the guiding hand of an unseen sprite, I climbed up on the embroidered footstool and took down "The Stress of Life". Curled on the divan, with the light from the goose-neck lamp aimed at the page, I began to read.

The book took a week to finish. The more I brooded, the more I drank Southern Comfort and chain-smoked, the less I slept and the more I read. Selye became a pal. I loved his words, sure that with him I would find a solution. The key was to neutralize conflict before it neutralized me. Unfortunately, I was just a little vague on what my conflict was.

***

The spring of my second year in medical school my chronic insomnia caught up with me. My ribs stuck out and my hands shook. One morning after breakfast, I broke the Mr. Coffee pot, a tiny sliver of glass fell to the floor, piercing the top of my foot. Tears spilled out of my eyes as I hobbled into the bedroom, a paper towel soaking up the dot of blood.

Late for work, impatient, unsympathetic with how lost I appeared Nick did not know what to do. The exaggerated look of worry on his face pissed me off.

"What's wrong?" he asked. "Is it me, did I do something?" He folded one end of his tie into the loop he'd made. It was too short.

He shot an irritable look at me, as if it were my fault, then ripped it lose and started again.

"No! Why do you always personalize things?" I yelled so loud my temples throbbed. My head felt like a bale of hay, the tight wiring around it about to snap. The glass lodged deeper into my foot.

I had Liz dressed and ready to go; now she stared wide-eyed at me. For her sake, I tried to control my voice. "I'm sorry. I don't know what's wrong." With a feeling of terror, I realized that the quiver of life, the hope for joy at the core of each of us, was stretched to the breaking point.

The magical mystery tour of being "special" was more like a train wreck. Boiled down to more clichés it was too many "hard knocks and no free lunches." But each time I fell, I'd always been able to get up again convinced by that little kernel in my brain that kept telling me, "don't give up yet, don't give up, there's still more out there just around the corner." Even at those times when my mind became my own worst enemy, a hellish place on earth to be, being drawn on that string into an unknowable future was irresistible.

Nick slipped into his suit jacket, pulling at his cuffs, he turned to me. "Look, it's obvious you've been working too hard, not sleeping enough. Thank God Spring Break is almost here. It won't hurt you to miss one day of school. Why don't you go back to bed? I'll take Liz to Nancy's."

I nodded, then picked Liz up and walked with Nick to the garage. While he tossed his briefcase on the passenger seat, I settled Liz in her car seat, smoothing her hair back and kissing her. She was so obviously Nick's daughter, with his perfect features and clear blue eyes; everyone always commented on what a beautiful, sweet child she was.

Solemnly she whispered to me what sounded like, "Please ask my daddy to put "Hansel and Gretel" on." This was a cassette we'd bought that she never tired of listening to.

"Did you hear that about "Hansel and Gretel"?"

"Way ahead of you."

Our eyes locked for a moment. "Thanks Nick, I'm sorry for yelling." I bent down to kiss him goodbye. There was no warmth in the kiss; a long suffering sigh escaped from him.

"I'll call you later."

As they drove away, I sat on the first step of the front porch, plucking at the yellow threads of my ratty terrycloth robe, smoking a soggy cigarette, more tears dropping on the bright green Astroturf covering the cement porch. The weeping willow tree in our front yard resonated with the drone of insects. In my fragile state it was deafening.

Nick had the interior balance of a gyroscope, a genial detachment, no need to relate outward. The sense I had of an unused, unwanted quantity in my heart almost overwhelmed me, like an *idiote savante* whose genius for math is never discovered.

There was my conflict.

***

I spent the day crying and staring flatly at the walls, my mind like a bombed out shell of a building left over from the fire-bombing of Dresden. The next day I awakened early feeling sick, as if razor blades were lodged in my throat. Time for a real doctor.

Numb with pain, I stared bleakly at Dr. Patterson's lined face, at the impassive, closed set to his eyes. He reminded me of Yoda-- bald, with tufts of hair at odd spots on his head, like stuffing torn from a pillow; unruly eyebrows that pointed aggressively at you.

"Here's a prescription for penicillin, take acetaminophen for the pain."

Back home, I moaned and cried, wished for a quick death. Days passed, blurred by the pain. Another trip to the doctor, more penicillin. Then a slight shift in the pain's intensity, as if someone were applying leeches to bleed off the poison. Dr. Selye visited me in my delirium. Complete with white lab coat, gray hair, intense demeanor, taboo cigarette hanging out of his mouth as he spoke. "This illness, this conflict Sophie, it will kill you, you must neutralize it." Neutralize what, I wondered? How can you help yourself if you don't have the necessary insight into the problem?

Recovery was slow, I stared at my haggard face in the mirror and saw nothing but dark circles under my eyes, a pale waxen effigy of the former person I'd been. It rained for two days straight while I moped around in a black turtle neck and ratty running pants cut off mid-calf.

When the sun finally came out, I sat in the backyard next to the fragrant lilacs draped across the fence while Susie and Liz gamboled about chasing birds and butterflies. Smoke from my cigarette curled around my fingers in the still morning air as I drank from a steaming mug of Starbuck's House Blend.

By the time Spring Break was over I felt much better and was able to sleep through the night. The fever had burned out whatever madness was eating away at me, restoring a sense of calm. My grades were higher than expected and I did well on the USMLE1, a progress test medical students have to pass before applying to residency programs.

In the short interval before school started again, there was time to be a better wife and mom and bask in the glow of my newfound equanimity. Apparently, conflict had been neutralized.

***

Then the madness of third year descended. The first three months remain a blur of impossibly long hours during the Internal Medicine rotation. It became an endurance test: can you take in the huge volume of information needed to diagnose and treat disease in humans; can you develop the necessary proficiency required for clinical procedures? Like military basic training, can you deal with house staff and residents who are constantly in your face and derive pleasure from giving you any number of shit jobs to do?

Until we figured out a routine, our family life verged on the non-existent. In order to spend any quality time together, Nick and I took to letting Liz stay up until well after eleven. Then I'd be out the door again at five a.m. Thank God Nick's schedule on the faculty was more flexible.

I started the Hematology and Medical Oncology rotation in October and life became slightly saner. The study lab opposite Jameson's office drew several others from the same rotation. Once we'd been dismissed for the day we'd meet up there and chatter away like magpies about what we'd just learned.

Raj Khan didn't join in at first. He was always on the periphery doing research at one of the computers, giving off a shy kind of loner vibe. His mellifluous Texas twang blew me away it was so unexpected in a man with such smooth Asian features.

Eventually we gleaned a few facts from him, though it was like pulling teeth. His mother grew up on a farm not far from Hereford, Texas. She met his father, Naveen, an émigré from New Delhi, India while they were students at Texas A & M. Naveen was killed in a car accident shortly after Raj was born and mother and son went back to the family farm where he grew up. In the sixth grade he tested in the genius range on standardized IQ tests and went straight into ninth grade the following year.

A little over six feet, he was broad-shouldered and strong looking. Even with the alleged genius IQ, one couldn't help but think of him behind a horse and plow digging mighty trenches in the flat Panhandle farmland. His finely textured skin was a dusky pale that contrasted sharply with his black hair. Behind the wide-eyed gravity of his expression, I sensed a strong intelligent control, a natural reserve. He rarely smiled and his flat, expressionless face, with those somber black eyes hidden behind the thick lenses of his glasses, did not stir much interest at first. A solid family man, he talked on his cell phone with his wife as often as he could during the day.

It's funny how proximity exerts such a powerful force on humans. In college I'd read about a sponge made up of semi-discrete cells—like the animalcules that Anton von Leeuwenhoek first saw under the microscope. They can't live separately but can change their anatomy by shifting cells around: a never ending intimacy.

As the days passed there was no one I spent in closer proximity to than Raj, our schedules were similar enough that we were together constantly. Once the ice was broken our friendship blossomed, we never ran out of things to talk and laugh about, easy and natural in each other's company. Beneath his shy exterior, he was bright and witty, completely down-to-earth and always ready with a good story. Like how he decided to become a doctor.

"Mom told me this story that Dad had told her about my grandfather. His name was Sadar and he was a doctor from the Uttar Pradesh province of India. A man in his village came to see him. When asked what his ailment was the man replied, "Sir, I have pissed a piece of tomato skin.

"The man unfolded his handkerchief and handed my grandfather what remained of the tomato skin, swearing that it had travelled through his urethra into his stream of urine.

· "While Sadar had never encountered such a problem among any of his patients over the years, he knew how it might happen. He also knew that without miraculous medical intervention, of which there was none nearby, for their village was remote, the man would probably die. As predicted, within a day the poor villager had a very high fever and severe diarrhea. It was in the early forties during World War II, there was little to do but ease the man's suffering.

"My grandfather was curious and decided to perform an autopsy after the man's death. He soon discovered exactly how a piece of tomato skin had migrated so far afield. In people suffering from diverticulosis, the diverticula, or little pouches, extend out from the wall of the bowel. Burrowing through the bladder the diverticula had erupted sending contents from the bowel into his patient's bladder."

What woman wouldn't be charmed by such exotic stories? I was young and naïve about many things, as bad as "Cunegonde" in Voltaire's "Candide" sure that she was living in the best of all possible worlds and that humans, at heart, were noble creatures. And doctors weren't really the assholes they often appeared to be, they were just focused on healing folks. Right?

After Raj finished the story about his grandfather, he flashed a dazzling smile at me radiating such uncommon warmth that I should have immediately grown wary. Ninety-nine-point-nine percent of the male population I came into contact with daily looked right through me or if they did look, smirked and you could see they were thinking, 'hey, you are dog shit compared to the Olympian heights I've reached.'

Imperceptibly at first, then crashing through to my conscious thoughts, Raj began to dominate my life. One day after school I drove to HEB to pick up a few groceries. Maneuvering through traffic, I kept replaying the conversation we'd had earlier. He'd taken his wallet out to show me a new picture of his twin girls, Jane and Jennifer.

His face broke out into a huge grin. "They're so goofy, they make me laugh so much, and what good babies."

He handed me the picture. "Oh, they're so adorable." Eighteen months old and dressed only in diapers they held on to a redwood bench. They stretched toward each other, mouths pursed as if about to kiss. Above chubby cheeks their black eyes shone with the same liquid intensity of Raj's eyes.

"I never knew my father but mom says that we all three look just like him." Raj had looked at me with this kind of plaintive expression and suddenly I felt a thrill of intimacy surge between us. That's what first got me, knowing how absolutely no one else around us had the time, much less the inclination, to show any emotion at all.

Rushing through the automatic doors at HEB, I lectured myself, recognizing a little late the danger of getting too close to someone at school. *Put him out of your mind Sophie.*

***

The Hematology and Medical Oncology rotation was the thread that kept our little cohort together, but we'd also come to rely on each other. Dealing with patients and the myriad challenges they present kept us constantly on high alert. The philosophy of "watch one, do one, teach one" was a scary premise for clinical procedures; you needed people to watch your back.

The group included Owen Lambert, Raj, Rebecca McGowan, and Terry Martin. One afternoon we sat together on the cheap orange

Naugahyde couch and chairs next to the vending machines in the basement of Texas Memorial. In recent days there was very little that we didn't do in lockstep according to the dictates of our current guiding light, Dr. Ginger Newton, oncology resident.

Rebecca planned on being a surgeon. Whenever she wasn't cross-stitching homilies like "Home Sweet Home" she used silken thread on a scarf to practice surgical sutures and knots. Tiny, with a child-like body, she topped out at four-feet, nine inches tall. She'd need a stool to stand on to reach the people she operated on. Highly intelligent with a photographic memory, she also had a very intuitive knack for correctly diagnosing what was wrong with any given patient.

The first openly gay man I'd ever met, Owen was also something he called "hypomanic" which must be code for brilliant and incredibly witty. We'd been great friends as undergrads at UT in Austin, sharing a lot of the same science classes. Almost every weekend we went to see whatever movies were showing on campus, even the foreign ones by Fellini, Truffaut, Polanski and Bergman. Thirsty from chomping popcorn, afterwards we headed to one of the bars along the main drag that served ice cold pitchers of Lone Star beer of which we could consume several.

Owen had the soul of a poet and was quite the raconteur. I'd often scribble quotes of his into my Moleskin notebook like the start of a poem he once wrote while we were in the chemistry lab. "Ode to a Bean Burrito:" *The brain often secretes clouds of toxic thoughts billowing from one synapse to another the way the anus spews forth a steady volume of methane, depending on what you've eaten that day.*

Our conversations often reached such a feverish pitch we sounded like two people with ADHD, talking so fast and flitting from subject to subject. Possibly we were drunk too. After getting his BS he worked as a paramedic for several years before choosing medical school.

That day in the basement he drank from a Red Bull and spoke through a mouth filled with Cheetos, the mass consumption of which probably accounted for his being a tad overweight.

"The world as we know it could very possibly come to an end at the stroke of midnight December 31st, 1999. It's not that far off. What do you guys think? A hoax of monumental proportions?"

"Christ, you don't believe all that Y2K bullshit, do you Owen?" A thin, short man with a lot of nervous energy, Terry Martin was deeply scornful of Owen's preoccupation with "unscientific" phenomena. There was no love lost between them. At six-foot three inches and with a solid two-hundred and thirty pound frame, Owen could definitely be overbearing.

With a short dismissive wave of his hand, Owen's initial assessment of Terry had been that he lives in the existential hell of being totally pussy whipped.

His wife Janet had a good three inches on him and an enormous bosom. She was the soprano soloist in their church choir and such an egomaniac that she had recorded her version of the aria from "Madame Butterfly" on the ring tone of Terry's cell phone. I loathed her.

Owen was on the defensive. "You just never know, look at what happened to the dinosaurs, the great dying off."

"What? That doesn't even make sense. I bet you believe in crop circles and aliens too."

Tuning out their conversation, looking for an exit where I could go for a quick smoke, my glance came to rest on Raj. Chewing on the end of a Bic pen, he sat comfortably slouched in his chair, legs parted wide in an unconsciously suggestive posture. My eyes lingered a moment too long on his body before swiftly moving my gaze up to meet his. Nothing escaped his attention, his eyes twin beams of intensity aimed at mine.

Turning away from me he drawled, "Screw this. It's Friday afternoon, nothing's going to get done. Who's up for TGIF at Captain G's?"

Owen wiped his mouth with a napkin and lumbered up out of his chair, pulling Rebecca with him, "Come lovey, he says it's Miller time. Terry?"

"Nah, gotta get in the wind, Janet will be pissed if I don't come home. Besides, I'm on call this weekend with Newton."

Raj looked at me, "Can you make it Sophie? I'll call Chris; see if she wants to come."

We each flipped open our cell phones and called our respective spouses. Nick would be in a staff meeting until late, he told me to go without him; he'd pick Liz up at Nancy's. Chris had cramps and couldn't find a sitter on such short notice.

Just south of the medical center at the Grantham Street Mall Captain G's Woodbine Bar catered to a younger crowd: eager corporate types, students and newly minted lawyers from St. Mary's law school. Whether or not there was a real Captain G, whoever owned the place had a good eye for nautical relics. On the right as you walk in past the hostess station, a massive piece of a ship's prow is anchored on the wall. A mermaid carved into the weathered wood smiles down on you, her naked boobs, the nipples erect and a faded red, are thrust forever forward. Many drunks have fondled her and come away with splinters.

Owen and Rebecca waved at another group of med students

guiding us through the maze of people toward their table.

Just as we passed the bar I spotted Erin Albright, a girl I'd been friends with in high school. Pushing through the crowd, I made my way over to her, giving her a hug. She was pretty drunk already, her boozy breath tinged with the smoke from her Virginia Slims wafting over me. Although we were the same age it was obvious that drugs and alcohol had taken their toll, giving her a gaunt, hardened look, not helped by the heavy black mascara and eyeliner. Deep lines were carved on either side of her nose and mouth; her teeth were yellow and stained. I had to force myself not to stare at her bare arms that were dotted here and there with tiny red scabs. What the hell kind of skin disorder was that?

"Sophie, how fun to see you! Meet my friend Jared." She gripped the thigh of the man seated next to her. Wearing dirty jeans and a Grateful Dead T-shirt, his greasy black hair hung down his back in a thick braid. He had the smooth, hairless red-hued complexion of a Native American, one obviously enjoying the same dissipate lifestyle as Erin.

Over the raucous din we carried on a short conversation, then suddenly Raj was at my side.

"I ordered your drink, Lone Star draft, right?"

Slurring her words, Erin asked, "Hey, is this your hubby?"

"No. A friend from school. Erin, Jared meet Raj."

"Pleased to meet you."

Raj stared hard at Erin, I could almost read his thoughts, *You were friends with these skanky people?* Sensing Raj's disdain Jared's blood-shot eyes went all cold and steely looking; male strutting and displays of testosterone were imminent. With a cheery goodbye, I dragged Raj back over to where Owen and the others students were seated. Conversation was impossible above the blare of music and shouted conversations. I gulped my beer down just as another round arrived. "After this, I have to go."

Raj reached for my hand. "Me too, but let's dance first."

Not really a dance, just an excuse to breach the normal constraints of distance. As we moved on to the dance floor, I felt no sense of the music, overwhelmed by Raj's presence, his arms around me, the masculine scent of his cologne, the lilting music in the nearness of his body. Dizzy with lust, painfully aware that I was almost nine years older I tried not to read much into the dance.

"Relax," he said.

"Easy for you to say."

"Do it anyway." He pressed my head to his chest. "Just close your eyes and breathe in and out..."

For a brief moment I let my head rest on his chest, gave myself up to his warmth and strength.

***

At home, later that same night, I woke up at two and touched the back of Nick's neck, my hands cold. He pulled the covers up to his ears, sinking down into his pillow, closed to me. Nick has a recipe to help me with my insomnia: "Picture this Sophie: mountain streams, crystal clear water reflecting the surrounding evergreens, lush green meadows beyond, dotted with mountain wildflowers. There is a delicate mist in the air; it's virgin land where wild animals roam free. You have to try something really soothing, nothing that will excite you."

Picture this instead: Raj's naked body astride mine, he was deep inside me, the tip of his penis working hard against the entrance to my womb like a child begging to be let back in. I wanted to be lost in the warm blackness of his eyes, to feel his tongue moving over my body, between my legs, to feel the grip of his strong hands on me, to surrender and be possessed by him.

Like a child sucking her thumb for comfort, I stuck two fingers between my legs, pressing them deep inside that smooth wet surface, moving them slowly, rhythmically, hoping to quiet that sudden aching hunger for Raj.

***

The Trauma Center's cafeteria was filled to near capacity; several people came off the buffet line and stood searching the room for a place to sit. Raj and I were lucky to get a seat not far from the kitchen where the racket of plates being dumped into bins was enough to guarantee no one would linger.

I had no appetite for the fried fish, limp carrots and rice on my plate. Cisneros always had that effect on me, there were times when it was like a vision of hell with its vast entrance and the constant drone of the automatic doors opening and closing, opening and closing—bring me your tired, your poor, your horribly disfigured. In the parking lot that morning I'd seen a man who looked like his face had been put together by a demented artist. A one-eyed Cyclops with a nose battered to one side, his upper lip was completely gone revealing a gaping red maw and stumpy teeth. Poor man, all I could feel was terror and revulsion. If I looked like that I'd wear a veil over my face.

Putting my fork down, I stole quick glances at Raj as he ate, trying to forget the man in the parking lot. Though I hadn't sketched or painted much since starting med school, as I stared at his face I was so taken with his pale beauty, the black hair and eyes, the porcelain skin. The play of light on his strong features reminded me of a lambent chiaroscuro I'd done years ago of Lincoln's somber face.

What to say, what to say? I didn't want to ruin his appetite talking about the man without a face. "Did you check out the lady in the wheel-chair just outside the entrance to the cafeteria, over by the gift shop?"

"This sounds like the start of a joke."

"No but it was one of the weirder sights of the day. Left leg amputated to mid-thigh. She obviously didn't like her prosthesis because she had it in her lap, leaning across her shoulder with the foot—complete with shoe and sock—sticking up in the air. It put me in mind of the contortions people trying to have sex in a VW bug would have to go through."

He burst out laughing, wiping his mouth with his napkin. "How did I miss that one?"

"Dunno."

"Okay, I know something you don't know."

"What?"

"A high school kid was admitted from the ER this morning."

"Raj, how could you have heard about any other patients when we've been with the same patients all day? Are you telepathic?"

He gave me a cheeky grin. "Older woman, supposed to be really smart—connect the dots, where can't you go?"

At my quizzical glance he said, "I heard about it in the men's urinal earlier. Dr. Beckett, the ER doc, was talking with another doctor, I think his name is Reynolds."

"Eavesdropper. What were they talking about?"

"A senior at Callaghan High School, Michael Norman—ring a bell?"

"Nope, never heard of him."

"He's *only* the star quarterback who almost single-handedly led the Wolverines to their first ever undefeated season last year. Kid came in complaining of recurrent pain in his left thigh just above the knee. His coach thought it was another sports injury but Beckett had it X-rayed and they're pretty sure it's a sarcoma.

"Oh my God, that's awful, poor thing."

"Norman is something a little more special than your regular jock. Not only is he a great football player but he's a National Honor Society merit scholar, a complete shoe-in for an academic and football scholarship to UT-Austin, where he wants to go. What a shitty deal. They'll have to amputate don't you think?"

"Depends on how invasive the tumor is."

We were both silent for a few minutes, lost in thoughts of how cruel life could be.

"By the way, what I just said about older women, I don't really think of you as an older woman. Maybe when I first met you the idea of someone thirty-four seemed older, but not now, after knowing you."

Where I expected to find rough edges in one still so young, I found instead this delicacy and insight. At twenty-five he had an old soul, as if it had been in his family for generations and gone through several reincarnations; open and questing like mine.

**

Raj arrived the next morning at first light and caught up with me in the study lab. Out of the jumble of stuff he was carrying he withdrew a tattered copy of "Lust for Life" by Irving Stone and one of the Black-Eyed Peas CDs.

"I thought you might like to borrow these. The book came all the way from India courtesy of my father, a Penguin original. It's supposedly the best biography ever written about Van Gogh."

The CD slipped out of its jewel case and rolled across the

conference table, knocking over my Starbuck's cappuccino. Coffee immediately spread across the table in front of me. I leaped up, grabbing for my papers, cursing under my breath, then laughing.

Raj stared at me. Behind the thick lenses of his glasses, his expression was so frank, so honest and compellingly clear, yet impenetrable. What was behind that smoldering gaze? The sudden knowledge that I was in love with him overtook my body like a fast-acting drug, leaving me damp and breathless with confusion.

***

Late one Friday afternoon we all fell in step behind Dr. Newton as she checked in on her cancer patients. Most of us thought Ginger was a good doctor, yet behind her staccato words, her manic buoyancy, you sensed that she was running away from a dark edge. Her jittery, impatient behavior made us all nervous; each one of us had been on the receiving end of her acid tongue. She wore a lot of make-up which did little to hide the fact that when her face was in repose her somewhat hooked nose, hollow cheeks and pointy chin made her look like a witch.

Stopping so abruptly in the hall that we nearly ran into her, she rattled off the different types of lung cancer. "The two main ones are non-small cell carcinoma and small cell carcinoma; someone went all out giving those puppies names. Between seventy-five and eighty percent of people diagnosed with lung cancer will have non-small cell, almost always your lifelong smokers. The more aggressive one, small cell lung cancer occurs in fifteen to twenty percent. In the later stages prognosis is grim, six months, maybe eight."

Our last patient, Steve McKay, was a man who had just undergone surgery to remove his larynx. A lifetime two-pack a day smoker, he had Stage III cancer of the larynx with axillary lymph node involvement. McKay was still knocked out from the anesthesia and as Ginger perused the surgical notes in his chart, she said, "He'll be using a mechanical larynx in no time at all and the prognosis after the chemo and radiation is really quite promising. Whether he'll stop smoking or not is another matter."

It was scary enough seeing so many people with lung cancer, but the guy who'd soon be using an electrolarynx and sounding like Stephen Hawking was the worst. Lagging behind everyone when we left his room, I kept surreptitiously feeling my neck for suspicious bumps, vowing to quit smoking as soon as possible.

Little clusters of family members spilled out of some of the rooms into the hallways. They cast prayerful looks our way as if saying, "Please, please can't you do something, can't you save his life?" Their sorrowful glances tore at my heart and made me want to stop and reassure them. But it was nothing compared to the time we spent in Pediatric Oncology. The only way I could survive knowing what could befall helpless children was to strip away all of my expectations about life for Liz and face my fear of losing her head on. That while I kept it uppermost in my mind to cherish every minute with Liz because she could be gone—like that—I had to envision losing her, a world without her in it. Prepare for the worst, expect the best; we all walk a tightrope through life.

Still, at the very core of my heart I knew how insanely strong I could be in the face of any threats to her.

After Ginger dismissed us Raj and I headed back to the study lab. There were several medical students milling around in the hallway opposite Jameson's office. Just released from a histology exam, they were all jazzed up, comparing answers, and listening to Eminem on a boom box. One or more of them had been smoking marijuana, the odor, mingled with sweat and something citrusy, trailed after us.

I made the mistake of making eye contact with one of them and feeling safety in numbers he gave me a leering once over, his pink tongue darting out to lick his lips. The disgusting lizard-like spectacle barely penetrated I was so depressed at the thought of leaving Raj for the weekend. It had started to rain earlier which added to my depressed mood.

In the conference room, without speaking, we gathered our books and papers. Then suddenly a boom of thunder cracked so loudly across the sky it made the window pane shake slightly as if it might fly out of its frame. The ever present keening wail of ambulances added a further note of tension to the charged air.

Thunderstorms had been predicted for most of central Texas that day but the violence of the storm came as a shock. Raj walked over to the window staring out as the wind and rain raged on; trees in the distance swayed wildly back and forth their leaves flying off like the tiniest of birds. An eerie howling from the wind rose in pitch as if the world outside was vibrating on its axis.

Standing next to Raj, I watched the storm pelting the earth in lacerating sheets of rain mixed with hail. There seemed an odd rhythm to it as if something beyond the mass of bruised plum clouds was orchestrating it. The room grew steadily darker, then lightning flashed with such intensity I felt a crackle of electricity tumble through my marrow.

A seam opened up in the curtain of rain. Following Raj's glance to the circular drive below, I could just make out Chris waiting for him in their Toyota.

With that jolt of reality I turned quickly from the window. "You better go, she's waiting for you." I sensed that he wanted to say something but couldn't find the words. Don't look at him Sophie; don't open your mouth again.

If he knew my true feelings he'd back away and apologize for misleading me; explain that he was happily married.

"Right. I have to leave." He moved away from me, picking up his backpack, slipping out the door and down the hall.

I was just about to lock Dr. Jameson's door when Raj gently pushed me back into the darkened room. He turned me so that my back was pressed against the wall, knocking askew one of Jameson's framed diplomas. With his body molded to mine, he buried his face in my neck, whispering, "God, Sophie I've wanted to touch you for so long."

My heart stopped. I mumbled something unintelligible as his lips touched mine. The release from the tension of silence filled me with an unexpected joy unlike anything I'd ever felt before.

"I adore you," he whispered, his breath moving against my hair.

"Raj?" A voice from out in the hall.

We jumped apart; Raj flipped on the lights.

It was Ginger. She came barreling through the doorway, running her hands through her hair as if she were at the end of her endurance. Her makeup had all worn off and she looked witchier than ever. She'd have to be brain dead not to suspect something.

"Oh, hey guys, can you believe this storm? I thought we were going to lose power there for a second."

Clearly there was something else on her mind as she pressed her face to the other window, lost in a distant reverie, her posture forlorn. She didn't even respond when we said goodbye.

***

It was nearly four when Susie nudged me, ready to go back

inside the house. The night was cold; the woods beyond the wire fence had changed character in just a week. Now, mixed in with the live oak, there were starkly naked trees their spindly branches raised to the heavens. The muscadine grape vines were brown and grey, with clumps of tiny desiccated grapes. Echoing calls from the primates at the zoo across the canyon struck a mournful chord.

I wrote Raj's name in the dew on the redwood table, then slowly wiped it away. The wait for Tuesday seemed interminable.

Chapter Three

Monday morning driving to the babysitter's house, Liz and I sang "You are my sunshine, my only sunshine."

"Again mama!" I grinned at her reflection in the rearview mirror, her face so earnest and her voice so sweet and strong. She sang all the way up the sidewalk and to the front door as I rang the bell and bent down to kiss her goodbye. "You're the best sunshine ever sweetheart. I hope you have a wonderful day."

Nancy Metcalf opened the door and gave me a peck on the cheek in greeting while Liz ran off into the house.

"Did you have good weekend?"

"Super. How about you?"

"Um, maybe not super..." Dennis Martin, Terry's little boy who Nancy also watched, appeared in the doorway, "I need you NOW."

"Yes sir young man, how about using the magic word?"

"NOW please."

With a grin she stepped back across the threshold, "Have a great day Sophie."

Nancy adored children and they in turn adored her. A tiny, nervous woman, she wore her short brown hair in a cap of curls that frizzed out around her face, giving her a charming, gamin look. There was something riveting and adorable about her mannerisms, the way she moved and talked with such precision made you want to stop and stare as if you were watching a rare exotic bird. She was delicate and fragile, appearing almost anorectic. This was deceptive, she was always eating.

Her husband Jack worked in Information Technology at the medical school. He was Nick's racquet ball partner; evenly matched for height and weight, they were both fiercely competitive. With his simian brow, deep set eyes and pugilist's nose, Jack was not a handsome man, but his face had character. Fortunately, their daughters, Amanda and Nellie, looked like Nancy.

Back in the car I was grateful for the few minutes of silence on my way to work. Enough to settle my racing thoughts of Raj and tomorrow night. Could I really go through with this? Judging from the sheer intensity of my feelings this proposed infidelity had taken on the importance of a developmental step as critical as developing speech. Would it more likely be a cruel act of self-destruction on my part?

Yesterday on impulse I had pitched my painting of Charlie in the backseat of my Volvo. Despite my extreme ambivalence, I meant to finally have it framed, then hang it--where? In the utility room with the face to the wall. As I glanced at the painting in the rearview mirror it suddenly struck me how much he and Raj looked alike.

The painting was good, one of the best I'd ever done with a perfectly balanced play of light and dark and just a hint of the Satanic in Charlie's eyes. The background was mostly black shading into red with the slightest intimation of a crumbling structure surmounted by gargoyles. It was even better than the one I'd painted of Picasso that I'd sold for four-hundred dollars.

Maybe it was the early morning light shining in on the portrait that gave it such an eerie resemblance to Raj.

How did the thought of Charlie still have the power to make me feel so uneasy, to knot my stomach and reduce me once again to a childlike dependence? For an instant, I glimpsed clearly that former fearful child I'd been, shamelessly subservient, do with me what you will, only love me.

I come from a big Catholic family, with four brothers and sisters. Both of my parents were hard-working, but also high strung, nervous sorts, moody and unpredictable. Mother was alternately very strict and unyielding, then oblivious at other times. They labored under the constraints of a demanding religion, go forth and multiply and God help you if you don't send all of your children to Catholic schools.

As a partner in the law firm of Bartholomew, Wright and Tunney, my dad worked close to sixty hours a week. Mom also worked at the firm as a paralegal, she was only part-time but always ended up working a lot more hours.

We were never a close family and now everyone is scattered around the country. Scott, the oldest, became a priest and ended up in a parish in Baton Rouge, Louisiana. Mona got married right out of college and moved with her husband to Chicago. I was the middle child. Ted lives in Provo, Utah, he married a Mormon girl he met while skiing at Park City. When mom and dad retired and moved to San Miguel de Allende, Mexico, Sara, the baby of the family, moved with them. Now she's married to an expatriate artist she met there.

My father was a total mystery to me, probably most kids' parents are. A strict constructionist of "do as I say and not as I do," he rarely did anything untoward. At least that we knew about. His friendship with Charlie Thompson, owner of Charlie's Bar and Grill, seemed way out of character.

When one Saturday he took me and my younger brother Ted to the bar and grill, all he said by way of explanation was that they were "business partners." I pictured unsavory characters and shady dealings but for the most part the place was no different than a family diner.

The first time I saw Charlie he was leaning across the scarred wooden countertop talking to a man seated there. With his luminous black eyes, rakish smile and perfectly toned, muscular body, he seemed to shimmer with radiance. His nose was fairly big and slightly hooked, set above a full, sensuous mouth. The planes of his face were angular; his skin was pale and smooth but still hinted at a five o'clock shadow along his jaw.

My dad caught his eye and Charlie made his way over to us.

Tongue-tied with embarrassment, the blood rushed to my face and I quickly lowered my gaze. I couldn't believe this was the man my dad had come to see. His sheer physical beauty worked on me like a drug; when we shook hands he held mine for a fraction of a second too long. My whole body pulsed with electricity the same way it did when Scott, Mona and I held hands while Scott touched a live wire on an old radio. At seven years old it was a little like being Frankenstein when the lightning struck, power surging through your body.

Seated at the counter, Ted and I drank Cokes and munched on French fries after dad and Charlie disappeared down the hall to the office. With the uncanny prescience of a ten-year old, my brother said, "I saw the way you looked at him; you want to have sex with him."

I slapped him hard on the side of his head. "You say stupid things like that again and I'll tell Father Martin."

He looked suitably cowed.

In the car on the ride home that afternoon, after a few beers, dad waxed eloquent. "Yeah, Charlie's a bit of a strange duck. Probably French, you know some of them harken back to the troglodytes, those prehistoric cavemen and women around Les Baux in France. That explains his being so hirsute."

Ted piped up, "What'd you say, dad, he's got a "hair suit"?"

"Almost but not quite," he spelled the word out. "It's just a fancy word meaning someone who is really hairy. As in Charlie's always showing off his manly chest, he must have gotten that tan in Aruba."

Ted fell into such a fit of laughing I thought he'd choke.

***

Dad visited Charlie fairly often and usually invited me to go with him. After a few months I began showing up during the week without Dad, dragging my friends along to his place there on Broadway. Charlie always took the time to stop by our table and say hello. My girl-friends would sit up straighter, pat their hair and push their boobs toward him, flirting outrageously with him. It certainly helped business if you could charm the pants off of your customers and keep them coming back.

I asked him once about his family and what his wife was like, surprised when he explained that the bar was pretty much his family. "I was married for a little while, but it didn't take and she eventually found someone else."

Now, knowing what a psycho he was, it occurs to me that he probably murdered his wife and left her body parts in garbage bags in the dumpster behind the bar and grill.

Even when my friends had other things to do, I'd stop by and visit him. One afternoon Charlie asked me if I'd like to go for a ride with him. He left his assistant manager, Albert, whom I adored, in charge. Al was an older black man who had the widest, warmest smile and a short beard filled with curly black and gray hair and this deeply sonorous voice laden with honey. Not very politically correct but I could just picture myself sitting on the front stoop of a farm house in Virginia, listening to him sing and tell stories about the Civil War.

Charlie kept his baby-blue Triumph MG parked out back in

the alley. What an awesome car that was. We used to get on the freeway with the top down and Charlie driving like a bat out of hell, my hair blowing wildly in the wind.

His house wasn't far from the bar and grill and on one of our outings we drove by to see it. Nestled on a corner lot with a smooth green lawn of St. Augustine was a red brick rancher with white shutters on the windows. Encircling the house like a frothy petticoat were blooming masses of hot pink and white azalea bushes.

I didn't even give it a thought when he asked me to start meeting him at his house in the afternoons, bypassing the bar and grill all together. Incredibly naïve about the world, had you told me that prior to having sex a man's penis had to be as stiff as a flag pole, I'd have called you a liar. The word "pedophile" was unknown to me.

Had I no common sense though? I came from a big Catholic family with parents who treated me well. Maybe being in the middle of five children I sometimes felt lost in the general scheme of things. But this thing with Charlie, it was mostly curiosity and vanity, there had to be something special about me that an older man would be so attentive?

The first time I went to his house, Charlie gave me a quick tour then we sat down in the den and drank Lone Star beer. For months now my older sister Mona and I had been sneaking smokes out in the backyard while we waited for mom and dad to get home from work. When Charlie offered me a cigarette, I knew just what to do, holding my hand steady while he lit it for me. We smoked and talked about books and people and some of the characters who came into his bar and grill.

One afternoon we stood in the hallway as we were about to leave and something passed between us. An awkward silence followed; his house wasn't that far from the freeway and suddenly I could hear the roar of traffic in the background. I shifted from one foot to the other, feeling tongue-tied. He was tall, over six feet, and thin, not exactly ungraceful but clearly not entirely at ease with such long arms and legs and big feet. He must have been working on his car earlier because he smelled like a mix of car grease and English Leather. The silence lengthened as the powerful masculinity he exuded enveloped me. Then echoing up from that instinctual well in the most primitive part of our brains, the brain stem, I suddenly knew what it was that he wanted.

Stumbling around in my head, searching for a comment to bridge the uncomfortable gap, I grabbed the door to the garage and went rushing out, breathless with this new insight into our friendship.

What could I have been thinking to continue seeing him? Like an empty-headed moth to the flame, I should have run fast and hard in the opposite direction. But I didn't and after a while he gave me a key to his house; we met as often as his schedule allowed. Waiting for him at his house after school, I'd smoke a few cigarettes and snoop around, opening drawers, reading his mail, even checking out the medicine cabinet.

There were stacks of old magazines in his office, I'd sit at his desk and thumb through old *Time* and *Business Week*. The room was small and had a lot of stuff crammed into it, a drafting table under the window and what looked like a small engine on newspapers in the corner. A glass-fronted bookcase held an eclectic choice of books, Dickens, Shakespeare, biographies of Churchill, Roosevelt, Kennedy; the lower shelves were chock full of paperbacks by the likes of Tom Clancy, Ian Fleming, John Grisham, and Clive Cussler.

***

One Sunday afternoon when his place was closed, I took the

bus to see him, hopping off on the corner of Broadway and Tulipa Avenue, and then walking the five blocks east to his house.   Charlie was in his front yard spreading mulch on the trees and shrubs.   Dressed in a light blue knit polo shirt and cut-offs and wearing scuffed loafers with no socks, he looked younger than his thirty-two years.   I followed him over to the garage as he put the wheel-barrow and shovel away, then washed his hands in the small sink.

"Let's go inside and get some iced tea."

His slightly sunburned face heightened the sheen in his dark eyes and brought out the tiny laugh lines around the corners. Something sexual in my gaze must have made him bold; he leaned down and kissed me.

Nothing more than a peck but afterwards I felt a little awkward.   We sat down opposite each other in the den and drank our tea.   It was icy cold strong tea with lemon and just a little bit of sugar, I gulped it down.   Then nervous, unsure what to say, I stammered out a total non sequitur, "So!   You're friends with Richard Adams, I see him at the grill a lot.   You mustn't believe he was guilty of that rape." Adams was a senior at my high school.   The year before a girl had accused him of sexually assaulting her.   Nothing came of the accusation, but once people get a notion in their head it so often seems to take on the veneer of truth.

Charlie had been flipping absently through the latest issue of *Fortune 500* magazine; he closed it, tossing it aside.   "Does that bother you?   I'm absolutely positive he's innocent.   He asked me about you once, you know."

A jolt of fear and excitement rippled through me as my mind conjured up an image of his rugged handsome face, his piercing eyes raking over my body.   I'd run into him once, not long ago, after slipping out the back door of the bar and grill on my way home.

He leaned against his motorcycle smoking a cigarette. The comradely singing and shouting of the Hispanic cook and the dishwashers drifted toward us. The lively tune they sang lightened my step and made me feel happy as I moved across the asphalt.

Beyond the lacy pattern of leaves from the Dutch elm trees I caught a glimpse of the sky, a shimmering eggshell blue. The stench of rotting food in the nearby dumpster hovered in the moist, inert air, flies buzzing eagerly around it. A beetle scurried across my path, as if intent on a particular destination, sunlight glinted off of its carapace and off of the chrome and glass and green leaves surrounding us.

Richard and I watched each other warily until he gave a slight nod in my direction. He had the most sensual and expressive face with brown eyes that bored right through you into your soul, learning the knotty truths and lies that you hid. I loved his face, always wondered about the question in his eyes as he held my gaze so intently.

Then with a curl of his lip he flicked his cigarette away, got on his motorcycle and powered up the engine. A shiver went through my body as he drove off, not from fear, but because I was so drawn to him.

Now, with Charlie, I forced that more than slightly erotic picture out of my mind, like someone working with a slide jammed in a projector.

"It's hard figuring out the truth, but you being friends and all, you'd know. He's nice, I see him at school." I didn't want to talk about it anymore. Guilty of rape or not my attraction to him left me unsettled.

Charlie gave me a probing look. "Are you aware that there are cultures where you might have been married at this age; perhaps even had a child or two? Muhammad was a big one for the young girls and so was Joseph Smith, the founder of the Mormon religion. It's a mistake we make in our society being so puritanical, preaching abstinence. The toll it takes is often tragic.

The world is overpopulated; resources are finite. Still we end up fucking like rabbits and breeding willy-nilly. We have only the illusion that we are in control of our lives. So we give lip-service to being civilized and enlightened but in truth the world is an only slightly muted madhouse of barbaric ethnocentrism and political chicanery the likes of which are no different from thousands of years ago. It's a seething cauldron out there."

"What's chicanery?"

"Devious deeds, lying, cheating, bribing. Congress, in a word."

"Dad says the same thing."

His smile was fleeting. He stared intently at me, reminding me of pictures I'd seen of Rasputin. Those eyes were so compelling, drawing me toward him. "You wouldn't even be safe in a harem guarded by a Eunuch—castrated male—not that perhaps you'd want to be that safe. Young girls were known to have taught their overseers a thing or two about how to provide them with sexual satisfaction in the sheik's absence. And don't forget young boys were often put to good use in the absence of female companionship."

His voice dropped to a mere whisper. "So you see what we are doing here is only what humans have been doing since time out of mind. The urge is so strong."

When he reached for me I slid into his arms. He pulled me onto his lap, his hands under my skirt felt warm against my sheer nylon panties as he gripped my butt, pressing me tightly against him. We kissed, his tongue twisting around mine, the heat rising inside of me.

***

I had not set out to lose my virginity and embark on a secret affair that thrust me down the rabbit hole into the world of a man who might as well have been the Marquis de Sade. He cast a spell over me. To this day I don't know why my parents couldn't read my mind, see the changes in me and intervene on my behalf. More likely I was a very good actress and desperately trying to be grown up. I'd always held my own counsel, kept secrets to the grave, something probably learned from my lawyerly dad.

After a bit more coaxing from Charlie, I finally agreed to spend the night with him.

My friend Anna Travis was a hell cat back then. She said whatever came into her head and if it was profane or insulting then too bad. Her boyfriend was an older kid who'd dropped out of high school and worked the day shift at a Pac-N-Go. To make extra money he sold baggies of marijuana to the kids who hung out at his store.

Anna's parents were divorced and her mom worked two jobs just to keep the bills paid; her philosophy was that the world was a wild, wicked place and Anna would one day have to find her own way in it. Might as well be now. We'd been friends since the second grade and always covered for each other. When I told my parents I'd be spending the night at Anna's house they said fine. The subject was closed, they'd raised me to be a good Catholic girl and felt sure that would keep me on the path of virtue.

Traffic on Broadway was the usual lusty TGIF affair and most of the passengers on the bus wore smiles and chatted amiably. Getting off the bus I felt overwhelmed by the butterflies in my stomach and kept telling myself I could back out at any moment. Dragging my feet and kicking stones along in front of me, it took a while to finally reach

Charlie's house; by then it was nearly dark. His house was ablaze with lights as I hurried up the sidewalk, taking a moment to compose myself before I rang the bell.

The evening couldn't have gone more smoothly.

We sat talking after dinner at the table in his kitchen. When the dishes had been cleared away, when the candles had burned down to fat nubs that I twisted and molded into new shapes, Charlie brought out a bottle of champagne from the 'fridge and plucked two fluted wine glasses form the cupboard.

Chianti with the veal Parmesan, now champagne. He expertly popped the cork, then tipped one of the glasses, pouring it until frothy bubbles threatened to spill over. Light from the candles cast shadows across his face, he looked very handsome and sexy, his dark coloring set off by the crisp, long sleeve white shirt, buttoned at the wrist, black hairs curling around the starched cuffs.

"For you." He handed me the glass then poured another, "Shall we toast?"

"What shall we toast?" I asked, draining my glass, holding it out for more.

"To new beginnings." He answered, refilling my glass.

I drained that one too, with a sudden quaking feeling inside. Was I really ready for sex? Too late for misgivings or second thoughts, I couldn't back down now.

When the bottle of champagne was empty I stood up, so dizzy and unsteady on my feet I knew I had to lie down. Charlie stood up also, holding my arm, steering me toward his bedroom.

I'd been in there before and admired the heavy dark furniture, an antique armoire and chest of drawers and the carved headboard. A black leather loveseat sat against the far wall beneath a window covered by plantation shutters. Dim light came from the torchiere floor lamp next to it.

We stumbled toward the bed, kissing and then falling together on top of the burgundy comforter. With my brain so dulled by alcohol, all of my sensory nerves narrowed to that small place inside my mouth, Charlie's thick, hot tongue so soft against the warm yielding surfaces. Then something unfolded inside my body like a timed-release capsule and out spilled an aching sense of desire, of sexuality. Sensing a new eagerness in me, in one motion, Charlie leaned down and picked up the hem of my blue polka dotted summer dress, effortlessly lifting the whole garment over my head, tossing it aside. My bra and panties offered no resistance either; all I wanted was to lie with him in bed, to have his warm, muscular body next to mine.

My legs parted easily, overcoming in seconds a lifetime of modesty. I felt his firm hands on my thighs, his mouth burning the soft flesh between my legs, his tongue probing me, then moving up to that round button of flesh, whose name I didn't even know, but whose use I was well acquainted with. He worked it with his tongue until I climaxed with arching spasms, soft moans escaping involuntarily from me. Then damp and unresisting, I was a supplicant, entreating him to take me, drunkenly bold and eager. When he entered me there was only a moment of pain as I adjusted to this new fit, exultant over these new sensations.

It was everything I had expected from sex, initiating me into that undercurrent of passion that had swirled around me all of my life, but which until then had always eluded me. What had been concealed before was now apparent in the way Charlie moved; the way he touched me, in the way his body tensed just before climax, his oblivion as he gripped me to him, then called out my name in moaning surrender. "You're mine now, Sophie, you mustn't forget that," he whispered to me.

I took his cautionary advice lightly.

We slept. When I woke up hours later, I was dizzy and thirsty, but too lazy to get up. Charlie stirred next to me, moving over me again, his lithe, tan body, dark with black hair, dwarfed my pale, slender frame next to his. "Turn over." There was a tone of command in his voice I'd never heard before.

He entered me from behind and without knowing any better, I thought this was normal, "Does that hurt?" he asked.

"Not too bad." He pushed in deeper still, and then settled; I felt stinging moisture around the rim of my anus and wondered if it was blood. He slipped a hand underneath our weight, reaching long, slender fingers to probe inside my vagina, then up to massage my clitoris. Slowly his passion began to rise again, was communicated to me by the motions of his body, by the urgency in his hands, the way he thrust into that dark well inside me. A corresponding urgency rose up in me until I lost all sense of myself, my control disappeared as he rode me wildly, drawing me higher and higher with him into that field of perverted energy, consumed, filled in every spot that had been bleak and empty before. Gratefully I yielded, becoming part of some greater mystery that this powerful man endowed me with.

That night I learned that passion was a force in me that would brook no stifling; a force not for those weak and weary or who would come to it tentatively, apologetically, or seek to smother it.

Never once did I consider that something had been done to me that I hadn't been totally complicit in. The next time we were together, I was as eager for sex as the first time. He had hypnotized me sexually with the force of his personality; I surrendered totally, allowing him to overpower and obliterate me, absorbed, consumed, needing his darker mystery, his strength and command to make me feel alive. I obeyed him slavishly, came to be afraid of him, but I never loved him as I had once thought I would, not after discovering how black and empty his soul was.

One New Year's Eve I'd been waiting at his house for him to come home from work. If I'd wanted to I could have stayed all night, my parents had gone to Austin for the night and wouldn't be back until in the morning.

When Charlie arrived he was tired and a little drunk. I had a cold and we both agreed it would be best if I just went home to bed. Just before we left, I dropped my purse on an end table and ran to use the bathroom. Charlie was standing in the kitchen waiting for me when I came out, his face dark with anger. The only time he was ever like that was after he'd been drinking, alcohol could sometimes make him so mean and ugly he had once threatened me with a tire iron because some little thing set him off. When he was like that, I was terrified of him.

"So who's this Thom guy, you been fucking around on me?" He grabbed my arm, twisting it painfully behind my back as I started to reach for my things.

"What do you mean? I have not." I jerked my arm away from him angrily then saw the picture of Thom Murphy, a boy in my class. He'd given it to me just before the holidays and I'd stuck it in my purse and forgotten about it. Charlie must have been searching through my purse.

"Liar. What does this line mean, `I loved her, they loved her' what the hell, he think he's some sort of poet or did you let he and his friends gang-bang you?"

Before I could even explain that I hardly knew Thom and had no idea why he'd written those words on the back of his picture, Charlie turned slightly away from me. I thought we were done but instead he swung his fist, striking me on the cheek. I cried out in pain as I went flying to the floor, then crawled into a corner, cowering and waiting for his anger to subside.

Battered and bruised but thankfully nothing visible to the outside world, I recovered quickly, or so I thought at first. For months afterwards I suffered from ringing sounds in my ears and occasional bouts of dizziness.

Another time, in a drunken rage with me, he pushed me down the four steps leading from the kitchen into the garage. I thought I'd broken my ankle but it was only sprained. Recovering his sanity quickly because of my initial howling and screaming in pain, Charlie apologized over and over, promising never to hit me again.

It's a funny thing about women and physical abuse. When it happens to you from someone you have an intimate relationship with, it's so incredibly easy to rationalize if that intimacy has stunned you into passivity. You understand the crippled ego that is behind that person's behavior, in fact you're a prop for that ego, and you have this martyred, saintly self-image for putting up with that kind of shit. The other side of the coin is that you also feel trapped, too cowed by the brutality to try and escape. Women can be so compliant and forgiving; they take beatings in stride, unaware that it destroys their soul. My relationship with Charlie painfully extended my self-awareness into something abnormal as if a bulldozer had been clearing new ground for development and cleared too far, destroying the dense protective layers of impenetrable forest. Innocence lost.

Charlie and I were together for three years in all, until I went away to college. When I was a junior in college I heard that he had been killed, stabbed in the alley behind the bar and grill. The cops were never able to point the finger at anyone and eventually wrote it off as a robbery gone wrong.

After we parted company, I didn't have sex again for years, a curious backlash of my relationship with him. Everyone I met was pale and colorless by comparison, unwilling to play the games of psychological (and physical) abuse Charlie had made second nature to me. At school, surrounded by nubile young women, their sexual relationships superficial and easy, I felt my loss of innocence keenly; hating Charlie for having robbed me of it.

The news of his death came as quite a shock, not because I cared for him; by then I hated him. But some things become immutably mired within your soul: soul murder.

***

I'd finally reached the medical school and found a place to park. Before exiting the car, I turned to stare for a moment at the painting of Charlie. True, Raj might look like him, but I knew Raj was nothing like him, he was rock solid, gentle and kind.

Chapter Four

Pulling out of the driveway Tuesday morning, the frenzied beat of a song on the radio moved through my body as if someone were tattooing it into my being; I felt feverish and had begun to perspire. The day of reckoning was at hand.

A Chinese woman named MeiLing Wan lived in the corner house, a custom made home trimmed in glossy red and black; the edges of the roof curved gracefully upward in a distinctly Oriental motif. At the crack of dawn every day and on moonlit nights as I returned home she was always in her vegetable garden, moving among the furrowed rows. Dressed in black peasant pants and a dark tunic, her long gray hair braided and falling across one shoulder, she reminded me of a figure straight out of Mao's revolution.

Would my life ever be that uncomplicated? Like Voltaire's admonition to tend your own garden, in other words, 'mind your own business peasants'. That probably didn't include dangerous liaisons with younger married men.

Raj and I met up outside the cafeteria. After getting coffee we spotted Owen Lambert, threading our way through the tables to join him. He'd finished eating and was surfing the internet on his Compaq laptop.

"Morning guys. Have a seat, join me. No breakfast today?" The cafeteria was known for its breakfasts: heaps of crisp bacon, scrambled eggs, and buttery toasted raisin bread, washed down with their dark roast coffee.

"I already ate." That was a lie. My stomach was tied up in so many knots at the prospect of cheating on my husband that I doubted I'd ever be able to eat again. Then to add to my worries I remembered that of Owen's many talents the top two were how intuitive he was and how observant. The idea of Raj and I, together, in love—he could so readily tune in to that frequency. We had to be careful.

***

The morning flew by. Cameras were set up in the operating room to record Michael Norman's surgery and we were able to watch it in real time in a classroom on the first floor.

Vascular surgeons were amputating his left leg above the knee and the lead surgeon, Dr. Olivetti, an Italian who spoke with just the slightest accent, kept up a running commentary while he worked. Michael was fortunate that no other cancer had been detected.

Halfway through the surgery Ginger joined us. With a viperous glance my way, she sat down in the empty chair next to Raj You'd never mistake her for a *femme fatale* but when she gave Raj such a high wattage smile, her eyes drilling into his, I'd swear she was channeling Scarlett O'Hara at her most saccharine.

The room was fairly dark because of the TV monitor but above Ginger's head one inset light cast its glow straight down on her. All the world's a stage: her soliloquy was fierce and intimately spoken, her body language unmistakable as she leaned toward Raj.

"I had a patient like this kid; it's been about five years ago. Greg—that was his name--Greg Paulsen, a nice looking guy, like you. The sarcoma had already metastasized to the lungs by the time he was correctly diagnosed. He went ahead with the amputation and was scheduled for chemo and radiation, but his chances for survival were slim. After he left the hospital I lost contact with him and assumed that he'd died shortly afterwards. Two years later he came to see me, this robust guy with Norwegian heritage, sporting a heavy red beard, he looked like a Viking."

Inscrutable and silent as the Sphinx, Raj stared at her while she talked. "Famitonex was an experimental drug available in Germany, very toxic to the human body and ultimately never developed commercially. But—he went for it. Said it nearly killed him, but it also killed all the cancer. He used a forearm crutch instead of a prosthesis and had great mobility."

The rest of the people in the room, suppressing the urge to tell her to shut up, crossed their legs, coughed loudly, and shuffled their feet under their chairs.

Oh God, I thought as I watched Ginger and Raj, she knows. It was that day of the storm, when she saw us in the study lab. Why else would she have given me that look? Why else would she glom on to Raj like he was her newest best friend? I could see the wheels churning in her head, what does this kid Raj have that Sophie can't get at home and do I want some of it?

For whatever fucked up reason the default expression on my face is an eager smile and if my vestigial tail were visible it would always be wagging like Odie's. All qualities that immediately put people in mind of "bimbo al bordo." That first, and lasting, impression had happened so often that I took for granted not registering on people's radar.

Deluded. So much for being careful.

I kept an extremely low profile later that afternoon when Rebecca and I met with Ginger and two other oncologists, one from MD Anderson in Houston and the other from the Scott-White Clinic in Temple, Texas.

They were submitting an article to "Oncogene" journal on the results of a clinical trial for Versanimide, a new drug targeting atypical cases of acute myeloid leukemia. Rebecca and I had examined and drawn blood at specified intervals from all the San Antonio participants and recorded the results in the AML database. Ginger was the lead author and somewhere at the end of a long list of contributors I'd get to see my name and Rebecca's in teeny tiny print.

The meeting ended early and I was on my way out the door and heading home by five. Ginger had insisted that I have all of the graphs and charts done up in Microsoft Power Point for the Versanimide trial results by noon tomorrow for inclusion in the final draft of her article.

It would take me all of half an hour to get it done, but I needed an excuse for going back out to the hospital that night. Or wherever I might end up; certainly not the hospital.

Even with Charlie I'd rarely had to lie outright to my parents. "I'm off with Anna or Holly or whomever." These omissions of the truth had always sufficed. But lying to Nick? All those early years at Ursaline Academy had left my brain addled with all-purpose guilt.

Nick nodded absently when I told him I had to go back up to school. There was nothing unusual about my leaving, as a medical student it happened often enough. To show how mundane the topic was, he turned away with a smile, caught up again with the pulsing tunes that held him in their sway. As he tapped out a rhythm on his jeans, I wondered, but not deeply, at this music in his brain that drowned out much of what was around him, an interior metronome that kept him hypnotized.

Dinner was leftover pot roast and veggies from the freezer, nuked in the microwave. Afterwards, exhibiting the logistical skill of adulterers who had gone before me, I removed the dishes, deposited them in the dishwasher, brushed my teeth, chose a fetching blouse, dug through the tangled mass of chains, thread and earrings in my jewelry box to find a safety-pin for my favorite, too-tight jeans, and still had time to rest on the green couch in the den with Nick and Liz and Susie, watching the news. I was inwardly amazed at this insouciant, not-a-care-in-the-world demeanor.

Then finally, mentally kissing the floor in front of me five times, praising Allah, it was time to go. With real kisses all around, even for Susie despite the fact that I had just seen her lick where the sun doesn't shine, I left my family standing in the doorway leading from the kitchen into the garage. They waved goodbye to me as I backed the Volvo slowly out of the garage, down the driveway, turning into the street. Liz's grin was wide and happy; see mommy go meet her lover.

The interior of the car lost heat quickly as I waited for Raj in the parking lot of the mall. Some guy on the radio was interviewing Jack Berendt, the meteorologist for KSAT, about the blue norther from Canada that had blown into town earlier that day.

Berendt was a vapid, smarmy guy whose pompadour was as glossy black as a raven's feathers. Once, a few years back, on the 10:00 o'clock Live News, after the station had gone to a commercial break, somehow the camera man had taken us back to the studio for an instant. We were treated to a close up of Jack gazing like Narcissus into a woman's compact and patting his nose with a powder puff.

The memory brought a smile to my face, easing some of the tension tightly coiled in my neck. From the six-pack of Lone Star longnecks just purchased, I grabbed a bottle and opened it, drinking half of it down, my fingers turning numb from the added cold.

Then finally I saw Raj's car in the distance. Afraid that I had invented his presence, afraid he would disappear like a mirage, I forced myself not to blink until he parked next to me. He hesitated for a second before getting out as we stared at each other silently through the jaundiced glow of the halogen lights.

A sudden pang of shyness seized me. What should I say to him?

After he was settled in the seat next to me, I started the engine, asking, "Where to?"

"Dunno." He saw the beer, removing a bottle for himself, opening it. "Let's just drive around for a while, out toward Helotes. Damn it got cold fast."

"No kidding, an arctic blast ripped through the car when you got in."

Turning right, out of the parking lot, I maneuvered the Volvo past an old Chevy Impala with Distrito Federal, Mexico license plates. It was so crammed with people that I wondered if they were refugees just arriving in town. Mexico City was a long way off.

Impatient to put the slower traffic behind me, I shifted into overdrive, leaving the city behind.

My focus returned to Raj, to fleeting observations as I drove, his strong, handsome profile, how lights on the dashboard reflected off of his glasses, a tiny mole just below his ear that I'd never noticed before. His presence with me felt like the solution to a problem I had not yet fully articulated.

It seems so odd that our lives have to unroll in such a linear fashion, there's no fast-forwarding or rewinding, you can't splice in a new outcome. If in fact, arrayed on the periphery of my mind, was the insight that there was a problem in my life and it had to be resolved, why couldn't the solution have been something quiet and dignified? Instead of what it turned out to be, so very messy and infinitely painful to everyone involved.

"Did you have any trouble getting away?" I asked.

"No, being in med school is its own excuse, right? We've always got stuff that has to be done."

We drove aimlessly; I felt easy and confident behind the wheel, happy there wasn't a lot of traffic. Lights from the city fell away and the countryside became hillier, covered with live oak trees flashing by the windows. Raj flipped through my CD folder pulling out "Aerosmith" then loading it in the player.

Reaching for his hand, I squeezed it. "It's really good to see you."

He grinned, "Yeah, finally." His face was in shadows, he kept shifting his glance from me, to the CD player, to his beer, then staring out the windshield at the darkness beyond.

I exited from the highway, taking a back road and then headed down a two-lane road with no other cars in sight.

"Would you mind? I'm going to have to stop and go to the bathroom. The beer goes right through me."

"No problem."

A gravel road leading off into the woods looked promising. I turned right and then pulled over to the side. Leaving the headlights on, I jumped out of the car, and ran a little ways in, stopping behind a tree, uneasy because of times in the past when I had come away from such nature calls with a few ticks. There was a slight mist hovering a few feet above the ground, swirling around the base of the trees like something spooky and malevolent out of *Nosferatu*. Hoping Raj couldn't see me I squatted down and peed. Then peering down between my legs I finished up, watching dreamily as steam from my urine rose in the cold night air, mingling in rippling currents with the mist.

Back in the car the digital clock on the dashboard alerted me to how fast time was passing. Desperation made me assertive. "You don't want to ride around all night do you?"

"No. Where do you want to go?" He was staring out the window on his side, talking to his reflection in the glass.

Patiently, I asked, "Do I have to say it?"

He turned back toward me, I couldn't read his expression. "I can't say it. It has to be your choice."

God, why did I suddenly have an image of *Lost Boys* and having to "invite" the vampire across the threshold of your home? How easily hypnotizable I must be to have yet another man lure me into his butterfly net.

He rested his hand on my shoulder, his fingers tracing a pattern on my neck, making it almost impossible for me to concentrate.

Take a deep breath Sophie; try to force your over-stimulated nerves to relax. But I was in such deep, unknown, treacherous waters, would he think less of me if I said that all I wanted to do was go to a motel and get into bed with him? I should have thought this part through more carefully.

"Do you want to go to a motel?"

He left off rubbing my neck, grabbed my hand and kissed it, grinning at me, his voice husky. "I thought you'd never ask."

We stopped at the Texas Star Inn, just off of Highway 87 and FM 1499. I rolled the window down and looked around. It seemed a desolate, isolated place like a back lot ghost town at Universal Studios, complete with a sound track of coyotes baying at the moon.

Clustered together were the motel, a Shell gas station and Katarina's Cantina which had several trucks parked out front. Beyond the bar another road twisted up into the hills, with a house overlooking the highway. More lights twinkled in the distance like dancing fireflies.

Raj disappeared inside the lobby to pay. Fighting the urge for a cigarette, I breathed in the misty, cold air filled with the tang of cedar and juniper. Minutes later Raj hopped back in the car, folding the receipt into his wallet. "Drive around to the back, it's upstairs."

Once inside we both paced nervously. There were two double beds divided by a nightstand with a lamp bolted to its surface. On the wall between the beds, above the lamp, was a Remington reproduction, a scene of Cowboys and Indians caught in one of their perennial clashes. We laughed nervously at the picture and the two beds; one was enough, two superfluous.

I opened another beer, passed it to Raj, then took one for myself.

"Thanks, I meant to bring some wine but time got away from me." Perhaps paranoid, he peered out from the curtained window, watching the parking lot. There was nothing but hilly woods beyond the motel and few other cars. "It's quiet, almost too quiet. And no music either, not even a radio, we'll do better next time."

Next time? We hadn't even gotten to the first time. Unsure how to proceed, I sat down on the bed feeling enormously stilted, "Yeah, music would have been nice."

My jeans were too tight for me; the safety pin was cutting into my flesh. Slipping under the covers in the bed closest to the bathroom, I undid the safety pin and hid it in my pocket. Raj turned off the lamp on the nightstand, but left the other light on, then climbed under the covers beside me. We kissed, fumbling awkwardly with each other's clothes.

No matter how crazy you are about a person, the first time you make love is never great. There were so many fantasies crowding us in bed, nothing turned out well.

When I felt the shaft of his erect penis pressing against me, I pushed back to covers, kissing his stomach then taking his dick in my mouth, sucking gently.

"No, come here."

"I'm sorry." I moved back into his arms. His black eyes were as impenetrable as beads, his face damp with sweat, his cheeks flushed, the long black hair curling around his neck and face.

Looking past his shoulder I caught my reflection in the mirror on the bathroom door, startled by my wildly tousled hair, the lipstick slightly smeared across my mouth. The eyes looking back at me were like twin glass eyes for the blind, made of green malachite, incandescent.

He sat up, gently brushing the hair away from my face, speaking earnestly. "Don't be sorry. I didn't mean that to sound sharp. See, what I mean is this first time I want to see your face."

The delicacy of the situation touched me. I wondered if it was a mark of his Indian heritage, that he found it debasing for me to do such a thing our first time.

We lay back down on the pillow, facing each other, silent, embracing. I searched his eyes for answers, knowing the warmth they conveyed was what had first captivated me. Now, before all that was to happen between us later, we were still able to think in simple terms of satisfying our need for love from one another.

***

Back home by ten I tiptoed into Liz's room, tucking her red and black quilt more snugly around her, kissing her forehead.

Then in the bathroom, brushing my teeth, washing up, I wondered, did Raj and I hope for the same thing? That tonight would be a dismal failure and the fantasies assailing us would subside, allowing us to go on with our lives.

From the wooden hooks on the back of the bathroom door I took down my favorite pink silk nightgown throwing it over my head, and moving silently to the foot of the bed I shared with Nick. Feeling more grounded, I tried to figure out how best to unobtrusively reenter the flow of my marriage, sort of like a prisoner breaking back into prison.

Nick didn't leap from bed to hurl accusations at me; he only burrowed further down into the warm covers. Susie was just a tight warm knot of fur in between us, not even stirring as I slithered in between the sheets. So far, so good. Too thrilled and excited to even contemplate sleep, I lay there glowing like a radioactive element, surprised that this did not jar Nick out of his sound sleep.

Nothing had changed. Behind my closed eyes, all I could see was the light in Raj's eye, drawing me to him. The glow of perspiration on his pale, finely textured skin, the black hair on his chest curling beneath my hand, the fresh scent of soap, a slight hesitancy in the way he touched me that revealed a sense of awe for what we felt. Like all unwary lovers, I didn't see the danger and eagerly looked forward to the next time.

***

At precisely noon the next day I stopped by Ginger's office to drop off a disk with the Power Point presentation she wanted. Arching her right eyebrow, she looked out at me form the gnarly depths of her soul as if to say, I know you, I know what you are up to with Raj.

Terry Martin saved me from the awkward moment when he knocked briefly on Ginger's door and stepped inside. "Sophie, I'm glad I found you. Did you still want to meet Dr. Monroe? After lunch she'll be seeing patients on the fifth floor."

Phyllis Monroe was the new head of faculty for Infectious Diseases. Terry and I wanted to do an Infectious Disease rotation next term. We were especially interested in pandemics, fascinated by the 1918 H1N1 influenza virus. Some estimates at the world wide death toll were as high as fifty million. Conventional wisdom was adamant about one thing: not so much *if* another pandemic like that could happen, but *when*.

Dr. Monroe, originally from the Centers for Disease Control (CDC) in Atlanta, was an M.D. as well as having a Ph.D. in Genetics. A tall slender woman with curly black hair, she had a mole above her mouth on the left side that had black hairs growing out of it. It looked like a tiny spider and I was surprised she hadn't had it removed.

In spite of Owen's assertion that Terry was the most pussy whipped guy he'd ever met, Terry had a solid, mature presence, the confidence and demeanor of someone who'd already received his medical degree. Dr. Monroe took to him right away, talking about her two patients with TB. With Terry's obvious keen interest and probing questions, I soon found myself trailing after them as she invited us along.

We had to gear up in masks, gloves and paper gowns when we entered the patient's room. With his severely compromised immune system and resistance to normal drug therapy for TB, the precautions were as much about protecting him from germs as it was to protect us.

The other patient, a black woman with the odd name of "Kinshasha" was HIV positive as well as having tuberculosis. A street person with no apparent family ties in the area and an admitted alcohol and drug abuser, she was in a downward spiral that would ultimately lead to her death.

The most interesting patient was a man originally diagnosed

with meningitis who actually had equine encephalitis from a mosquito bite.

The infection laid siege to his central nervous system, leaving him helpless in the face of violent seizures and psychotic behavior. He'd been in the hospital for a month, with several setbacks but now seemed on the road to recovery. A thin, wiry man of thirty-eight, he was married with no children. He'd taught history at San Antonio Community College prior to being hospitalized, but the damage to his CNS meant he would probably never teach again.

As Dr. Monroe examined him he looked at me with the confused, frightened expression of a broken man who couldn't get back to a place of light in his mind. He reminded me of a psych patient I'd once seen who'd had one too many jolts to the brain with electro-shock therapy. It did nothing to quell his bipolar disorder and after an unsuccessful attempt at suicide deprived his brain of oxygen, he lost whatever had been left of his mind.

***

At the end of the day Raj and I met up in the basement at our lockers. It was the first time we'd seen each other since the night before. Once was obviously not going to be enough; everything inside of me seemed to shift and melt at the sight of him. With a boyish shyness, he looked around the locker room, then smoothed the hair at the back of his head. When he gave me a smile of incredible warmth, his eyes glowing like black coals, any resistance I had ebbed away.

We got our things and headed out of the building toward the parking lot. Waiting at the red light, Raj leaned against the silver street-lamp, giving me a curious sidelong glance. He wore a beige sheepskin coat, unbuttoned and navy-blue twill pants and a maroon sweater vest over a long-sleeve white shirt. For the past week he'd been working on growing a mustache. According to him most Indians have very little body hair, but when his mom's Irish-English background was added to his particular gene pool, voila, one hairy guy. The mustache was shaping up nicely though he kept tugging at it self-consciously. We watched each other quietly. I wondered about the transformation from friends to lovers. We'd been so at ease with each other, uninhibited, unaffected as friends and confidantes.

Smiling sweetly down at me he asked, "Do you think you could meet me again at the same place next Tuesday?"

Without hesitating I agreed to meet him. The light changed, his hand at my elbow, he steered me across the street. A gust of what felt like Arctic air pummeled us forcefully, bringing tears to my eyes. I looked up at the gray sky overhead. Oddly, for the first time in months, I felt free, no longer torn and almost buoyant in that wild wind.

The Catholic Church two blocks away tolled the hour, in a weird, mystical way as if offering up a warning meant only for me: repent you sinner. Then the guilt was gone and it was as if time stopped for a moment, was protracted, stretching out like a rubber-band, engulfing me with an unexpected sense of love that I had denied myself for so many years. We moved slowly against the wind, fighting to get across the street, then hurrying into the protection of the eight-story Cisneros Trauma Center.

Stopping to catch our breath, it came to me how precarious our situation was, how easy it must be to see the bond that stretched between us now.

***

The second time we returned to the Texas Star Inn was not as awkward. Once settled in the room, we talked easily; I sat facing him at the end of the bed with my legs crossed Indian-style. Raj had brought a baggie full of marijuana and expertly rolled a joint that we passed back and forth.

"After graduating from high school my mom took me to India to visit my aunts and uncles. I have enough cousins to populate a small town.

"Panhandle summers are so fucking hot, worse than a desert, you pray for the occasional cyclone. But New Delhi gave me instant culture shock. There's this smell, a combination of wood smoke fires, animal shit, and curry mixed in with the sickening sweet smell of camellias and plumeria. Not to mention the sweat from wall to wall humanity.

"The heat and humidity act like a convection oven heating it all into a noxious brew. And my God, there are flying bugs as big as mice. One of my cousins, Amir, introduced me right away to *bhang*, a type of cannabis. It's been around forever, since way, way back into Marco Polo's time and beyond. Even the Muslims would use it in their hookahs.

"We smoked every day after that, otherwise I'm not sure I would have survived. It's funny because sometimes I crave the taste of ice cold beer, but I didn't have pot again for over a year and never really missed it. They should legalize marijuana."

"Wow, I've never heard you talk quite so much so fast before."

He grinned and passed me the joint. I drew the smoke into my lungs and held it for a beat, then exhaled, "I totally agree, it's less harmful than alcohol. But it does give you weird dreams. Last time I smoked—it's been several years at least--I dreamed that there was a disk drive in my forehead and I had to load up an operating system every day."

"Form follows function. We're always inventing stuff that mimics us: cameras, TVs, computers." He stubbed the roach out in the ashtray, squinting as the last of the smoke curled around his face. "But they'll never legalize pot, even though it has a long list of medicinal uses. There's always the better sex angle too. Not that I'm any kind of addict, for dope or sex. I don't have to have sex every day like some guys."

Where ever he'd gotten the drug, if he'd brought it back from India or grew it on the farm, it was very strong. Insights usually barred from perception rippled through my thoughts. Marijuana always seemed to cast the world in a more benign light. Wars waged and won or lost, the moments of cringing insecurities and black, bleak self-loathing muted into the background; a kinder, gentler surcease from the pain.

I had a sense of being ushered into that revealing, mysterious substrate beneath the workaday world. Could Raj really say that at twenty-five he knew completely the terra incognita of his sexuality? Was I a ravenous aging woman to his less ardent needs?

The pillow I rested my head on smelled incredibly fresh as if it had been set out in the sun and soaked up its pristine radiant energy. Yes, I was definitely stoned.

"The second time is always better." Raj whispered to me later as we came together. Without his glasses, it was always my fervent hope that I was a Renoir-like blur. Tenderly, he removed the gold chain and tear-drop pearl I wore. "Everything has to go."

I traced a finger over his full mouth, the lips moist and rose-colored, the tiny black hairs of his mustache curled delicately on the soft skin above his mouth. I watched his eyes, they were so black you couldn't see the pupil; the whole iris seemed focused on me with such a burning intensity that I lost myself in him, became him when I felt him deep inside me. We moved together slowly at first, then quickly, desperately, the boundaries between us eliminated.

And like the sponge with the semi-discrete cells, my body seemed different after sharing it with Raj. Unseen forces work away at the blood red interior chambers of our hearts, binding people to each other in irrevocable ways. Of course, I did not know it then, who recognizes the subtle, shape-shifting changes taking place? Until it's too late.

Still quivering inside, I snuggled into the crook of his arm, stretching out lengthwise next to him, entwining my legs with his, running my hand slowly down the side of his body from mid-chest to his hip, resting my hand on his thigh. "Your body is so wonderful."

He was close enough I could feel the words vibrating in his throat. "I really like yours too."

Wrong word, love, love me as much as I love you, Raj. Then as if reading my mind, he murmured, "I want to marry you and run away somewhere crazy, the Florida Keys maybe. Live in Marathon. I'll be smarter than your husband though, I won't let you out of my sight."

In the bathroom later, cleaning up, he pulled me to him in front of the mirror. We watched each other silently, finally he said, "You're beautiful you know, and so sweet."

Ah, that old honey trap. No, I wasn't so sweet. Wasn't he really just a small-town boy dazzled by an older woman? Was he even aware of what I loved most about him? That centered core of silent intensity, alive with accessible emotion, an intuitive awareness of the world that seemed close to genius. A gravitas that neutralized the differences between us.

I stared at his face in the mirror, then at my own, trying hard to believe him, to see what he saw. Instead all I saw was that black hole of insecurity. An odd thought crept into my skull, could that black hole reflect outward as something positive in a person, a burning charisma drawing people to you? Was that what I saw in Raj, did we share the same adjustment to pain?

"I love you."

"I love you too, Sophie. God, I can't believe how easy that is to say. I told myself I wasn't going to say it but I did it anyway. Chris knows."

At my look of horror, he added, "No. She doesn't really know. But she's wary."

"Are you still sleeping with her?" None of your business, Sophie.

"We hadn't for a while…"

I put my hand over his mouth, couldn't bear to hear the rest. Like oil oozing up out of the earth, jealousy pulsed through me, a black, thick tar that clung to my soul.

Just like Ginger, she knew. I was certain. A soft-spoken man of few words, a man who'd grown up on a farm, tied to the earth in a deceptively simple existence. For all his bashful charm, the impassive face, there were cunning and powerful emotions just beneath the surface. A wife who knew him well would know something was different.

What, if anything, did Nick know? Nothing, nor did he suspect anything. Flashing through my mind was the image of he and Liz waving goodbye to me that first time as I backed out of the garage, intent only on meeting Raj. The thought of telling Nick, of shattering his happy countenance, was unbearable.

Then unbelievably Raj said, "I'll leave her, if you'll leave your husband."

That struck to the very core of my worst nightmare. Impossible. There couldn't even be a discussion of that. "I want to Raj, really, but I'd never know how to tell him, just the thought of it terrifies me."

Again cutting right to the essentials he said, "Someday you'll have to learn to quit being so nice. Do you think he's going to like it any better if he finds out some other way, without your being up front with him?"

I hated lying, hated sneaking around. Altruism may be one of the cornerstones of civilization, but a wide vein of cruelty sits coiled inside as well. I had standards, a code of behavior, not Mother Teresa for sure, but I had a lot of empathy.

Grudgingly I pulled on my jeans, tucking my red T-shirt in, then I sat on the floor, slipping my socks on and buckling my sandals, "You don't understand, there have been things that happened to him in his life, it's not that easy. I've got to go. We'll talk about this later."

"Quit being so analytical about it Sophie. Don't analyze it, just do it."

How seductive having him tell me what to do; the force of his personality drew me in with no hint of danger in succumbing to his will. More than anything, I didn't want to leave the magic, protected circle of his love and have him go back to his wife.

***

Mornings I would awaken and lie still in bed, waiting for my life to fall back into consciousness, for the lurid, strange dreams of the night to abate, and reality return. Each morning the pieces in the puzzle of my life, my secret love, shifted and changed, revealed new pathways being paved in my brain, a new dimension wrought by dreams. Those evanescent, silent sculptors of who we are, as if we go to sleep at night specifically to be reshaped and molded like mysterious pod people.

If we don't wake up in the middle of a dream and recount the details, entrench them in memory, they are will 'o the wisps destined for the cutting room floor.

Then fully awake it seemed as if I'd been rehearsing for this moment all of my life, learning my lines from some off-stage prompter.

The days were as unsettled as my sleep. I would dress for work, dress Liz, make breakfast, devoting only a third of my attention to the tasks at hand.

My husband's cheerful conversations during breakfast, his sense of security that all was right in his world, were a painful indictment. Liz would crawl into my lap while I munched toast and drank black coffee, she'd snuggle next to me, pressing her soft baby skin against my cheek, planting wet kisses on my face. The sheer joy she brought me, the sensuousness of her presence inevitably brought Raj's face to mind, making my heart skip wildly, reminding me how much I loved him.

Like an alcoholic desperate for a cure, each day brought new resolve. Today I must put this madness behind me. I would see Raj as he really was, like any other man, inaccessible to me because of my responsibilities.

But then all of my resolve would fly out the window when I'd see him in the halls at school, walking toward me, a deceptively serious look in his eyes. Then he'd grin his cocky, lopsided grin, I'd remember what it felt like to have his hands on me.

This secret life was killing me. My thoughts echoed loudly through my mind; any louder and they'd be audible. The fluttering beneath my breastbone, the adrenaline swirling through my veins, all made me feel as if I'd been trapped in the "fight or flight" response to danger with the switch stuck in the "on" position. In this constantly heightened emotional state the world came at me in vibrant hued 3-D. Every thought, action, word I heard, scenes I witnessed—yes, thank you even clinical procedures—become electroplated on my brain.

Was this love or madness? Too many excitotoxins—cigarettes, caffeine, alcohol, drugs, MSG, red and yellow dyes, why was I like this? With the current level of stress in my life my cortisol levels must be sky-high. Much higher and I'd be like those people found dead from spontaneous combustion.

Perhaps I had an adrenal tumor?

It made sense that adrenaline was key to memory and that stress would played such a big part; oxidative stress and inflammation were behind many diseases.

Years ago I'd been jogging through Brackenridge Park early on a Sunday morning. There'd been a car parked on the side of the road and as I passed a man leaped out and grabbed me. He picked me up and carried me back to his car. The driver's side door was open and he tried to stuff me in the car. I arched and kicked the roof of the car, gaining leverage and then slipped out of the sweater I'd been wearing. He lost his grip on me and I turned and ran away as fast as I could. If he'd been sober, I might not have escaped so easily.

The point being, forever more in my mind, the park was a very dangerous place to be.

At lunch I sat in my Volvo in the parking garage smoking a Marlboro and drinking a jumbo hot coffee laced liberally with cream and sugar. With the windows rolled down cold air streamed into the car, dispersing the smoke and clearing my head enough to realize that

I'd reached a crisis point.

Because of the twenty-four hour, seven day a week stress of being in medical school, students had access to a staff of adjunct psychologists who held office hours at the Counseling Center every Monday, Wednesday and Friday during the afternoon.

I kept the campus-wide directory in the glove compartment of my car. Squashing out my cigarette in the ashtray, I dug out the directory and flipped through until I found the number for the Counseling Center. How is it that menu options on voice mail are constantly in a state of flux, can't they get it right? The options were hellishly long considering their goal of treating students in crisis; I wanted to smash the phone on the dashboard a thousand times screaming *fuckyoufuckyoufuckyou*.

Finally reaching a human, a perky woman named Molly, I made an appointment with the first available therapist.

Dr. Hitchens had an unfortunately long face with arched eyebrows so far above his eyes that he appeared to be in a constant state of surprise. To make matters worse his nostrils were huge, if he looked heavenward during a downpour he might drown. Prematurely balding and devoid of facial hair, he seemed pale and unfinished like a woman who needed to put on her make-up. His eyes glittered coldly at me.

With only fifty minutes of his time at my disposal, it was necessary to talk fast. The situation required quick results, not years of analysis. There was the obligatory brief sketch of my family, Nick and my previous relationships, mainly the corrosive impact Charlie had on my sexuality and self-esteem.

After several false starts I said, "I gave up a long time ago trying to find Mr. Right, he doesn't exist. I married Nick for all the right reasons: he's a good, responsible, loving man.

"But I'd been on my own so long it was hard to adjust to marriage. I didn't want to give up the male friends I had. And vowing to be faithful in body and soul was like taking a vow of chastity for me. One man for the rest of my life? How unfair that life as you'd known it was over. Why couldn't I adjust, did other people feel the same way?

To begin with, neither of us were strong enough personalities to dominate the relationship. But I found out fast what a bitch I could be, and he just took it without fighting back. I got pregnant and that made things better, we adjusted, were settling in. I was really, really trying to be a good wife."

Suddenly the effort to think and speak at the same time left me breathless so I quit talking, wringing my hands and shredding a tissue.

Hitchens leaned back breathing through those nostrils as big as a horse's, I could picture him neighing and shooting twin streams of frosty air out. Then it seemed as if he was trying to stifle a yawn.

Owen had said he'd never do psychiatry because he hated listening to whiney-assed people tell the same story over and over again. "Boring, boring. It would be only marginally better than being a dentist. Here's an interesting factoid, dentists supposedly have a high rate of suicide."

Bored or not, the doctor suppressed his yawn and carried on.

"There's an inordinate amount of unresolved neurotic conflict here Sophie, conflict that has to do with defenses built up in response to the tensions surrounding your earlier life. They could be significantly reduced with extensive analysis. There had to be compelling reasons from your childhood long before Charlie for you to allow that kind of relationship to develop in the first place."

That conflict word again. Was there a pattern here? Yes, I

had done this before Charlie. It was a trick I'd learned in childhood to keep myself from being bored. It was so astonishingly easy for me to get addicted to sleight of hand with my brain. A kind of autohypnosis that kept me lavishly entertained.

"You're right, I can see that there's a pattern to all this."

"It's impossible for you to recall the genesis of these conflicts without talk therapy, perhaps hypnosis..." Was he that desperate for a narrative to hang his hat on?

He droned on and on until finally he said something that made the visit worthwhile.

"You are only responsible for your own emotions, no one else's. Your husband is an adult and while your situation is regrettable, we all have to deal with whatever hand is dealt to us."

I'd let the burden of Nick's ego rest squarely on my shoulders, where it didn't belong. What a startling insight, how mature and liberating. Nick was a grown man and would have to deal with what life shoved at him, just as I had to deal with it. Speaking of *Atlas Shrugged*, that was an eye-opener.

Great in theory, difficult in practice. Easy to be glib, but to hurt someone that deeply was total anathema. To go against a concept as deeply ingrained as the sanctity of my marriage vows and the need to protect Nick's ego? Impossible. It would be as if a Hindu had suddenly given in to his hunger and sat eating the sacred cow standing in his doorway. Right back where I started from.

Going behind Nick's back was rotten but easier than hurting him. Maybe one more time with Raj and I'd get over this attraction, come to my senses. Acting on strong impulses relieved you of the pressure, returned you to psychological alignment. Selye again, neutralize conflict. Obsessively, the way I used to race through the

"Hail Marys" and "Our Fathers" after confession with Father Martin, I repeated those two words like a litany, "neutralize conflict, neutralize conflict."

Back at school there was a little note stuck in my locker "WHERE ARE YOU?" written in all caps and a zillion question marks trailing after it. As I waited at the elevator, the doors opened and Raj stepped out.

With a sense of calm I hadn't felt in weeks (maybe there was more to the shrink business that I'd given it credit for) I fell into step with Raj, stopping to get a drink of water from the water-fountain.

Wiping my mouth I turned back to him. "I got your note."

"Where've you been?"

"To see a therapist. This is making me crazy."

"You haven't told Nick yet have you?"

"No. I will later."

"When?" There was a hint of anger in his voice, petulance. He had begun to feel a sense of sexual monopoly, expressing jealousy and animosity toward Nick. My confidence in his devotion was high.

"I don't want to ruin Thanksgiving for everyone. It's just two days from now. I'll tell him this weekend.

We made plans to see each other early Friday night, after Thanksgiving.

Then irrationally, unrealistically, confident of his devotion or not, I promised myself to end it with Raj Friday night. Nick trusted me completely; there wouldn't be any reason to tell him, to hurt him. By Friday it would all be over.

Chapter Five

Thursday morning I woke up early, my eyes flying open like one of those bizarre, immobile China dolls. Instantly I picked up the thread of my thoughts from the night before, as if they'd been waiting for me on my pillow while I slept. The up and down of an emotional seesaw: you must tell Nick about Raj, you can't tell Nick about Raj.

It was hard for me to gauge how he might react. Without any sense of boundary or substance, without a subcutaneous layer of moral fiber holding my life together, I thought of myself as invisible, see-through like a pane of glass. How can a stick-figure affect real human flesh and blood? I could not picture a wild, angry scene with Nick. Then what? Something muted and crushing, infinitely more painful.

Slipping silently from bed, with a quick peek in on Liz who was still sound asleep, I padded through the den then across the cold linoleum of the kitchen in my thin nylon slippers, Susie trailing beside me, eager to be let outside. The air was brisk and cold; I joined her on the terrace for a moment, breathing deeply, the crisp air waking me more fully.

Back inside, Susie took her accustomed spot on the cushions on the window seat while I made a pot of coffee. Thankful for the silence, still on my seesaw, obsessing, I set the oven, prepared stuffing, rinsed the turkey, greased the Dutch oven, all the while resentful that I could take no pleasure in these tasks. We were spending the holiday with Angela and Dave McIntosh and I felt no sense of excitement at the prospect.

My eyes were scratchy with the need for more sleep, my mind warped and misshapen as I wrestled with how to tell Nick about Raj. Each thought seemed to elude analysis, sort of the way my father's squab had eluded him once at dinner. Slipping greasily from under his knife and fork, it flew across the table, as if still under its own power, landing on my plate. Would that I could put this problem on someone else's plate. The relief I'd felt from talking to the doctor was short lived. Psychologically fragile at that moment, I could see inside my head, how the gossamer strands of my personality seemed to be unraveling like the hem falling out of a young girl's skirt. The image frightened me, my anxiety mounted. How could I face dinner at Angela and Dave's with my head so full of Raj? An unrelenting pressure seemed to be building; soon I'd explode and end up speaking in tongues of my love.

Hitchens had a point about conflict. Why did I put myself into situations that jeopardized my mental health? How does self-torment with its echoing, intrusive, constant background noise become a permanent state of being? Is it incurable? Does it have a name in the "Diagnostic and Statistical Manual of Mental Disorders" (DSM III)?

There was more to the black hole than just Charlie, it had been with me a lifetime, maybe I'd been born this way. Yes, with each successive psychological burden, a greater stimulus was needed the next time to fill it, then the greater my capacity became. It was a vicious circle, you withstand a lot of psychic pain, but it becomes like a voracious animal, constantly wanting to be fed, expanding its horizons.

Charlie's "seething cauldron" best summed it up; a veritable tsunami of bedeviling thoughts. I travel amid shadowy labyrinths, a flashlight in my hand, hoping to find the broken part, to shine light on it and cauterize the wound.

Oddly, in some ways it ultimately promised better mental health by delineating the structure of personality for me, Socrates' famous quote, "Know thyself." Medical school had been the perfect antidote, a giant puzzle to fill the vaulted chambers of my mind; I prayed I wasn't sacrificing that for Raj.

***

In spite of my misgivings Thanksgiving dinner went well. We provided the cooked turkey and additional wine; Angela and Dave took care of everything else.

Dave McIntosh hailed from Boston, he and Nick had been friends in grad school at UCLA. They'd lost touch when they went their separate ways to do post-doctoral work, pleasantly surprised when they both ended up in San Antonio.

Dave exuded Boston Brahmin ethnocentrism, blunt, distrustful, and suspicious of the slow, friendly pace of the southwest. Easily one of the most outwardly charming men I'd ever met, he had a wickedly funny, sarcastic wit, often at your expense. His black hair, slightly graying at the temples, the straight, aristocratic nose, military bearing, and searing, magnetic blue bedroom eyes made him fatally attractive to women. He'd long since grown used to the power his physical presence exerted and wore the knowledge with a barely concealed hauteur.

Angela was English with milky skin and red hair. Pleasantly plump with soft, rounded curves, she was brisk and forthright and loved to talk. She and Dave had four children, three red-headed, freckled boys, Rusty, Billy and Charlie. The fourth, Miranda, was a fey, eerily beautiful child much like her father.

All the traditional turkey-day food was served on gleaming gold-trimmed, ivory and dark blue Rosenthal china. Dave gave a simple Thanksgiving blessing, then amidst a flurry of dishes passing between hands, of parents admonishing children not to take so much, of nervous voices claiming they were starving, everyone began to eat. Above the din of silverware and the tinkling sound of crystal wineglasses was the spontaneous conversation and laughter of children and toddlers.

Angela threw down her napkin and hurried off to the kitchen. The house was overly warm and her face was flushed when she returned, "Almost forgot the yams, you can never have enough yams, not to mention the nuked marshmallows on top."

Settled at the table again the conversation flowed in a desultory fashion and only become animated when Angela commented on the recent legal imbroglio at Texas Memorial. The parents of a two-year old boy who died during a routine appendectomy had filed a wrongful death suit against the hospital.

I was content to sit and listen, watching Dave and Angela and Nick as they each talked in turn, quarreling about money and lawyers and doctors. Nick's face was red, he'd had too much to drink, his eyes glistening with the alcohol, his demeanor intense, caught up entirely in the conversation. At one point he turned to smile at me, hoping perhaps to draw me more into the conversation.

All too soon dinner was over and the children scattered about the house, then settled in the den, screaming in excitement over their video games. We remained at the table, drinking more wine, then coffee, our faces lit only by the soft illumination of candles, the muted rheostat lighting.

Thanksgiving indeed. I'd made it through dinner without being overcome by gauche behavior, something along the lines of getting drunk or weeping, perhaps confessing my sins in front of everyone.

From the silver coffee pot on the sideboard, I refilled my cup, stopping for a moment to admire once again the excellent reproduction of Paulus Potter's "The Farm" on the wall above me. The original painting hangs in the Hermitage in St. Petersburg, Russia where for some odd reason it is titled "The Urinating Cow." Even with a cow pissing right in the center of it, it is a scene so bucolic and reminiscent of a simpler way of life that it always delights me.

Seated again, I lost myself in a daydream that Vesuvius had poured forth a ton of molten magma, freezing us together forever in these pleasant surroundings. Centuries from now, when archaeologists discovered our perfectly preserved bodies, Raj would only be a hollow echo in the sand that had once been my mind.

***

The windshield wipers moved rhythmically back and forth as we made our way home on nearly empty streets with Liz conked out in the back seat. As we merged onto the freeway the rain suddenly stopped and the wipers made a sound like a squeegee on a window pane. The discordant tune shook me out of my reverie and I came close to telling Nick about Raj. But even with all I'd had to drink, the inhibition against revealing my infidelity was enormous.

Instead I put my hand on Nick's shoulder and gave him a pat, staring at his profile. How was it that he'd suddenly decided to grow a mustache at the same time as Raj? That seemed a little freaky.

We smiled at each other then lapsed back into our own private thoughts. Why was it that we never seemed to connect? We were like the classic physics example of billiard balls bouncing smoothly off of each other but with no point of intersection, Venn diagrams.

It felt as if there were something quite tangible missing from the "us" of us. How could our brains be configured so differently, was he that much smarter than me and thus clearly not accessible?

You'd think that by the time your third year in med school rolled around you'd be way over the one-size-fits-all, cookie-cutter approach to humans. In college I'd met these two brothers from Papeete, Tahiti. They were good kids; Gauguin got it right with their smooth, dusky skin, dark hair and eyes, their blocky bodies.

Humans are constantly putting out feelers for sexual compatibility and I have to say, these handsome guys registered a flat zero on my chart, seemingly totally asexual. They apparently didn't like us that much either since they only lasted one semester before heading back to Papeete.

On his five-year *Beagle* voyage Darwin encountered many native populations. The Fuegians, natives of Tierra del Fuego, convinced him that the evolution of *Homo sapiens* in far-flung remote corners of the world had many divergent paths. I can't say that out loud in public, mainly because a lot of the students here at the school are members of the religious right and completely denounce Darwin. That's how it is in Texas. They are none too keen to speculate with me about the mysterious unseen forces impinging on human behavior. We know a lot more than we used to, but definitely don't have the full picture. Not that I'm trying to let myself off easy for my behavior with Raj.

The world is so complex, you want to be connected, vulnerable, engaged, it's what we're all looking for.

***

All day Friday Nick was on the phone making final arrangements for his trip to New York City in early December. He was really psyched about the three-day seminar at Columbia on new developments in brain research. Eric Kandel was presenting a paper on his most recent research on the *Aplysia* snail and the physiology of memory. Nick really admired the guy and used his "Handbook of Physiology" extensively in the classroom.

More than once as Nick enthused about the man's work, how he was drilling down to the most basic constituents of memory, I longed to go to New York with him. Kandel's goal was to deliver up from the depths of the brain the holy grail of insight: where those memories lie and how they got there. They are laden with chemical code that could foreseeably be unraveled like the double helix of DNA.

And if it were so, if he finally achieved what he hoped for, would there come a day when I could trace back in time the very origin of an impulse that sent my life spiraling out of control? Could I look deeper into Raj's soul?

How far inside another person's mind can you go, how far can empathy go?

If I slipped into Raj's skin could I tell you what he saw and felt? The interior of his mind had so many layers. Most people you meet in everyday situations so often seem as shallow and superficial as the cellophane wrapping around a package of cigarettes. What you see is what you get. Raj, on the other hand, had an alluring depth.

He possessed an odd eccentric mix of small town mentality and the kind of sophistication that curiosity and awareness bestows, he was versatile, malleable, open and willing to experiment; he had a knack for getting immediately to the heart of an idea, avoiding the superfluous. Totally inner-directed, attributing more importance to what he did than what those around him were doing, he was nevertheless unhappy with their settling for mediocrity when he was so impassioned. He was deceptively subdued, quiet, but intense. He got things done.

Yet another layer was earnestly intent on the wellbeing of his children; he possessed an ingrained sense of loyalty. On a baser level, in the blindness of youth, he was not above stealing another man's wife away from him, of deserting his own wife when in the throes of love. He could be jealous, selfish, petty, and relentlessly caught in the grip of his need to prove himself.

But aren't most men like that?

***

Raj and I met early Friday night at the Red Robin off of North Loop 410. Neither of us could stay long and while we drank beer and ate French fries we talked briefly about how our Thanksgiving holiday went.

"The panhandle got dumped with a foot of snow. My step-dad was shoveling snow yesterday morning and started having chest pains. He and my mom spent the holiday in the emergency room. I guess it was nothing.

"My mom was crying so hard when she told me, mostly because she was so relieved. But still, I can't stand the thought of how she'd feel if she lost him too, like my dad."

I felt a pain rise up in my chest at the thought of something similar happening to Raj; losing him would be unbearable. Suddenly I realized that I had no more choices, the decision had been made for me. How stupid of me to have ever thought it was even in my hands. Something previously coiled and inert inside me had come alive at Raj's touch; there was no backing out now. Somehow I would have to find the strength to tell Nick.

"I can tell you haven't told Nick yet. When are you going to accomplish that little chore?"

"I know, I have to, but there's Christmas coming and he has this trip to Manhattan planned. I'll tell him when he gets back, I promise. What about you?"

"That's not a good idea, the longer we put it off, the worse it's gonna be. How about we make it a Saturday night special?"

"You mean tomorrow night? No, I can't..."

"Yes you can. We'll both do it."

He finally talked me into it and afterwards we stood talking in the parking lot next to my Volvo. Twenty feet up the light fixture shook in the wind, the cone of light it shed wobbled and seemed like something alive. We were both shivering but reluctant to leave each other. Raj peered in through the back window and asked about the painting of Charlie on the back seat.

"Nice painting? Who is it?"

"Just a man I knew a long time ago, a good subject for a painting." They'd done a good job at the frame shop I'd taken it to. Between the canvas and the brown wood of the frame was a narrow strip of gold painted wood that brought out Charlie's dark, brooding eyes, the hint of dangerous depths. I was ambivalent as hell about the painting, considering the subject matter. That's probably why I hadn't been able to take it back into the house.

Raj gave me a measuring gaze, sensitive to the neutral tone of my voice.

"Obviously someone important to you?"

"No."

***

Saturday night special, Raj had said. Wasn't that what happened every Saturday night in San Antonio? Jealous lovers and guns; only more often than not the hot-blooded Hispanics used knives. And just two months ago the general counsel for the medical school was at dinner with his wife at Dauphine's on Broadway when something ticked her off and she thrust her steak knife into his chest.

Such an enlightened time we were supposed to be living in why did there seem to be so much more violence? In our second year of med school Owen had thought about writing a thriller. "Do you suppose that the serial killer genre is passé by now? Might I slip one more into the mix before it's completely done in?"

Everyone agreed that the niche would remain wide open so long as *Homo sapiens* dominated the planet.

Declaiming in a jocular manner he said, "We should all screw relentlessly like the peace-loving bonobos and perhaps after a few generations we'd breed true, without the need for violence."

My hour of truth had come. Susie was staring out through one of the panes of glass in the bay window, the breath from her nose forming parallel lines of steam on the cold surface. The dishes were done, Liz asleep, Nick relaxing in the den.

I raised the window in back of me a few inches to expel the cigarette smoke then sat at the kitchen table, my feet propped up on the window seat. Susie turned and licked my toes, then rested her soft warm nose charmingly against my ankle.

Most of our house was hidden by the tiny forest that had grown up around us. The previous owner had been raised in New York City in an apartment on a street where there had been few trees, the ones he saw everyday were choked and stunted by city life. Over a ten year period he'd landscaped the house with nearly forty different kinds of trees, mostly fat evergreens densely packed together, allowing us an unusual sense of privacy and seclusion.

From where I sat there was a slight gap in the foliage through which you could see into our elderly neighbor's living room home. His drapes were open and he sat alone watching television; I felt an ache of sorrow for the loneliness that seemed to envelop him. Last year Roland had called Nick from out of town and asked him to check on his wife Enid, who hadn't answered the phone all day. Retrieving a key from its hiding place beneath a rock in the mulch surrounding the oleanders, Nick had entered the house and found Enid in her bedroom. She'd died of a heart attack while dressing, one stout leg, marred by ropy veins, encased like a fat sausage in Sheer Energy L'Eggs pantyhose.

You could go so quickly, I had to seize this opportunity to be with Raj, didn't I? The knife twisted deeper in my gut as I put Nick in Roland's place, alone and mourning night after night. Would he shrivel up and die when I was gone? No, Nick would not kill himself; I was not indispensable. Christ, who needed such morbid thoughts; things were bad enough already, with or without a Saturday night special.

I inhaled from my cigarette, taking a stream of smoke deeply into my lungs until it hurt, as if trying to fill that black hole inside, to finally be whole again. Would having Raj do that? Was it right to expect another human being to so utterly complete you?

Using my cigarette, I nervously sculpted the ashes in the ashtray into designs, an arabesque, the peace symbol, an arrow. There'd been wine with dinner, and now there was a bottle of Lone Star next to me, none of which offered any comfort as I strained to hear what was playing on the television in the next room.

My heart hammered in my chest, tripping along with alarming palpitations, adrenalin squirting continuously into my bloodstream. My head pounded, blood engorged my cheeks, waves and waves of hot flashes swept over me. I got up, walking reluctantly, as though to an execution. Susie lumbered down off of the cushion, her nails making a "tick-tack, tick-tack" racket as she padded along on the linoleum behind me.

Nick was working on a New York Times crossword puzzle and watching a rerun of Seinfeld on television. He looked up as I came in, smiling at me. All evening long, after every encounter with him, I would tally up his fond words and facial expressions, knowing they were limited, would be gone forever tomorrow.

My tactic was to reveal myself in tiny increments that might be more digestible. Drawing a deep breath for courage, I began.

"Nick, there's something I need to talk to you about." His expression soured. For any given argument we might have, if I started the yelling his tactic was to cede victory to me immediately. He hated criticism and would rather cut me off at the pass before I could hit my stride. Not that I had ever been all that critical, but it made me crazy not to even get my point made. This would be much worse than a wife's nagging.

"Remember when you tried to reach me on my cell phone Thursday? How later, when you asked where I'd been, I said I'd gone to the dentist?" He had a polite expression back on his face now, thinking perhaps this wouldn't be so bad after all. "Well, I lied. I was with Dr. Hitchens at the counseling center. I've been having a lot of problems at work. Problems dealing with how I feel about Raj."

His expression turned quizzical as he tried to fathom who Raj was. "Raj? Not that ugly kid in your class? What do you mean?" He looked genuinely puzzled.

I let the insult pass. "Just that. Sharing so many hours of the day at school with him, we've gotten really close. Too close and oh, God, Nick I don't know what to do, I care an awful lot about him, he feels the same way about me. It's tearing me up inside not being honest with you."

"You've talked to him about it?" Then I could see his mind

shifting gears. The color drained from his face, I wanted to run from the anger I saw in his eyes. "Have you slept with him?"

The way some people can go from placid to murderously hostile in mere seconds has always amazed me. That must be what happened with the general consul's wife, luckily there were no weapons lying around. My own hostility was so well concealed from me it might as well have been in a time capsule, buried far beneath the surface of the earth. As a mediator, an appeaser, you never get angry; you're too busy trying to stop the flow of other people's anger.

I couldn't tell the whole truth, so I lied. "No, I haven't yet, but it's hard not to give in to the temptation. Nick, I know how that sounds, I don't know how else to say all of this. It's just one of those stupid things that happen when two unhappy people..."

"I didn't know you were so unhappy."

Men! God, in my next life let me be a lesbian. Maybe he'd suffered so much from rancorous relationships in his own family growing up that his only defense was to tune out all stimulation, hear nothing but the beat of his own inner drummer.

Thinking back over the past months of agony, I conceded that perhaps too much had been kept inside, again that high threshold for psychic pain. Then I remembered one night last summer, coming home from work, brimming over with excess manic energy and intense frustration mixed with anger, mixed with no sleep, mixed with a crying baby who was getting another ear infection, mixed with the nagging worry that the stress of school would become too much.

I had gone straight out to the back yard and picked up the ax, then split logs until I was too tired to raise my arms.

And when I'd gone back inside Nick and Liz were seated together on the couch. He drank a beer and kept laughing at some absurdly inane sitcom, oblivious to my turmoil.

In a flash I could see the chore ahead of me, of trying to be honest with people, to rip apart the seamless facade of my own defenses, and give voice to all of those emotions locked away. It was like staring up at a blank forty-foot wall, knowing you had to scale it to survive, but unable to find even a tiny hole to grab on to hoist yourself over.

"Actually I wasn't really all that unhappy, not with you, us. I wasn't looking for anything, my life was perfectly fine. Or so I thought, until this situation just overwhelmed me."

Nick nodded but refused to meet my eyes. I could imagine what he was thinking, *Goddamn, you just get a toehold on security, start a family, get away from the rat race of dating, of lousy relationships, and now this.*

My body felt like a pillar of guilt and pain. "Well say something," I pleaded, "We need to talk."

His voice was low, choked with emotion, "What am I supposed to say, 'Goodbye and have a good time?' That's bullshit. You'll do what you have to do."

"I just said, I don't know what to do." How do you explain what you are feeling to someone who appeared not to suffer from the slings and arrows of tormented emotions, someone whose emotional equilibrium seemed always vigilantly maintained, or perhaps, more to the point, so muted and low key as to be below the level of awareness? I had not deliberately choreographed this disaster. To make matters worse the doctor of physiology reached for my pack of cigarettes.

"Nick! No, don't do that, it's been years since you quit."

Ignoring me, he lit up anyway, tossing the Bic lighter on the coffee table in an angry, aggressive way. "It's not worth the effort anymore." With an ironic grin on his face he said, "Some days I still dream about smoking, spending the entire night looking for cigarettes I've misplaced. Now I have an excuse to start again." The grin left his face and he looked sorrowful.

His face was slack and gray, closed to me. "I'm really tired, maybe we should talk about this in the morning, when we're both more alert."

I went to bed, waking up again at midnight. Nick was not beside me. In the den, light from the gooseneck lamp cast a sickly ocher glow over Nick and the couch. There was a half empty bottle of Chivas on the floor next to the couch. An ashtray overflowed with cigarette butts. He was asleep, a cigarette butt in his hand, it had miraculously gone out without burning him awake or falling on the carpet and burning the house down.

I slipped it from his fingers and tossed it in the ashtray, then covered him with the ivory afghan, fretting over how he was going to feel in the morning.

A knife-edged pain arced through me as I thought of his disappointment in me, my disappointment in myself. I struggled not to give into those feelings, knowing how easily they could undermine my resolve to leave.

We didn't talk Sunday. He was hung over. Always enormously disciplined in his routine, in spite of his hangover, Nick jogged for his customary four miles, showered and shaved then dressed in clean jeans and a work-shirt. From there he buried himself behind the Sunday newspaper, with the television on, volume all the way up so God could listen to the pre-game twaddle too. There were distinct signals of, "I want to be alone."

Most of my Sunday was spent tiptoeing around the house,

wringing my hands like a mad Lady Macbeth, not even bothering to get dressed or clean up beyond brushing my teeth and flossing. I tended to Liz as if by rote, thankful she was too young to require explanations.

During the football game Sunday afternoon my cell phone rang. Nick was glued to the game and had not even heard it ring. Two Bloody Marys and a bowl of cashews had restored him to the land of the living and he was as loud and boisterous as ever during the game. Liz was so used to it she had fallen asleep on the couch next to him. I raced to answer the phone, suddenly positive it would be Raj.

"Hey Sophie, it's Raj. Have you told him yet?"

"Yes, it was horrible, as bad as I thought it would be. What about you?"

Unfortunately, he hadn't been as discreet with Chris in the telling. He came right to the point, blurting out to her that we'd been having an affair and that he wanted a divorce so he could be with me.

"What happened?" It hadn't occurred to me before to wonder how he would break the news to Chris. Men are so much ballsier than women; they get straight to the point without equivocating. They don't wring their hands and lament, what to do, what to do? If it's a lethal blow that's needed to kill the monster, they've got the nerves for it.

"There was a lot of arguing and crying and shit, what you'd expect. Listen, I'm at a bar on Somerset watching the football game, Dallas is ahead. Can you come?" The same game Nick was watching.

"No. Are you going back?"

"Of course, all my books and study materials, everything, Christ, my whole life is there."

I heard a noise from the other room, terrified that Nick would come in and catch me on the phone, guessing immediately who I was talking to. "I've got to go, I'll see you tomorrow." I hung up, filled with a deep sense of foreboding.

More coffee, more cigarettes than I needed, I sat at the round oak kitchen table, inanely admiring it, fondly remembering my grandfather Marcus who had given it to me. Susie was just a warm auburn ball asleep on the cushions on the window seat. It felt warm and snug in my kitchen, but I knew I was no longer safe, yet had I ever been? Living with a black hole deep in the center of your being meant that you never felt safe.

I stared balefully out the window, watching the gray winter sky, the leaves blowing wildly across the lawn next door.

Chapter Six

The following Monday at school, just as I sat down in the hospital cafeteria to grab a quick bite for lunch, my cell phone rang. It was Nick, "You'd better come to my office Sophie, there's something we need to talk about."

"Sure, what's wrong?"

"Just come, now."

Something in his voice alarmed me. I snapped shut the cell phone, muttered an apology to Raj, Rebecca and Owen, then hurried away, keenly aware of their eyes following me.

Nick's office was reached through the gross anatomy labs. Stealing myself against the stench of formaldehyde and something else, something putrid as if all the dissected cadavers had pickled the air, I made my way past huge jars of organ specimens. There were bizarre, misshapen embryos and other pale, bloodless organs with ragged edges of floating tissue and membranes that looked like the handiwork of *Jaws*. My black Saucony running shoes squeaked on the cold tile flooring; I shivered, it was always freezing in the labs.

When I walked in to Nick's office he shut the door behind me and stood leaning against it, his eyes closed. "Is it true? All Chris Khan told me?" His voice wavered; he seemed close to tears, shutting his eyes tight to ward them off.

Regaining his self-control, his eyes opened, flashing angrily, "Dammit, Sophie, I didn't even know who Chris Khan was. It took me five minutes just to figure that out. You've already slept with him."

A statement, not a question, his face was so pale and grave; his lips were bloodless like the specimens in the jars. "She said you want to divorce me so you can be with him; I had to hear it from a goddamn stranger. Is it true, the part about divorce?" His voice broke off suddenly.

More than once I'd heard stories about certain fanatic followers of Islam. During Ramadan these overzealous worshippers, their emotions whipped into a frenzy of madness, indulged in self-flagellation, striking themselves with whips embedded with razors. Nick's pain struck me like that now. Cursed, blessed, whatever, that deep strain of tenderness women need for nurturing children burned through me with a white-hot intensity. And the doctor's credo: first, do no harm.

Then anger at Raj welled up inside for the way he had treated Chris coupled with a blazing anger at her for running to my husband. Still other emotions ran counter to those: not everyone minced around like you Sophie, did you think this would be a civilized little minuet then you bow and change partners?

Trembling, I sat down in the cane chair opposite his desk, suddenly overwhelmed by the consequences of my behavior. Stick-figure emerging out of her chrysalis. So tell me, what kind of inept Creator would form a species only half conscious of its behavior, the rest of it submerged in an inky black snake-pit that you had to fish around in blindly, grateful when a few nibbles of insight rippled the surface?

I stared numbly around Nick's cluttered office, at the stacks of medical books and Xeroxed copies of journal articles strewn carelessly here and there; at his impressive, neatly framed diplomas and awards. A Norfolk pine and a dieffenbachia were perched precariously on the narrow windowsill to the left of his desk, beneath them a stack of paper towels soaked up condensation on the inside window where heat from the ducts met the cold windows. On the credenza in back of Nick's desk were snapshots of us in happier times visiting the zoo at

Brackenridge Park.

Nick watched me silently, pain etched across his face. What would it take to make me feel such pain, to feel human, losing Raj? Raj wasn't mine to lose, except spiritually. There was no way I could go through with this. Nick's pain was too much for me. With my mind made up, I went to him, my arms encircling him.

"No, we're not getting divorced. I lied Saturday night because I didn't want to hurt you. But lying is like a nuclear chain reaction, one lie begets another and another, destroying everything around you. I'm so sorry."

His arms went around me in a hopeful gesture. I held him tight, trying to draw out his pain, deflect it away, grounding it in myself.

"If it's going to be this painful for us, I'll give Raj up. We'll work on our marriage; we'll save it. That's what's important, right?"

He wiped moisture from around his eyes, nodding, not trusting his voice.

I glanced at my watch, "Ginger's going to be even more pissed at me than usual if I don't make it up to pediatric oncology in the next sixty seconds. I've gotta go. We'll talk more at home."

Still pale, visibly shaken, Nick made an effort to speak normally, the words thick with stifled emotion, "Sounds good.

***

The new acting chief resident from Johns Hopkins was an expert on recurrent childhood lymphoblastic lymphoma. Ginger shot me a deep frown for missing her initial introductions. I mouthed an apology then picked up the thread of Dr. Luke Walsh's conversation.

"Childhood non-Hodgkin's lymphoma at an early stage has the best cure rate. We know more about this childhood cancer than just about any other with the exception of maybe leukemia. Unfortunately, drug companies have not focused their energies on pediatric cancers."

Raj stood in back of me; I could feel his body heat, could feel his eyes boring a hole in my back. I glanced at the faces of all the other med students around me, listening raptly to Dr. Walsh. Forcing myself to relax, I took a deep breath and sank to that inner spot of equilibrium that usually got me through the crisis points of life; there was a bedrock of sanity in there somewhere, right?

Back downstairs, dumping my books off in my locker, I took out my Moleskin notebook and sat on one of the benches writing, waiting for the place to clear out and for Raj to come.

As soon as I saw him I lost it, hissing at him, "Christ Raj, Chris called Nick and told him everything. He's extremely upset, what did you say to her?" Why couldn't I picture him trying to break his marriage off in a way that would be the least painful to Chris?

His face was earnest, faint smudges of purple were visible under his eyes, as if he hadn't been sleeping well. "It just didn't work out the way we planned. How was I to know she was going to call your husband? We argued about getting a divorce again last night after I got back from watching the football game. Later I went for a walk, when I got back around midnight she was sitting on the couch aiming my .22 rifle at me. She was going to shoot me, rather than let me leave her." He looked nervous and chagrined, a thin sheen of sweat adhered to his face. No wonder he hadn't slept last night.

Did I blame her? In the same position would I roll over and play dead, or fight like hell to keep what was mine? Oh my God, what if she had killed him? Instantly my mind was filled with gory images, mixed in with all those serial killer novels I'd read. People murdered for kicks, for far less than what Raj and I had done. Neither of us had expected such a calamity. We stared at each other, silently measuring our commitment.

Other students arrived, slamming their locker doors loudly, talking and laughing. You learn to communicate without words when circumstances bar intimate conversation. Something first learned with Susie, the appeal in her eyes, so direct, her expression emotional, beguiling, smart, coy, enormously focused to get the message across to me, eerily communicating without words better than some humans do with them. Raj was like that. He found so many ways to convey a veiled meaning in superficial conversation, or just with a certain look. Away from Nick, staring at the face I loved so much, my confidence in being able to put this all behind me wavered. Even now, as intuitive as a woman, he knew that I was faltering.

"Look, I promised Lou I'd help him in the lab tonight. I'll call you afterwards."

"Okay."

***

At home, while I settled Liz in the den with toys and Susie, Nick immediately grabbed a Stella Artois beer from the fridge. His earlier emotional reaction to Chris' phone call had been replaced by anger. "So do you mind telling me how this all happened?" He sat down in one of the armchairs opposite the fireplace, looking around. "And where the hell are all the ashtrays?"

"Nick! The only place in this house I smoke is the kitchen. Otherwise I smoke outside. I don't want Liz breathing second-hand smoke. Besides you quit."

"Give me the goddamn cigarettes."

I turned the ceiling fan on and opened the damper to the fireplace, hoping to deflect some of the smoke away, then settled across from him on the couch, "You want to know what happened?"

He gave me a disgusted look, "Of course I do."

"It's just I can't believe you could even ask that. If you had been paying attention instead of being locked inside your head somewhere, you would have known there was something wrong here long ago."

The look on his face said he didn't understand, "Christ Sophie, after Liz was born, with the way you changed so much from how our marriage was in the beginning, I thought the only way for us to survive was for me to leave you alone."

That was the crux of our problems, his strange willingness to forbear any situation so long as it was not actively disruptive. My marriage was the reverse of the Sleeping Beauty theme. The magical prince didn't want to be awakened.

"You're such an ostrich, Nick. Being a new mom brought my life into much sharper focus. While on maternity leave I had time to think about our relationship, wondering whether we got married too quickly. You were probably still shell-shocked from what Barbara did."

Barbara Thomas was a flight attendant who worked for American Airlines. She and Nick had lived together for two years and planned to marry. Two months before the wedding she ran off with a pilot. Four months later Nick and I were married.

He looked disgusted; you could see his mind working, Typical fucking female mentality to bring up something that bears no relation at all to the current conversation.

"What has she got to do with this?"

"A lot. I was always made to feel, maybe not on purpose, but I felt it all the same, that I was just another interchangeable doll with her, that so long as there was a nice warm body at home, a generous set of mammary glands, anything beyond those superficialities didn't much matter. There were times when I wasn't even sure you could remember to call me by the right name."

"You were never the bitch she was." He spoke with such force that I began to feel better, this was progress, he was making a distinction between the two of us.

"That's kind of a non sequitur. Did my not being such a bitch make it easier for you to slip away to wherever it is you go inside your head? I can't get a grip on you, I can't get inside you, connect with you. Things don't seem to gel with us. Just how bad were things with Barbara? I always had this eerie feeling that you brought the same style of relating with her into this relationship and just superimposed them on me. Now how was that supposed to make me feel?"

"I admit that maybe I haven't paid as much attention to you as I should have, but is that so bad that now I have to face losing you and Liz?"

He had me there, how strong was my commitment? Relationships can be so bizarre. For every subtle verb, subject, noun, for every sensitive turn of phrase you utter that correlates perfectly to the emotions you struggle to express, they often fall on deaf or indifferent ears. Men are trained in the same language but I suspect they speak a slightly different dialect. You don't perceive this right away; it may take years of communicating. So who adapts? Why women of course, it's easier to go from micro to macro, from subtle nuances to big, bold, brash, immediately explicable statements.

Still, I talked and Nick gave a good impression of someone listening. All that had built up over the past five years began to pour out, my voice emboldened as the words tumbled out. Were men just not as psychologically dexterous as women? Did I expect too much to be loved and known in my own right instead of someone lazily, inflexibly allowing the mental image of a woman from a failed love affair to remain fixed in place? My standard of women, by Nick Trudeau.

Later, while I cooked dinner, he stood out on the patio in the cold, smoking and drinking more beer, pacing, thinking in that inimitably intense way of his. Wrestling with everything we'd said, he said, she said. So much could get lost in translation in those types of conversations.

Nick ate little at dinner and immediately afterwards went to bed.

All I could think about was going to bed, of curling up on the new foam and feather mattress cover I'd ordered online for our bed in the hopes that it would help my insomnia.

Little Miss Perverse Liz, who normally was out like a light at eight, didn't drop off to sleep immediately but wanted to keep hopping out of bed, tiny pink nightgown clinging to her slender body as she ran into our room to show me that she was still up, then giggling and running away again. She chased Susie, riding on her back, then yelled at me to chase them.

Trying to keep my fragile composure, desperate for the oblivion of sleep, I grabbed her, "Oh no you don't, come here this instant Liz." It would definitely be an Ambien night.

"No! No!" She giggled and ran off again, leaving Susie in the dust. I caught her, scooping her up in my arms, "Your daddy is very tired and needs to get his sleep, so you have to be a good girl and go to bed too."

Finally, by eight-twenty she was exhausted enough for sleep to snatch her away, leaving me free.

***

I'd left school at noon and fell asleep on the couch in the den, sleeping until five. My on-call shift started that night at seven and I scurried around the kitchen getting dinner ready for Nick and Liz.

They arrived home at six-fifteen, just as I was heading out the door.

Liz frowned at me. "If you're leaving I want to go too."

I picked her up and gave her big hugs and kisses. "No sweetie."

Nick glared at me. "Where are you going? Meeting up with that asshole?"

"No, I told you this morning I'm on-call, you never listen Nick. Anyway, there's some Michelangelo's Lasagna warming in the oven and a salad in the fridge. I probably won't see you guys until sometime tomorrow evening."

He gave me a grudging look, squinting.

"Sorry, you're right; I do vaguely remember it now."

***

The evening flew by allowing me to forget the mess my personal life was in. Work had always offered me a chance to escape from the ruminating that I was prone to. Even as the hours passed furiously by, I only felt more energized, all resistance having ebbed away.

The ER was so backed up with patients—was it a full moon that night?—that Dr. Jaworski shifted me down to there to work. The triage nurses sent me a few patients whose complaints were fairly routine.

One elderly woman I saw had two inflamed sebaceous cysts next to her vagina. "I can't hardly sit down it hurts so much, it must be infected."

After numbing the cysts with two Lidocaine injections I swabbed the vaginal flora onto a slide to be later cultured. Then I made a small incision with a scalpel and squeezed the pus out from the first cyst, there was quite a bit of cheesy looking gunk. Without cutting very deeply I excised the other cyst; it came away cleanly and I dropped it into a specimen jar. That one needed two tiny stitches.

Her name was Ida Fowler and at that moment her face was puckered up in pain, her wrinkles pulled so taut that she looked like a dried up prune.

"You okay?"

"Yeah, I'm fine. The internet said that you could get a staph infection from these things. What about that flesh-eating bacteria I've been reading about?"

"No way. You'll be on antibiotics for ten days, plus you need to take Betadine sitz baths at least three times a day. Your regular doctor can take the stitches out."

At two in the morning I went up the ICU to check on Dorothy Hammond, a woman who'd been admitted earlier that evening with severe hyponatremia.

The notes in her chart were enough to get my heart racing. Her sodium level had gone down to 115. It may not seem like a big difference but sodium levels have a very narrow range in which they can fluctuate, the normal is 135-145. The emergency room physician had written "Why isn't this patient in a coma?"

I read further. She told the ER doctor that a few weeks back she'd had a pretty bad kidney infection and started wetting the bed at night. This continued to happen even after the infection cleared up. Her doctor prescribed DDAVP Nasal Spray which is a type of synthetic vasopressin given to young children with enuresis (bed wetting). Within twenty-four hours after starting the medication she was so sick she could hardly stand up. Her husband brought her to the ER.

A second blood sample was drawn to confirm the dangerously low sodium level. The ER doctor, Cody Brown, had the on-call ICU doctor examine her as well. Discounting the DDAVP, they then consulted with Dr. Donald Hall, a nephrologist. Diagnosis: self-induced hyponatremia by drinking too much water, thereby diluting her serum sodium. Recommended treatment: Saline solution at no more than 0.33mmol per hour and potassium supplement for muscle cramping.

The ICU nurse in charge of Mrs. Hammond was busy with other patients. Dorothy was awake while I examined her, the words from her chart ringing through my mind. *What was so different about this patient that she had been lucid instead of in a coma, which with a 115 sodium level would almost certainly have been the case?*

She complained of spasms in her abdomen and that she couldn't sleep. "I'll see if we can give you something." Stepping into the hall I called the on-call ICU doctor, giving him a status report.

Stifling a yawn, he mumbled, "She can't sleep? Neither can I. Give her a Phenergan suppository."

After that I crashed in the bottom bunk of the on-call room managing to get almost three hours of sleep. Fortified with stale coffee that tasted like Turkish mud, I grabbed a quick bite to eat in the cafeteria and then was off to the clinic to see patients by 7:00 a.m.

By eight-thirty that night, finished with my shift, racing out of the hospital, I remembered Dorothy Hammond. My curiosity got the better of me and I ran up the steps to the ICU on the fourth floor.

The room was empty. I looked around confused, thinking I had the wrong room. At the nurses' station I asked where she'd been moved to.

Dolly Rosen, the day nurse, was nice enough, and by all accounts a good nurse, but she was at least seventy pounds overweight. She wore a short black wig that made her white skin vampire pale.

"I'm sorry, Mrs. Hammond didn't make it. After lunch she went into cardiac arrest. Dr. Ito and the crash cart team did everything they could but it was just too massive a heart attack. She also had CPM with severe neurological damage."

Central pontine myelinolysis. The worst case scenario with hyponatremia. She was only forty-nine.

"Will there be an autopsy?"

"Um, don't think so." Her fingers flew across the keyboard of her computer. She peered at the screen. "Looks like someone from Wallenstein Funeral Home picked her up around six."

***

Nick was still up when I got home, probably ready for one more round of tearing our marriage apart bit by bit to find where it had gone so wrong. Liz was in bed.

Susie hopped off the couch where she'd been sitting with Nick, wagging her tail, face all soft. I kissed her and rubbed her tummy stealing glances at my husband, trying to measure his mood.

"Care for a glass of wine?"

"After the shift from hell, yeah, I'd love one."

We had a couple glasses of wine while I told him about Mrs. Hammond. He listened intently always interested in my experiences with patients, asking all the right questions and agreeing with me that there should have been an autopsy. Then around midnight he went to bed.

I had just finished brushing my teeth and washing my face, when I heard my cell phone chirping in the kitchen. It was Raj.

"Are you alone, can you talk?"

"Yeah, what's up?"

"Chris is at the store, she'll be right back so I don't have much time. Please don't back out on me now Sophie. I know you, I know you're staying for Nick, but that's not the right thing to do. I love you and want to be with you."

"Raj I love you too and I want to leave, really, but I didn't know it would be this hard. Nick told me tonight that he invited his parents for Christmas. Am I supposed to be Scrooge and ruin everyone's Christmas?"

"You can't go on being so fucking nice, not to mention indecisive! You said yourself it's tearing you apart inside; you've been to see one therapist. Promise me, you'll give it more thought."

"I don't know, I don't know, I can't think clearly."

"Think about this. When I got home tonight Chris told me she also called Dr. Cardiff."

"Oh Jesus, the dean of the medical school? Why would she call him?"

Raj took a deep breath and then exhaled slowly, I could picture his face so clearly, the deep lines of frustration.

"Because she wanted to know what went on at the med school that something like this could happen. They can't kick us out over this can they?"

"Shit no, but still, the dean? My god, that's so embarrassing."

This was going to escalate into something neither of us could handle.

***

I wandered half-awake into the kitchen surprised to find that the table was set and a fresh pot of coffee in the Krups machine perfumed the morning air. On the stove was a pan filled with scrambled eggs next to a platter of buttered toast and bacon. Susie sat on one of the chairs at the oak table; ears back, warm brown eyes alight with the prospect of bacon. I gave Nick a hug, his hair was still slick from his shower; the scent of Paco Rabane cologne clung to him. "What's up with the lavish spread? You're sure energized this morning."

"Guess I mostly drank my dinner last night, waiting for you t0 get home. I woke up starving. Let me get you a plate."

"Thanks."

With coffee in hand, I sat down at the table. It occurred to me that there was a certain ease to living with someone with whom your emotions were not always at a feverish pitch. There were no brooding head games, the kind of dysfunction that can arise from the sexual tension between men and women. Still, you miss the pull of that tension when it's what you've been accustomed to before.

Liz appeared in the doorway to the kitchen, squinting in the bright light reflected off of the sunny yellow walls. Her hair was matted into knots where she'd slept on it, that white blonde hair, fine as silk. "Good morning sweetheart."

She smiled sleepily at me then laid on the floor next to my chair, resting her head on her fuzzy bunny, thumb in her mouth.

Nick joined me at the table, and then as if he'd been preparing this speech while he cooked breakfast, he began, "I know what we have to do to work this out. It came to me this morning while I was shaving. I want you to move out; we'll find you and Liz an apartment nearby. You'll need help with rent of course, and with Liz, I'll keep her this weekend, while you move, say until Sunday afternoon. It's the only way you can work this out, by yourself without any pressure from me." He refilled our coffee cups. Liz had climbed up in the chair next to Susie and was feeding her strips of bacon.

Pausing to gather his thoughts, Nick took my hand, "I love you Sophie and I want to stay married to you. But you have to be free to choose, free to find out how wrong Raj is for you."

Was that what had returned him to emotional balance, his conviction that Raj was so totally unsuitable for me, that once I was free to find that out, I'd inevitably choose to stay with him? That dense mass of emotions coiled inside, the core of my love for Raj, had taken on a life of its own and was beyond my control. Still, it wouldn't do to shatter Nick's hopes for our marriage.

The tension began to ease out of me as Nick went on with his sensible plan. "You'll have to miss morning rounds, I know you hate to do that, but you need to get organized, call around to a few apartment complexes. I'll take Liz to Nancy's."

Cringing inside, I told Nick about Chris Khan calling the dean of the medical school. "Don't be surprised if there's fallout from that, the rumor mill and all."

"I already knew. The resourceful Mrs. Khan called again yesterday to tell that she was going to call Cardiff. I couldn't talk her out it. By now I'm sure even Rosten knows." Walt Rosten was Nick's boss.

***

The morning had been productive. Out by nine-thirty I'd already located an apartment and signed a lease; I could move in Saturday. My second-floor apartment was in a relatively new complex with lots of trees, mimosa, weeping willow, magnolias and a few Italian cypresses. A small balcony off of the living room looked out on a park and playground. The bright green lawn stretched all the way to the next housing development, at least two football fields away.

Not having to tell anymore lies, with everything out in the open, I felt a huge sense of relief.

Back at home, dressed only in a pajama top and my oldest, most comfortable jeans, I packed a few boxes, and made a list of the most essential pieces of furniture to take. Nick and I had used Martinez and Sons Moving Co. in the past, pleased with their work. When I called, they agreed to move my stuff Saturday morning.

Around noon the doorbell rang. I stood on tiptoe and peeked through the little fish-eye in the front door, surprised to see Raj standing there. Jerking the door open, I moved nervously toward him on the porch. Roland was backing his Jeep Cherokee down his driveway; he braked and peered at us through the window on the passenger side. I waved at him, calling out a greeting, trying to infuse a sense of ease and nonchalance to this encounter with Raj, while inside I felt like Balcones Fault: two land masses scraping against each other in counter motion.

"Raj, what are you doing here? Nick could come home any second." If not that then Roland would undoubtedly tell Nick I'd had company.

Without a word he steered me back into the house, out of the foyer, then into the den where earlier I had built a fire.

As he surveyed the room my eyes followed his, seeing it all through his eyes, the plush contours of the new sectional green couch, admiring the way it perfectly offset the two beige arm chairs opposite. Bookcases, stuffed with books and knick-knacks, flanked either side of the fireplace.

"This is nice, really nice, just what I'd expect with you being a doctor's wife and all, not to mention how soon you'll be one too."

Surprised, seeing a side of him I hadn't seen before, I said, "He's not a medical doctor, just a Ph.D."

He spoke softly, the tone so ironic it was almost menacing, "Just a Ph.D., how modest. Yeah, I knew that. We couldn't live like this, poor medical student with student loans out the wazoo." His eyes glinted brightly at me in a manic, sexual way. What was this insecurity leading to? What sort of expectations did he have of me? That I was the solution to a problem he had not yet fully articulated either?

He was nosy, curious, moving through the house, peeking in rooms, looking at my home as if it held a key to me, defined me for him, explained why two such widely separated people--separated by age, by experience, by class--should become so linked.

In a baiting, almost sarcastic way, he said, "Must be love, huh? To give up so much?" He came toward me and it was obvious then what was going through his head.

"Raj we can't. Not here. Nick could come in any second to check on me." He grabbed me by the arms and kissed me. He was so broad and muscular; I was obviously no match.

When I pulled away from him, he grinned, coming after me again. Firmly, I said, "No, we can't do this, not here. I don't mind meeting you somewhere else." The fault line inside slipped a little further, tension mounting, but the slightest touch from him and I lost all resistance. Ever protective Susie chased after us, constantly at my side, ready to protect me, barking at him when he seemed threatening.

He grabbed me then, twisting my hands behind my back, holding them with one hand, while with the other he undid the top three buttons of my white flannel pajama top. He kissed my neck, then with his mouth and tongue traced a scalding pattern across my chest, moving further down to my breast, his tongue working my nipple. I could feel his erection pressing against me.

He undid my jeans, pulling them halfway down, his fingers exploring, then finally inside me, twirling and probing insistently, then outside again touching me so gently, pummeling my flesh, then harder and harder until I gasped, crying out for him.

At some level I was so used to brute male-domination, Charlie's defining behavior for me, that having been deprived of it, to find it again was like an aphrodisiac making me dizzy with lust.

"Hold still," he commanded in a tense whisper, as if mistaking my movement for trying to escape his embrace. Then he sought out my mouth again, his tongue invading me hotly. He undid his jeans, moving us in one fluid motion onto the couch in front of the fire. Susie, my wonderful watchdog, ambled over, sniffing us intimately, a tentative lick to Raj's bare ass, but we ignored her and she settled on the carpet next to the couch.

He was inside me moving deeper and deeper, taking possession of me like some mad incubus, the words of love he whispered tensely against my ear emptied my mind of concern, fused and focused me on him, with him. I forgot myself, could not figure out where I left off and he began.

Later, as we rested, he leaned against the back of the couch, his face red, bright eyes watching me. There were several black hairs on my white pajama top, telltale evidence. Raj noticed them first, "See what you do to me, I'm already starting to lose my hair."

"Too much androgen and testosterone, makes you more virile." He grinned, but was obviously not placated for the loss of more hair. I brushed the hair away from his forehead, wondering about this new mystery to him: that he took such wild chances and so willfully tempted fate; that he was emotional and undisciplined sexually. His desire would build and overpower him, nothing for it but to seek release, then go on again, normal, able to work, to think, until the next time.

"It's torture having you right there next to me at school sometimes, but it's torture not having you there also, when you didn't show up today it made me crazy. I was sure Nick had talked you out of leaving." His voice was so low, with such a deeply sexual timbre to it, at the sound of it the muscles of my vagina contracted around him, that smooth, slippery passage moistening again. He smiled in response to the movement, then went on, "Sometimes when we're in the midst of all those people, I want to reach across that short space between us and touch you, like this," he put his hand on my breast, caressing me gently.

"It's having to deny myself that makes finally being able to fuck that much greater. A game I play to see how strong I can be, how disciplined. Then I do something stupid like this."

"I love you anyway."

"I love you too."

When Susie sat up and looked toward the foyer, a lance of fear knifed through me. Her ears went back, the look in her eyes sharpened, a low questioning sound, half groan, half bark, escaped from her. I was sure Nick was home.

"Relax, will you? No one's here, quit being so nervous."

***

By late Saturday afternoon I'd moved into the new apartment, arranging furniture and unpacking boxes. Raj called inviting me over, Chris had gone to stay with a friend in New Braunfels and wouldn't be back until the next day.

Tangled strings of Christmas lights crisscrossed the floor, Raj was patiently untwining them; occasionally sipping from a Lone Star while I watched. Organizing everything for Christmas seemed an oddly domestic, settled occupation for someone preparing to move out.

Jane crawled across the carpet, hurrying toward the lights, eager to investigate this new toy. When she reached them she grabbed a set and stood up, her diaper drooping, showing the cleft in her bottom, "No Jane, take that out of your mouth. Sophie, catch her and put her in the playpen, all I need is for her to swallow a bulb."

As I sat back down on the couch, he asked, "So tell me again how much you had to pay in rent today?"

"Too much, over eight-hundred dollars, but I wanted a fireplace."

"You should've moved into an apartment here, it's cheaper and with fireplaces." He plugged in a set of lights, all of them in good working order, greens, reds, oranges, and blues blinking at us.

"Yeah, right next door to you."

Talking about money was awkward. Money had never meant that much to me so long as the basic necessities were taken care of. Was I being unrealistic? Being a single parent with a year and half left of medical school was not going to be easy.

"So do you like your new place?"

Yes. It's great. Now what about you?" I wanted to be as persistent as he had been with me about moving out but couldn't find the right words to say.

"I told you, I'm going to see a lawyer on Monday, I'll work on moving out then."

"Right."

Feeling uneasy—this was all a little too vague for me--I fell silent, staring at the large painting over the fireplace. Framed with black carved wood, it was a scene of a deer in the forest, painted with an almost impressionistic style.

Following my glance he said, "I painted that my senior year in high school."

"You're kidding." It didn't take a degree in art to recognize talent.

"No. I really painted it."

"Wow, it's good, you never said anything about being an artist."

"It just never came up." He flashed his cocky grin at me. "Too many more important things to talk about."

Why was I so surprised? Because he'd grown up on a farm? I had halfway expected the illusion, the myth of working class hero to be shattered when I examined his life more closely. So if a close examination of his life could shatter my feelings, what basically wrong and nebulous assumptions was I making about love and relationships that could allow so much conflict and turmoil in my life? That was too terrifying a prospect to look at very deeply. Did Raj and I just prey on each other's personality weaknesses?

But closer inspection preserved the illusion; there was dignity even with working class heroes. Nosing around his apartment while he worked with the Christmas lights, I noticed that everything was clean and orderly and comfortable. He and Chris's taste in furniture and how it was arranged, the adornments one uses to make a dwelling a home-- none of it was kitschy, the kind of plastic junk that made my skin itch and crawl. There were a lot of books around, mostly library books.

"Who reads so much?"

"Chris, she reads at least three books a week," Raj explained, a note of pride creeping into his voice, "She's really intelligent, has a high IQ."

***

The lights were out, Raj was in the bathroom, I stood in the doorway to the twins' bedroom, watching them. Jane was asleep; Jennifer stood up in bed and held her arms out to me. She was wet. I changed her diaper and then held her close, inhaling her sweet baby-powder aroma as she gripped my long hair in her tiny strong fingers. Her eyes grew drowsy rolling back the way Liz's did when she was ready to fall asleep. It was easy to love these two duplicates of Raj. Tenderly, I laid Jennifer down then kissed two fingers and touched them to her nose. She was asleep.

Why couldn't Raj and I just leap past the pain of what we were doing, leap to the other side, to a time when we were married, where life had returned to normal? If I let my mind wander, become diffuse, stretching the limits of my ability to probe into the fabric of the future, my intuition did not show a happy ending.

"Want another beer?" He called from the kitchen.

"Sure." Seated on the couch, I stabbed my cigarette out in a brown ceramic ashtray, still unable to relax, to feel like anything other than an interloper in this apartment.

Raj walked toward me from the kitchen. As I reached for the beer from him, he stopped just short of giving it to me, his attention riveted on something seen through the window in back of me. Seconds ticked by, the moment stretched out before me, was caught in some weird time warp as a web of tension seemed to draw us into its field, a shiver ran down my spine.

Chris had pulled up in their Toyota and parked in front of the apartment, was hurrying toward the front door. Raj's voice was tense, "Here, take this. Christ, she wasn't supposed to be home until tomorrow."

Jumping up in surprise, my beer toppled over into the ashtray, cigarette butts swimming atop the foaming liquid. Oh, Jesus, Jesus, now I was really caught, no back door, no place to run, no longer an innocent bystander in life.

She was shaking with rage when she burst into the living room, throwing her purse on the table. Her face was deathly pale, eyes darting around wildly.

It flashed through my mind that when you are overweight and unfulfilled and find out that your husband is cheating on you, that he wants a divorce, it must nearly destroy you. Like a rat in a trap, there you are stuck with two babies, without a job to support yourself--can life be any crueler, any more unfair? What do you do? How does it feel when your whole life is threatened like that?

The insight was harrowing, made my juggling neurotic conflicts seem tame by comparison. No wonder I had made it to my thirties without ever being real to myself.

Her murderous rage frightened me; Raj had mentioned a .22 rifle. God, how stupid we were, where was it, did she have it? My earlier inventory had not revealed anything.

Chris moved threateningly toward me, screaming, "I thought this would happen. How dare you come into my house, you whore! Is this the latest trick for you, stealing husbands?"

Her words struck me like acid, how could I have caused another person so much pain?

We were separated by the dining room table. Idly, I noticed that it was a nice one, Ethan Allen, nicer than mine. Gripping the side of it, I began edging my way around, hoping she would follow, allowing me access to the front door to escape. She followed me around the table as if she couldn't wait to get her hands on me.

"What kind of shitty plan did you use for luring him away from his family? Chase him around the cadavers in the gross anatomy lab?"

She faced Raj who seemed to have turned to stone, silent as the dead. Was this how family arguments went, was he a wimp to her greater wrath? Was he embarrassed by her outburst? Like so many men, did he shy away from confrontation? Or did her wrath invoke his sense of fair play: he was scum too, with no defense except to remain silent. Would I ever discover what was behind the silent gravity of those black, black eyes?

"Jesus, Raj couldn't you have taken this whore somewhere else besides to your own home. Then to show her off in front of my babies?" One still unaffected part of me wanted to affirm Raj's high opinion of her intelligence, even knowing how often high IQs and instability went hand in hand. Beneath the excess weight she was a pretty, potentially exciting woman.

She came closer to me, "Yeah, I see you now, flirting with him at school. He used to always say how nice you were. I should have seen it coming. Well, bitch, you may be pretty now, but he's nine years younger than you are and one day he's going to wake up and you're going to be old." She screamed at me, "Old. An old hag!"

I stood still as a rock. Her words cut through to the very heart of my worst fears. When youth is gone, how do you hold someone to you who won't go through that loss for years, won't you always be out of step with each other? Raj had been seduced by an illusion too.

Suddenly she grabbed up her purse off of the table. "I'm going over to the Shell station across the street. In ten minutes I want you both out of here. I'll be watching." She left.

Quickly, Raj grabbed a few things from the bedroom, then we hurried out to the Volvo, driving in stunned silence back to my new apartment.

Boxes abandoned halfway through unpacking, every free surface covered with bric-a-brac, my apartment was not exactly a "clean, well-lighted place." We dragged the mattress out of my bedroom and pulled it into the living room, dropping it in front of the fireplace. Raj made a fire while I spread fresh sheets and placed a lavender satin comforter over the top. My mother-in-law chose that inopportune moment to call, wanting to know what she could do to help Nick and me through whatever problems we were having in our marriage.

"When Paul and I were your age facing problems, we just worked through these kinds of disagreements."

Right, and the world was a lot different then. I could hardly be civil, even though as mothers-in-law went she was pretty decent.

"If things got really bad we could always depend on the pastor of our church to counsel us, to help out. Maybe that's the kind of help you need now." She droned on in this vein; while listening to her talk, I watched Raj roll a joint. He licked the sticky edge of the Zig-Zag paper then sealed it tightly. "Want some?" he whispered.

I nodded, depressed and greedy for oblivion. "Jean, I have to go. We'll talk later." Without waiting for a reply I hung up.

With two Buds from the fridge, Raj and I laid on our stomachs on the mattress facing the fire, listening to music from the radio. My eyes scanned the mess surrounding us; I had a high threshold for exterior disorder, but what about Raj? Obviously, if what he had been after was improving his situation that had not been accomplished.

"Sukiyaki" an old, old song I'd only heard a few times was playing on the radio. Even though the Japanese lyrics were incomprehensible, the yearning, plaintive emotion in the man's voice struck an odd, searing note in my soul.

Raj finished his beer and crushed the aluminum in his fist. He threw it at the fireplace where it clinked loudly against the red brick hearth, knocking me out of my reverie as it landed on the carpet.

Closer inspection indeed. Here it comes, now that we've wrecked two lives just so we could selfishly have what we want, it will become obvious that anyone who's sleazy and uncouth enough to throw beer cans around my living room isn't good enough for me. A low, but honest, thought. Familiarity breeds contempt.

The soft light from the crackling fire flickered across Raj's glasses, casting dancing shadows across his face. He was lost somewhere in thought, a heavy, closed presence, examining what we were doing, wondering if it would be worth the hassle. He was young, inexperienced, naive, easily caught up in his passions, did that make

Chris right? Was I more responsible for luring Raj from his family? The idea of being too old kept nagging at me, this was a relationship I would never be easy in, Raj was too exciting, too mercurial, without as much at stake emotionally. He had the regenerative powers of youth, while it was my misfortune to fall in love for the last time with a man so much younger.

My lungs felt char-broiled from the synergistic effects of beer, marijuana and tobacco. In the sterile new bathroom, I brushed my teeth and washed my face, then returned to Raj, climbing under the cool sheets, letting them draw off my confusion, clear my mind. I wiggled my toes, snuggling into the softness, watching Raj who stared moodily at the fire.

Just as I was about to break the silence, he stood up and without a word, closed the doors to the fireplace, disappearing down the hall, into the bathroom. In my self-centeredness I imagined that his thoughts and his allegiance were with me. In truth, he was only now dealing with the wrenching reality of losing his family, the integral thread of his life.

When he returned, slipping naked into bed beside me, we lay next to each other silently until he gently pulled me to him. We made love slowly in the dark; his body stirred an aching sense of longing in me. My heart and every secret within were laid bare for him to see.

What secrets will you hold from me Raj?

Chapter Seven

Sunday morning I awakened early, sun streaming into the unfamiliar room through the white curtains, bathing the jumbled mess of boxes with a sweet, benign glow, outlining the subtle, almost imperceptible animation of dust motes in the air. Where was I? For one wild moment I missed terribly the order of the house I had shared with Nick. From the neatly trimmed lawn to the dark shutters framing each window, it had satisfied my need for clean lines; as Samuel Butler put it, "for the intrinsic comfort of tidiness."

Easy come, easy go. From there to this tiny four-room apartment, decorated with my oil paintings. Without much furniture, the paintings gave the apartment the look of an art gallery.

Despite the early hour, it was hot, I'd thrown the lavender comforter off, lying naked on my side, the sun at my back, warming me. Just below my waist, in the center of my back is a large mole, Raj's fingers were lightly touching it, coming back to it, examining it. Lulled by his soft touch, sleep overcame me again.

Nick called early. Invited to brunch with a colleague, he wanted to drop Liz off first. Raj hurried to finish his breakfast, eager to escape, happy when I suggested he borrow my Volvo to preview cars advertised in that morning's newspaper.

Twenty minutes later Nick and Liz were at my doorstep. "Mommy!" Liz fell forward away from Nick's grip on her, arms outstretched to me.

Taking her into my arms, I kissed her, "How's my sweetheart, did you miss me?"

She nodded, "Uh huh, but Daddy and Susie and I had fun!"

"Good." She squirmed to get down and then went running off into the apartment.

Nick was dressed in a new black turtleneck sweater and brown leather jacket. His eyes seemed a darker blue, bright and piercing. "You look great, going someplace special for brunch?"

"Thanks. Just to The Omelet House on Hildebrand with Guy Dalton. He's still giving me grief over my graphs for the article." His glance became provocative as he stood appraising me in turn. It felt odd having him look at me like that. "You look good too." An uncomfortable silence followed as we stared at each other.

Liz and Nick were my family, it wasn't going to be easy walking away from them. In trying to escape it, my marriage seemed to have settled around me with a greater substance and reality than it had previously possessed. My eyes were drawn back to Nick's, to the pain just beneath the surface, forcing me to confront my failure to love him. I should have tried harder.

How could I though, when what I wanted, needed, was a force to rail against, to dance attendance upon in ever widening circles of despair, someone whose need to abuse, matched my need for abuse. The thought made me hot for Raj.

The noise of traffic from Loop 410 seemed louder in the Sunday morning silence, the speed of the cars shooting by made my brain speed up; tiny bits of dust were hurled at us, a cold breeze opened the hem of my robe, revealing my bare legs underneath. Looking away from me Nick said, "Well, I shouldn't keep you standing out here in the cold. By the way, Liz didn't sleep too well last night, she was restless, might be getting sick again."

"God, I hope it's not another ear infection."

"Tell me about it." He smiled ruefully, looked like he wanted to kiss me good-bye, thought better of it and left.

In the kitchen, I snatched Liz away from a box of canned goods she was unpacking, "Let me help!"

"Yes, you want to help Mommy, but Mommy wants to give you a bath." After undressing her, I made funny smacking noises on her cheek, then her neck; then puckering up my mouth continued with loud smacking noises on her tummy, like so many farting pigs. She giggled helplessly for a minute, and then slipped away from me running naked to the bathroom.

Settled in the tub, warm water sloshing all around her, Liz's attention was drawn by a bright green wind-up frog that plowed slowly across the surface of the water. It stopped and sank, she grabbed at it, wound it up again, giggling, following in its wake with her hand, making sputtering, motorboat sounds with her mouth.

Rubbing soap into a thin washcloth, I gently cleaned around her nose, which was red and running again. Another cold meant another ear infection, meant that intense guilt trip every time I stepped out the door to go to school; every time I left her at Nancy's.

Dressed in a sunny yellow sleeper, she was just swallowing a teaspoon of decongestant when I heard a knock on the door. "Daddy! Susie!"

"No Liz, not Daddy, sorry honey, I don't know who it is, probably Raj."

Raj came in through the back door, a swirl of cold air following him. He came down the short hall, emerging out of dark shadows, his face a mask I couldn't read. My cell phone rang just as he was shrugging out of his sheepskin coat, hanging it on the back of a chair. It was Angela McIntosh.

While she chattered on and on about how impossible it was for her to believe that Nick and I were separated, I stared around the room, suddenly seeing it through her eyes. Stacks of crushed, empty beer cans by the fireplace, the unmade mattress with the lavender satin comforter heaped in disarray. I could almost imagine the delicate sniff she would give the air around us. Obviously, she would find the whole place disgustingly redolent of illicit sex. I grinned lecherously at Raj.

The intensity of Angela's disapproval was palpable, slamming into me. I held the phone away from my head as her voice rose, Raj moved next to me, leaning his ear close to the receiver, as Angela hissed, "Don't be so selfish Sophie, there's more than just you involved here. You must think of Liz first."

Raj laughed, then said into the phone, "Sophie's got to go now, bye!" He slammed the cell phone shut. "What an uptight bitch. Where'd you dig her up?" His black eyes were intense with righteous anger. He turned to me and they softened a little, his humor returning, "Let me guess. She called to plead Nick's case. That you should go back to him."

"Right."

"Predictable."

So who would have suspected Angela of being such a busybody? Without knowing any of the details, she had automatically sided with Nick. I hated that kind of narrow-mindedness. She would never suffer the dissonance of conflict because she did not have the versatility to do so. No growth without friction.

Aware suddenly that my attention was elsewhere, Raj stood silently in the living room next to the beer cans and mattress. Sensing that he felt ill at ease, that like me he was finding it more difficult than expected to leave his old life, I put Angela out of my mind. We couldn't fuck all the time, but what else could we do with each other?

He wore jeans and work boots, a red-plaid wool shirt, his white T-shirt visible at the throat where black hair curled on the fabric. That handsome, so young face, the full mouth, his lower lip slightly red as he chewed it nervously, my hand reached out involuntarily to touch him. He was too far away.

As we watched each other across the room, I could tease the truth out of that jumble of emotions inside, that finding him, loving him, left me as much a hostage to fate as did being a parent to a vulnerable child.

"So nothing interesting with the cars?"

"Nah, I'll look more next week, right now I've got lots of reading to catch up on." He grabbed his black nylon backpack and rustled through it, bringing out his laptop. Liz was on the couch, laying on her side, drinking Citrus Punch Gatorade, watching a DVD of "Snow White and the Seven Dwarfs," her eyes glassy. Raj sat down next to her, giving her a goofy grin.

It was awkward for me with the mix of Liz and Raj, like trying to patch together a broken glass with pieces from a ceramic vase and pieces from a wine bottle, they didn't match. I thought of Jennifer from the night before, the way her arms reached out for me. The twins would be easy to love; they looked so much like Raj. Would the same be true for Raj and Liz?

"I'm going to get cleaned up."

Absently, reading the screen in front of him, Raj mumbled, "You do that."

In the bathroom, I looked in the mirror, taking stock. The effects of my dissipate life were beginning to show on my face, light purple smudges under my eyes, the definite emergence of tiny crow's feet at the corner of each eye. A little Nivea rubbed into the skin beneath my eyelids et voila, the wrinkles disappeared. For now.

As I climbed into the shower, relaxing under the hot, heavy spray of water, Chris' face appeared in my mind, her shouted words echoing through my brain. So I was to be a hag? Well, we'd see about that, there was hagdom and then there was hagdom. I was still young enough to believe in somehow escaping the tedious realities of aging.

***

The only other furniture in the living room besides the couch and mattress was a heavy Ethan Allen rocking chair. I sat in it, dressed in a virginal ivory cotton and lace dressing gown. Liz was in my lap; she hadn't touched her lunch, so I gave her a Sippy cup of warm milk. Tweaking her little button nose softly, she rewarded me with a wide grin. Her forehead felt warm to the touch.

Inwardly I groaned, another trip to the doctor, more time away from school. The Christmas break couldn't get here soon enough, I would spend the entire time with Liz, making up for the sorry ass parent I'd been these past few weeks. Her eyes rolled back in her head as she fought sleep, trying to stay awake long enough to finish the milk. But it was no good, she couldn't fight it any longer, with a tiny, barely audible intake of breath her eyes closed, a hand went up as if in protest, then gently came to rest on her chest. She was asleep.

Raj sat opposite me on the embroidered footstool, his eyes very black and warm like smooth obsidian, communicating without words, his love reconstituting my heart as if that organ had been torn and desiccated before. My legs were stretched out across his knees. His hands, hidden under the folds of my gown, were clasped together, resting on the edge of the rocking chair, the long index fingers extended, inside my cunt, covered with dewy moisture. He gently rocked the chair to and fro, fingers moving rhythmically back and forth inside me like a Chinese tickler.

***

Later, about one-thirty, Chris called Raj on his cell, her voice echoing across the room. Even at the best of times she often sounded shrill and strident, such a contrast to the low, intimate sound of Raj's voice. I stepped out on to the tiny balcony, closing the sliding glass door behind me. Jealous and insecure, I lit a cigarette.

A few minutes later Raj joined me on the balcony. It was cold enough that our breath came out in swirling streams of condensation. After staring off in the distance toward the medical center, Raj turned to me, "Would you mind giving me a ride home?"

"Sure, is everything okay?"

His eyes cut away from mine; he suddenly looked tired and worried. "She doesn't have any money to buy disposable diapers, there's hardly any gas in the car. She's afraid to drive too far in case she runs out. Diapers are too expensive at the convenience store, HEB's too far away. Jennifer's got a croupy cough again. You name it, I gotta go."

The reality of trying to switch partners mid-stream. With Liz bundled into her red parka we trooped silently out to the Volvo. On the drive to his apartment he remained cloaked in a heavy silence, closed to me, already looking ahead to what he must do to help Chris.

***

Back at home I flopped on the mattress watching Liz play with her dolls, making up stories for what they were doing.

Whenever I closed my eyes, Chris' face kept coming to mind, her brown eyes open wide in anger, the mottled skin at her throat, the deathly pallor of her cheeks; my realization of what she faced without Raj's support.

Raj. As if he'd left a hot burn mark in my flesh, I could still feel his fingers inside me as he rocked Liz and me back and forth in the chair. His eyes, bright and staring, probing like his fingers, into the innermost chambers of my soul, resting there, nothing hidden, a sense of intimacy that was almost shattering in its intensity, my lover, myself, where do you end and I begin?

My thoughts chased each other round and round gaining no more bright insight into my situation than a hamster gains ground as it ceaselessly runs on the wheel.

The phone rang, I jerked awake, maneuvering around Liz, who'd also fallen asleep next to me. I raced to answer it; a glance at the caller ID told me it was Raj.

"Hi. I'm coming back. Can you come get me?"

"Sure."

With Liz back in her car seat, we set out once again. On the east bound feeder road to Loop 410, a young kid on a Suzuki motorbike kept tailgating me. Then he revved his engines until he sounded like a jet taking off as he raced past me, his actions speaking loudly of his contempt for my cautious driving. And no helmet, the fool. It reminded me of an email Owen had sent a while back: pictures of a motorcycle crash on the autobahn somewhere in Germany, arms and legs strewn across the lanes. Subject line: organ donors and Darwin Award winners. One of those emails you wished you'd never seen, even for a normally unsqueamish medical student.

At the light I turned right onto Cheever Avenue heading for the Robinette Apartments. Built in the early fifties these were no instant ghetto apartments, they'd been made to last. In spite of the dated architecture the place had aged well, thanks in part to the forest of trees surrounding it. The moon was on the rise as I pulled into the parking lot, its pale yellow glow made the fat evergreens look like lumbering beasts.

Raj was waiting on the sidewalk outside his apartment. He squinted at the headlights, then bent to pick up his backpack and guitar. Not a good sign, where was the rest of his stuff? As soon as he opened the back door of the car to stow his guitar, Liz took one look at him and started crying, tears rolling down her cheeks. She dropped her fuzzy bunny out of reach, compounding her frustration. She gave a piercing cry, then stuck both of her thumbs into her mouth.

"What's wrong with her?" Raj asked, getting in the front seat with me. His expression conveyed little humor or indulgence. From one sick child to another, these two lives intersected, were too closely interchangeable, not the carefree interlude we imagined. Slowly the wheels turned in my mind; he was not omniscient either, nor as mature as I had previously thought. Not having foreseen the hassle this would be, the option of backing out of it hung manifestly in the air waiting for one or the other of us to pluck it into our conversation.

"Probably an ear infection." She was pulling on her ear; there were more tears in her eyes, ready to spill over.

At home, with a beer to appease him, I left Raj staring at the screen of his laptop, the light reflected in the lenses of his glasses.

In Liz's bedroom I sat down on the edge of her bed, with her in my lap. She'd had these crying jags before where she seemed like the most inconsolable person on the planet. Even as I tried rocking back and forth to soothe her, I knew this would just have to run its course. Could I wait until tomorrow to get an antibiotic?

After thirty-minutes, impatient, feeling abused and ignored, Raj came into the room. "Christ, Sophie, she is so spoiled, do you have do this at bed time every night?" We stared angrily at each other. How could he be so childish and selfish?

She stood up on her bed, blonde hair matted, face damp with perspiration, eyes running, nose running, she was an aching, wet mess in a baggy yellow nightgown with a tiny navy-blue cardigan buttoned against the chill. She took one look at Raj and her face crumpled, her mouth again caught in a tight rictus, tiny pink tongue curled; she screamed so loud I heard something pop in my right ear. Raj stared at me with somber black eyes.

I lost my temper. "What a bloody mess this is. Why the hell am I trying to do anything with you? I'm her mother, she comes first. This is never going to work."

Wrapping Liz in her coat and a blanket, I grabbed my purse and ran out the door.

***

Alan Perkins was the physician's assistant on call at the student dispensary that Sunday night. He did not comport himself with the dignity I associated with being a PA. Beneath his lab coat he always wore a black and red Harley Davidson T-shirt and cotton sweat pants, an outfit that you could get at Goodwill for about six bucks. The man was way short, no more than five foot five inches, and lean, but fairly muscular. He didn't so much walk, as barrel down the hall, arms pumping like he was leading an oompah-pah band. Ginger hair and bright blue eyes that blazed with intensity suggested an Irish-English background.

He looked at Liz's chart and said, "You're Dr. Trudeau's wife, aren't you?" The canny gleam in his eyes made it obvious what he was thinking: you're the one who left her husband to fuck a young boy toy. News travels fast.

From some bedrock of patience and sanity, I saw that, deeply introverted as I am, public knowledge of my sins was a given from now on.

"Yes, I am. He brought Liz in the last time when she had an ear infection. I'm sure it's the same thing now, I've listened to her chest, it's clear. She just needs the amoxicillin."

From the heap of clothes on the dresser in my bedroom I'd grabbed the first thing handy, threw it on and raced out to bring my lover back home. Now as Alan Perkins stared unabashedly at my boobs, I regretted choosing the scoop necked tight black sweater.

His pager went off. He dug it out of his sweat pants, stared at it, put it back and then resumed staring at my boobs. From his lab coat pocket he withdrew a pad and silently wrote out the prescription then tore it off with a flourish.

"Thanks."

"Don't mention it."

***

I arrived back home more than two hours later, surprised to find Raj still there. He was slouched against the couch, feet stretched out on the mattress, watching television, strumming Led Zeppelin's "Stairway to Heaven" on his guitar. We didn't speak.

Liz docilely accepted the medicine and more liquid decongestant, followed by a little bit of apple juice. Tucking her in bed, I smoothed the hair away from her forehead. "I love you little girl." She smiled, turned over and was instantly asleep.

Back in the living room with Raj my anger had evaporated. "Want another beer?"

"Sure, if you're having one." He kept staring at the strings on his guitar, avoiding my glance.

It was after nine by the time I sat down next to him, wishing he'd put the guitar away so we could talk. He played "Stairway to Heaven" again, his face an inscrutable mask.

"Sounds like the real thing."

He grinned at me and kept on playing for a minute or two, then stopped.

"When my mom and step-dad use to fight, I always had this feeling that I had to put things right again. Trouble was, they fought all the time, still do, like cats and dogs." His face was set; there was an almost ironic look in his eyes. He plucked a chord on the guitar; I remembered the last line, "And she's buying a stairway to heaven." Is that what I was trying to do?

He went on, "I thought I wouldn't be that way with Chris, with the babies. But fighting must be immutable in some relationships,' cause Chris and I were no different. Then I met you and thought that things could be better, only now, well, maybe it's all just too much."

How could he say that? I wanted to yell at him, to scream don't you dare tell me that this is all over before it starts. For a moment his easy come, easy go attitude toward me, his lack of will to fight for me left me breathless with pain. It wasn't worth it to him to put up with the interim period of chaos in our lives. Unspoken too, was the thought that at so young an age he had not understood that some choices, while maybe not the right ones, still had a firm grip on him, could not easily be eluded.

In trying to leave his marriage it had taken on greater substance for him as well. Leaving it was like watching someone kill a harmless animal.

We went through the whole six-pack while staring at the fire. Raj finally but the guitar down, "You didn't take too seriously what Chris said last night, did you? She told me she was really upset, but she's calmer now. She feels bad."

Upset? She could have killed me and been totally within her rights.

I wondered jealously if Raj and Chris had done more than just talk. The way he worded that apology, it hinted at more. Blood was thicker than water, even married blood. He'd gone against a deeply ingrained sense of responsibility toward family only to realize that things would not really be any easier with me. Why hadn't he seen any of this before? Was it only in action that our options, or our lack of them, were revealed to us?

It was obvious where all of this was leading. Quietly, I asked, "It's not going to work is it?"

"Doesn't look that way. I didn't even get hours in at the lab this weekend. And this is the first chance I've had to really focus on school."

We lapsed into a troubled silence, staring at the fire. I thought about Alan Perkins and his disrespectful and salacious manner. Why were women always the fallen angels? Did I have the courage, the mettle necessary to keep my head up or would I go slinking off to some dark corner to lick my wounds?

Raj wadded up the Classified section from the newspaper and tossed it in the fire, watching as it caught fire and was quickly consumed. "I was a Boy Scout you know, we know how to make great fires. The secret is oxygen, letting everything breathe properly."

Yes, everything about us was settled in his mind, as easy as getting a fire started. Suddenly I hated men. I crumpled my can and threw it at the fireplace with all of my might.

Hardly drawing a new breath Raj turned to me, "Well, since we've decided we're not going to be lovers, wanna fuck?"

I burst out laughing, falling back on the mattress laughing so hard my sides began to ache. That was the last thing I'd expected him to say. Raj moved toward me, taking me in his arms.

***

In the morning, refreshed from a good night's sleep and a shower, I felt differently. When he came out of the bathroom, a towel wrapped around his waist, his hair wet from the shower, the masculine scent of cologne clinging to him, all I could think about was how much I loved him.

But he had to do this; I could see that perfectly clearly. This was not the courtship phase of his marriage. He had two young babies and a virtually helpless wife. Right now he had to go home to his wife and family. There was no room in his life for me. He hugged me, "We're doing the right thing aren't we? I can't stay here with you and let you support me, and I can't leave her alone unsupported." I nodded, too stricken to speak, hugging him tight.

Neither of us had anything to say on the way to Nancy's house to drop off Liz. The amoxicillin was already working its magic, my sweet tow-haired girl was happy and chattering away.

Breathless in spite of this relatively innocuous encounter, I worried that Nancy would take sides—Nick's side—the way Angela had. Dennis was already there and Amanda and Nellie, more hyper than usual, raced around, shouting and laughing.

Nancy was her normal smiling self with no trace of aloofness in her manner. Nervously, I explained about Liz's ear infection. "The PA says she's not infectious, and the medicine is already working."

"She'll be fine Sophie, don't worry, I'll keep a close eye on her today and call if anything comes up."

I hugged her, "Thank you so much, you're a doll."

In the parking garage at the medical center, two of Nick's colleagues looked over and saw Raj and I getting out of the car. They hesitated just long enough to acknowledge me, then when they saw Raj they hurried away. Two nights ago I was still sleeping in my husband's bed, now today I show up at school with my lover.

***

My face burned scarlet as we rode the elevator up to the second floor of the medical school. We joined the crowd of students streaming into the Hoffman Auditorium for the first of Ginger's lectures on metastatic breast cancer.

Seating myself across the room from Raj, I thought about my newly discarded husband emerging out of his Toyota Highlander, probably stoop-shouldered with the pain of it all, making his way to work. I was at one with the untouchables in India, unclean, impure, a slattern, a pariah, and outcast from society. Imagining that I was a nun helped, or a novitiate who has to prostrate herself on the institutional linoleum, kissing it as she crawls along, leaving a trail of slime behind her like a doomed snail.

I couldn't wait to get away from Raj, from the taint that this illicit relationship had cast over me. But how do you do that when most of your day is spent in such close proximity?

Once inside and off and running through our day, whatever loose bonds apparent to the rest of the world, linking us in this lurid crime against society, began to evaporate. A certain figurative distance between us expanded and took over.

Out of necessity we became like those buttons on the newest vacuum cleaners, pressing it sucks the electrical cord in so fast if you don't watch out you get whip lashed. I had no idea that when the going gets tough, people can avail themselves of a similar button on their emotions.

Of course, all of this was going in the opposite direction, sort of like backing up on the space-time continuum to a parallel universe where the wave function hadn't collapsed yet and Raj and I hadn't started an affair, were still strangers.

***

With Raj so precipitately out of the picture, Nick and I focused on providing a united front for Liz, spending all of our free time with her. We talked a lot more than we had in the past and went out of our way to be considerate to each other. Narrowing my focus, I pushed thoughts of Raj out of my mind letting school consume me.

Late one afternoon, after a grueling day spent at the clinic at the Cisneros Trauma Center, I'd headed back to the medical school to check my mailbox and pick up two books from my locker. On my way out I passed the double glass doors that lead into the Dean's offices. Fortunately, Dr. Cardiff's personal assistant had intercepted the call from Chris complaining about Raj and me and didn't bother the dean with such trivialities. But Cardiff's assistant was known to be a gossip and word had quickly spread of Chris Kahn's extreme behavior in approaching a higher authority just short of God to help her deal with her domestic problems.

Dawdling longer than I should have, caught in a daydream about Raj, I stared out the windows at a construction site in the distance. The medical center was thriving and constantly undergoing expansion. Across the street and down a block, set against the backdrop of a cloudy, cold day, a crane hoisted materials to men working on steel girders ten stories up. The noise of a pneumatic drill on the ground below drew my attention. I watched a jolly green giant of a man at work, red bandana tied around his head to catch the sweat, his muscles rippling. How could anyone stand to hold that drill for such a long time?

Charlie Thompson's pre-pubescent experience with orgasm came to mind, making me smile. Stepping onto his aunt's weight reduction machine, adjusting the belt around his gluteus, leaning into it to make it taut, he flipped the switch on. It vibrated so hard, just like the man with the pneumatic drill, that within minutes he had his first orgasm, scaring himself silly as cum squirted all over his shorts. Charlie had been sure he was dying. "Why did my aunt have such a machine anyway? What genius thought you could vibrate fat away?"

Someone walked by, stopping to watch me. Shortening my gaze and focusing on the glass before me, I could see it was Rebecca. Perhaps finding my posture forlorn, she stood in back of me for a minute, then put her hand on my arm.

"You're a good person Sophie." I turned to look into her warm brown eyes, full of compassion. "At heart I know you're a good person." With that she turned and walked away from me. Tears stung my eyes, I tried to say thank you but couldn't get the words out.

It was obvious that everyone in our class knew what was going on between Raj and I. And if they knew, there were many who probably judged us harshly.

Sometimes it was all I could do to restrain myself from running through the medical school halls grabbing my fellow students by the lapels, trying to justify my actions to them. But I kept my silence, living inside my head thinking all the while in every encounter: don't judge me without knowing me.

Then ultimately I dismissed these pointless thoughts about the maelstrom at the center of my life, no one's life was perfect. We all have our fantasies. Some more intense than others, some that get acted on and others your only recourse is to sublimate them somehow.

There were hints all around me of people involved in their own sordid affairs. I just needed to a take a break from being so inwardly focused.

Chapter Eight

Thursday of the week before the Christmas holidays, I sat in the study lab at the conference table going over my final notes from the patient histories I'd taken at Cisneros. My last day at the Trauma Center everyone had been talking about the middle aged woman who'd been declared irreversibly brain dead after a head injury sustained in a car accident. Not wearing a seatbelt she'd gone through the windshield like a projectile. The family was just trying to decide when to take her off of life support—and should we parcel out her heart, lungs, kidneys and liver?--when she woke up fully cognizant of the world around her.

Just in the nick of time too, transplant doctors could be a mere cut above vultures in their never ending quest for organ donors.

Not to have too much gallows humor here but heads would roll from such a painfully wrong assessment of her injuries. Glad I was not responsible for that, at least not this time. Still, it scared me deep down inside as once again I realized the life and death responsibilities doctors have.

Just opposite the hallway Ginger's office door was open and I could see her staring intently at the whiteboard opposite her desk, trying to divine a pattern in the arrows and obscure words sketched there. She was lost somewhere inside a biochemical pathway of her own devising.

Raj stopped and chatted with her for a minute before coming into the study lab. Trying to appear nonchalant I glanced up briefly, gave him a thin smile then focused on my notes again. Talk about déjà vu: he'd walk to the back of the room, call me on his cell phone…and like "Groundhog Day" our affair would start all over again.

This time it was a paper clip tossed my way. It grazed my ear and landed in my lap, I picked it up and stared unsmilingly at him. It flashed through my mind that he was the prototype for the old saying "still waters run deep."

He smiled in a wistful, ironic way, his eyes glittering with apology, "I knew one day I'd fuck up and it would be big."

Clutching a tissue to his nose, he sneezed several times in rapid succession.

"Bless you. What do you mean?"

"Thanks. This. Us. Are you sorry?"

"No. For which part?"

"Getting separated from your husband."

"You know what they always say, an affair is only a symptom of a larger problem. We had problems before you."

We'd seen each other constantly at school in the last week, studiously averting our eyes. But now he grinned at me the way he used to, happy because I'd let him off the hook he'd been dangling on. "Well obviously that was true with Chris and me too."

No doubt, but the urge was so strong in all of us for life to be routine; that was how so many marriages lasted, people sucked into the hypnotic momentum of routine.

After that day, Raj would occasionally call me from his new Trac cell phone. He seemed to have a hard time breaking ties to people, knowing when to back off and be cold.

***

Even as everyone grew excited about the approaching holidays and the time we'd have off to recharge our batteries, my days were still incredibly busy. That was the only way to avoid constantly thinking about Raj. What do you do when your need for someone, your desperate love for that person is like a diamond broach lit up in neon and pinned atop your frontal lobes? How can you escape it?

Later that day standing in front of our lockers in the basement—Raj's locker was five lockers down from mine—we continued with the charade of ignoring each other. Then looking around to see that we were more or less alone he approached me.

"I saw you and Owen earlier, awfully chummy, weren't you? You going after him next? I thought you said he was gay."

A crack in the facade. For a moment I had a picture of Raj clearly in mind, surprised at this evidence of jealousy. I saw it for what it was though, he resented that I was free to come and go while he was forced back into a shaky marriage, now made hostile by his infidelity. Can this marriage be saved? Anything can be fixed if you try hard enough, it's not over until the Fat Lady sings.

In one of the few conversations we'd had recently he told me what the lawyer told him to expect if he followed through on his plan to get divorced.

"Think twice about leaving your wife, she's entitled to half of everything you own and almost always the mother ends up with custody. Judging from your current financial status, your hopes of finishing medical school would be down the tubes considering how much child-support you'd be required to pay."

Did he love his wife? He never said. He never lied to me, just omitted things. The lawyer's words echoed through my brain.

The basement always felt damp and smelled of bleach from the shower stalls and restrooms across the hall. That day the air seemed more acrid than usual with the remnants of cleaning solvents. Anxious to get away from that claustrophic atmosphere, I slammed my locker shut.

"What do you want me to do Raj? Mope around, pine away, threaten suicide, beg you to come back? As a matter of fact Owen and

I are going to Ginger's Christmas party together. Satisfied?" He couldn't see through my act, couldn't see how I ached for him, my advantage was that age had taught me to let go of those who do not want to be held. Still, his ego was hurt, so he needled me.

Silence, no rebuttal. The masculine wheels turned, creative thought, analysis, make this situation work for me. His thought processes were almost audible, "I gave in and went home too soon, too easily." A grim admission, but God, did it make me hopeful.

We'd worked hard to behave professionally toward one another. No one but Rebecca had actually said anything, though what people thought was often readily discernible by their expressions. I wondered about the fact that none of the residents in charge of overseeing our work had said anything. Must be like "cast the first stone" so long as no one caught us, or anyone else for that matter, fornicating in the janitor's closet, you're good to go.

***

Just before the Christmas break I had one more on-call night at the hospital and ended up staying for over thirty hours. The upside to that kind of schedule was that after only three or four short naps while on-call, when I finally went home, my insomnia disappeared and I slept like the dead.

Even so, my sleep debt had not been fully paid and I fell asleep during a lecture the next day. A fourth year student was summarizing a recent patient's history. The woman had arrived at the emergency room bleeding from her nipples. This of course had everyone else on the edge of their seats and normally I would have been avidly interested. I do remember she had advanced breast cancer and had just been too afraid to go to the doctor.

Thursday was our last day and by then those students flying long distances to get home for the holidays had already left. I saw my last patient at five p.m., a diabetic who'd had his right foot amputated and now had a severe case of cellulitis. I remember reading that John Wilkes Booth had cellulitis but back then they called it erysipelas.

Earlier, another patient had asked Dr. Charles Ratner, the attending physician we were on rounds with, why she always felt so much better after they'd drawn a few vials of blood from her veins.

Scribbling away on her chart he said, "I could understand if you had hemochromatosis and too much iron in your blood, but your blood tests were normal." He handed her chart to me. "Trudeau, you now have a new research project, help Mrs. Odin out."

Once I'd finished examining Otis Finn, the diabetic, making sure the drainage tubes from his surgery were okay, I ran down to the lab to follow up on Dr. Ratner's request.

Janelle Cisco was one of the phlebotomists. A tall African woman from Nigeria who spoke perfect English with only the slightest hint of an accent, she always wore a colorful Batik print scarf neatly wrapped around her head.

"Janelle have any of the patients ever said that giving blood makes them feel better physically?"

"Feeling good after a blood draw? Never. Guys especially, they just get pale and look like they're going to pass out. You'd know more about that than me. Is your patient a woman? Maybe she's got tired blood."

When an advanced query on the internet returned no hits, I leaned back in my chair, closed my eyes and thought about leeches and blood volume. Bloodletting was a popular medical remedy for centuries and is still in use today for rare conditions. People who unknowingly suffered from high blood pressure and who routinely had modest amounts of their blood drawn would have felt better. In those days salt was much more widely used to preserve meat and the extra salt people consumed would ratchet up their blood pressure even more. Dr. Ratner's patient was ten years post-menopausal with hypertension controlled with a modest dose of Lisinopril.

Menstruation's a kind of blood-letting; many women feel a lot better after their periods, purged and with the hormones back in balance. Chances are Mrs. Odin didn't watch her salt intake that carefully either. Having several vials of blood drawn would alter the fluid dynamics of her circulatory system more oxygen reaching down to the tiniest little capillaries. That could give her a sense of well-being.

Still, it was with a certain amount of trepidation, wasn't medicine an art as well as a science?—that I emailed my thoughts to Dr. Ratner.

After that I called it a day. It really was time to start focusing on Christmas.

* * *

And if I'd thought Christmas shopping downtown would cheer me up, it wasn't happening. Somehow I didn't fit in anymore, like a grown-up playing in a child's dollhouse. Friday I shopped at Dillard's buying Christmas presents for Nick and Liz and then had lunch in the coffee shop at the Menger Hotel. As I walked past the Alamo, heading for my car, many faces passed me by, young airmen from the area military installations, the beautiful Hispanic women visiting from Mexico, and myriad tourists from the River Walk. And of course there were the construction workers who so outrageously undressed you with their eyes, or made cat-calls, sucking on their lips in such a disgusting way. Normally I would return their stares, as brazen as they were. But that day I felt so raw and wounded inside, I wanted no reminders of my sexuality.

Then I turned a corner and caught sight of a ghost from my past. The summer between my junior and senior year at UT, I worked part-time as a waitress at Giuseppe's Italian Restaurant on the River Walk. My shift ended after the lunch crowd disappeared and afterwards I'd run to catch the bus home.

The gnarled and grisly man in the wheelchair was always parked in the same spot on the sidewalk as if that were his place of business. Covering his head was a greasy, sweat-stained brown fedora; spikes of dirty brown hair stuck out beneath the hat, hiding his ears. A yellowing cigarette butt dangled out of one side of his mouth. His legs were so scrawny they looked like Holocaust survivors' limbs, partially visible through a tattered, filthy muslin cloth. The sleaziest looking women always flanked him on either side, like sentinels from hell, their eyes flat, ringed with heavy black eye-liner.

What did he do their all day long? What went through his mind? Years ago I had him pegged as a pimp, a junkie, someone who sold dope to children. While I used to wait for the bus I would catch his eye and then dare to draw a little nearer. His eyes were brown, too big for his small, deformed face. The iris' appeared lost, like brown marbles floating in a bowl of milk. In my humble medical opinion I now deemed him a victim of pretty severe cerebral palsy brought on at the time of his birth, like that Daniel Day-Lewis character in "My Left Foot."

Despite that, there was an unnerving intensity in the way he focused on people. He always held my gaze the whole time I stood there, then again through the window as I seated myself on the bus, my face pressed to the glass.

His image would fill my mind, sparking my feverish imagination. As the bus wended its way through town, the fresh spring air would blow in through the open windows, rustling the hair of all the weary passengers. So young then, to me the air seemed filled with a timeless, dizzying mystery--like the man in the wheelchair. There was the fear and excitement of being grounded in something fiercely primitive, of knowing the future would unfurl like a magic carpet, full of heart-stopping secrets.

Unfurled to the heart-stopping secrets of Raj.

Was that raw feeling pressing against my brain because I had slept with Nick again last night? Slept with him and longed for Raj, such a sad, deflated aftermath of loss. Was that why such a profound sensitivity settled over me, why my sexuality seemed such a burden? The backlash of so public and painful an affair.

Even though I'd kept my apartment, Nick and I still spent a lot of time together. We'd had dinner at McAllister's Pub with Angela and Dave. Back home, Nick, slightly drunk, reclined on the bed with a crystal snifter half-full of cognac. Liz was sound asleep beside him, she would have to be moved to the guest room if Susie and I were going to have room to sleep. There were new sheets on the bed, dark blue with white stars and the planets revolving steadily, dependably around the distant sun.

Petting Susie, Nick said in a slightly caustic tone, "Sophie, I don't mean this to hurt you, but what does it say about a man who leaves his wife for two days, then goes running back to hide behind her skirts when things get tough?"

Naked from the waist up, seated at the vanity, my feet were resting on an open drawer. I watched him in the mirror and thought of Charlie's blasted, fragmented ego, of men who had acquainted me well with their psychotic urges. Nick was comfortably in touch with reality, dependable like the planets. Grabbing the cigarette in my red plastic Lone Star ashtray, I inhaled sharply, several times. With Nick's words, I regretted agreeing to spend the night, then not smiling, said, "You miss the point Nick, what does it say about me?"

"All right, I shouldn't complain, he's the fool, but it's my gain." Dependable like the planets, yet without a great deal of insight into people, there were some benefits to early exposure to psychotics.

"It took guts to go back to his wife."

"Bullshit. He's not mature enough or imaginative enough or versatile enough to stand the flak and create a new life, he took the easy way out, after pressuring you to leave me. He's doubly damned." He was silent for several minutes, dragging heavily on his cigarette.

Finally, he asked, "So are you ready to come back?"

And forfeit the independence I'm savoring, the richness of having the twin poles of my personality fulfilled: satisfied dominatrix with Nick, victim with Raj? No way. "Nick you know that's not such a good idea. It's too soon, I don't trust myself."

From a bottle of Shalimar body lotion I poured a small amount into one hand then rubbed my hands together, spreading the lotion around my neck and arms and breasts. Nick got out of bed, and then gently picked up Liz, carrying her into the guest bedroom, tucking her in bed. When he returned, he stood in back of me and removed the clippie which held my hair; it cascaded down, settling around my neck and shoulders in waves. Nick knelt behind me and reached around to cup my breasts, kissing my neck. "You smell so good, come to bed. Let's don't argue anymore."

Later, Nick slept next to me, sated and happy. As I drifted off to sleep I marveled that I'd been suffused with such a wicked eroticism that it reached out to encompass this relationship as well. Polygamy wasn't just for men anymore.

***

That Saturday night Ginger and her husband were hosting their annual Christmas party at their new home. Her husband, Trevor, in addition to being a cardiologist, was also associate dean of the medical school. Their new house was a five-thousand square foot showplace in Olmos Park formerly owned by the mayor of San Antonio.

Owen and I arrived a little late, walking up the wide front steps past the open front doors. The large foyer was tiled with off-white Saltillo tile shining like pearls lying in rich cream. Staircases on the right and on the left of the foyer rose to the upper story, their gleaming mahogany banisters intertwined with garlands of evergreen and California holly, all tied in place with red satin ribbons. In the center between the staircases stood a fourteen-foot tall Christmas tree, hundreds of brightly colored lights sparkled and twinkled at you, bringing back nostalgic memories of the magic of Christmases past. Four-foot high poinsettias lined the perimeter from each staircase to the tree.

A woodwind quartet, the four women dressed the same in black skirts and white blouses, sat close to the tree playing Christmas carols.

"Sophie, Owen, good of you to come." Ginger gave Owen a wide smile and a hug, turning away from me. The typical cold shoulder I'd come to expect from her.

She looked almost pretty dressed in Christian Louboutin stiletto heels, a full-length black silk dress, and a red and gold beaded black velvet Bolero jacket that offset her slim waist. Matching bright spots of red on her cheeks made her gray eyes shine.

Stopping for a moment to listen appreciatively as the women played "God Rest Ye Merry Gentlemen," Ginger whispered, "We can thank the nuns at Incarnate Word College for these young ladies; they rounded them up for me."

Effusive as ever Owen offered to help sing Christmas carols with them. "How long has it been since we've all sung any carols? What great musicians."

"Aren't they? We can sing later. Let me show you where everything is." She led us through the hall then into the den.

Three white linen clad tables, each with an exquisite ice sculptor of a swan in the center, were laden with food. There were platters of smoked salmon, turkey, ham, shrimp; another table was covered with different cheeses, Brie, Camembert, Gruyere, Edam, and finger-sandwiches, crackers and chips. Elegant crystal glass bowls were filled with luscious looking strawberries, pineapple, mango, blueberries and kiwi. The dessert table looked like a buffet one might have seen on the maiden voyage of the Titanic: cream puffs, profiteroles, Napoleons, fudge, a Sacher torte, and eclairs.

Ginger pointed to another table. "Help yourselves to the champagne fountain, or if you prefer something stronger, just ask Bob at the bar. That dish next to the crudités is real goose pate, the medical school paid for all this by the way, we didn't."

153

She dragged a cracker through one of the dishes, popping it in her mouth. "My favorite is the mushroom crab dip. Oh, and by the way, there are two bathrooms on the second floor at either end of the staircases, and one over there." She pointed toward the utility room where a man in a black tuxedo was opening more cases of champagne.

Trevor joined us, putting a hand on Ginger's back. "The dean's just arrived; you need to come meet his new wife."

At the champagne fountain, Owen and I filled tulip-shaped crystal glasses with champagne, drained them, and then filled them again, feeling like little kids with a new toy. We were both nervous and fairly desperate for a cigarette. With his hand at my elbow, Owen said, "Follow me. My nose has detected the scent of cigarette smoke emanating from just beyond the French doors leading to the terrace."

We joined a group of five other benighted smokers standing out in the cold, puffing away on coffin nails. Owen inhaled his in almost one gulp then saw Terry Martin and his wife through the window, leaving me to go chat with them.

Back inside, I moved among the crowd, feeling like I'd arrived in Oz, my eyes dazzled by the light refracted off of jewelry and crystal. The dean's new wife, Chloe, wore what had to have been a four carat diamond, it sparkled like captured fire and I couldn't take my eyes off of it.

Wine red Persian rugs partially covered the high gloss of wood floors in the living room. Exquisite tapestries shared space with paintings in ornate frames; the general theme was that of red-jacketed hunters, their horses caught effortlessly leaping across hedgerows, along with Springer spaniels in hot pursuit of a harried fox.

To rephrase Butler, the intrinsic comfort of rich and geometrically pleasing lines; the rich appeal of symmetry.

Back for more champagne to bolster my flagging confidence, I noticed that in this glittering crowd so many of the men were handsome, perhaps even brilliant, were they all cloned from the same Danielle Steel novel? And so often the wives faces were set in an expression of studied nonchalance.

Of the female doctors, several were obviously single; others were paired up with younger men.

With one exception. Dr. Randall, tall but still obese, an incessant nose-picker, so involved in his research that he often forgot to bathe or even to bother combing his hair. Behind his back, the other doctors referred to him as "tall, dark and slimy."

I pictured him as he was rousted from bed each morning, jumping into the same clothes he'd dumped on the floor the night before. His unfortunately gelled hair was somewhat spiked that night, reminding me of Johnny Depp. Curious to see what his wife looked like, I followed his movements until he stopped to admire a Gainsborough reproduction. And the fat babushka next to him was unmistakably his wife. They looked like a matched pair of June bugs. Dr. Randall was the odd man out in this eugenic conspiracy.

The first floor had been designed in an open way with few walls to interfere with the flow of the crowd around the staircases, through the kitchen, living room, formal dining room and study. There was a slow parade of people chatting happily. A fourth glass of champagne filled me with the unmistakable bonhomie of the season, that sudden sparkling sense of kinship you feel toward everyone at Christmas time.

The crowd standing around the entrance to the kitchen suddenly parted and a young man wearing a black turtle neck and khaki-colored twill pants made his way past them, champagne glass in hand, light bouncing off the silver frames of his glasses.

Catching sight of Raj felt like a blow to my stomach. He saw me, his eyes warming in a silent greeting across the room. My eyes were stuck, impaled as though by fish hooks with his, I couldn't tear my glance away. In his expression I read a slight apology which I understood when a second later Chris rounded the corner from the kitchen, looking rosy-cheeked and merry in a wine-colored long dress that was too little for her though it was obvious she had lost weight.

Unexpectedly, a surge of violent emotion swelled up in me-- bitter envy, jealousy, love--a pitched battle raged inside my body. With instant access to the "interior oracle" as E.O. Wilson calls that inner voice that guides us, it told me now was a good time to visit the powder room.

I hurried upstairs, slipping my black heels off to walk across the luxurious, thickly-padded yellow carpeting. Alone, with the muted voices from below drifting up to me, my own company seemed the best to keep.

In a bathroom as large as Liz's bedroom, I sat in front of a vanity on an armless chair upholstered in white damask. Nosy as ever, I looked through the drawers that opened on expensive silent runners; Ginger was as well-stocked cosmetically as the Estee Lauder counter at Macy's, not that it did her much good. Above the vanity was a brass chandelier with dozens of crystal pendants as shiny as Chloe's diamond.

The mirror in front of me reflected a woman in a red silk dress with a square neckline. All dressed up and no one to be with. Everything was in place, no goose pate in my teeth, but bad karma will catch you out no matter where you hide. It's dangerous to invoke the Furies, to dare try for a greater happiness.

Back downstairs, two glasses of champagne later, Raj's presence left me bristling with an uneasy tension, a painful awareness of him, a deep sexual angst. My whole being strained toward him, but what do hearts know of propriety and wives? Especially when floating in champagne.

Spotting Helmut Mantel out on the terrace, smoking and staring at the stars, I slipped outside.

"*Ola. Como estas tu?*"

"*Bien, y Ud.?*"

The mark of a high class *sud Americano*, always using the formal personal pronoun *Ud.*, they never used the intimate *tu* which I used so indiscriminately. Unless of course you were Catalina, the maid, and happened to be fucking the heir apparent, in which case it might be appropriate to get up close and personal language-wise.

Helmut was an Associate Professor of Genetics from Argentina. My first year in medical school, I'd been at a party at his house when he'd gotten very drunk. We sat together on the beige velour sofa in his den while he told me about his childhood in Buenos Aires. He came from a wealthy family complete with maids and nannies. His story oddly dovetailed with my experiences growing up. It seemed that when he was twelve years old one of the maids, Catalina, had taken a shine to him and vice versa. At night when everyone else was asleep, she would sneak into his room with lemonade and cookies and after this repast they would get under the covers and have sex.

Apparently he still carried a torch for her, he'd never married, and from his wallet he'd withdrawn a picture of Catalina. What an

Argentinian beauty she was, doe-eyed with curly black hair and porcelain skin.

Standing in the cold out on the terrace he began to talk enthusiastically about several unusual coincidences in Wilder's "The Bridge of San Luis Rey."

"I just reread it this afternoon. Our lives are flung with such abandon across the landscape, so random, yet oddly pre-ordained, if we could only see behind the mechanics. Is it really an expanding universe like a rubber band being pulled taut? If so, what happens when someone lets it go?" He stared wide-eyed at me, not really expecting an answer.

I wondered if he was completely sane, his intensity was so close to the surface, so unsolicited. Raj was intense too, but in a distinctly different way, more benign and intimate.

"Ever read Koestler's "The Roots of Coincidence" about synchronicity?" he asked.

I hadn't caught that one either.

"*Verdad?* You must read it. Jung believed that the mind has enormous capabilities to influence external events. What is that word the physicists call it, `nonlocal events', I think."

With such an intense preoccupation with coincidental encounters and destiny, Helmut must have known that something pivotal in his life was about to happen.

"Sounds interesting, I'll check it out." Crushing my cigarette out in the marble ashtray on the table I bid him a Merry Christmas.

Back inside, I spotted Raj across the room, making sure that as people shifted from room to room, I didn't shift too close to Chris. She turned and glared at me, possessively linking arms with her husband.

I longed to be in her place. Raj was the only man who had the power to silence my yearning heart, the man who swept away that black nameless sorrow inside. If somehow we could have vaulted from our two marriages into a perfect vacuum without the entanglement of children and wives, this was how I would have pictured myself with him. Our eyes would meet across a crowded-room, excited that soon we'd be going home together to share the same bed, the same hopes and dreams, the same emotions, the same life.

The noise level in the room had increased considerably as the normally staid merry-makers, fueled by alcohol, let down their hair; a few of the men had gripped their wives to them swinging them around in the foyer to the Strauss waltzes playing.

Even Owen and I danced for a while when suddenly I caught sight of Chris engaged in an intense conversation with Helmut. Despite those seventeen or so glasses of champagne seeing them together felt auspicious. Hadn't Raj told me how much Chris read, how high her IQ was? Maybe she and Helmut would hit it off talking about Nietzsche and Thornton Wilder. My mind kept weaving magical threads of intrigue as I pondered the possibilities.

Around midnight the party began to wind down. Women milled around in the foyer, donning their fur wraps. Cold air swirled into the room bringing with it the odor of exhaust fumes; you could hear the crunch of gravel on the circular drive as cars edged closer to the front door, picking up passengers who gaily called out their farewells.

Standing alone outside next to a copse of trees lit with fairy lights, I waited for Owen to bring the car around, staring up at the clear, starry night, feeling suddenly more virtuous and self-contained than I had all evening. Perhaps a bit more sober. A champagne-colored

Mercedes passed me, the woman inside was radiantly beautiful, her hair piled casually on her head, tendrils of curls loose at her neck, a silver fur draped across her slender bare shoulders.

The night was cold and clear with a rising three quarter moon as lustrous as a pearl. I turned away from a sudden gust of frigid wind, facing the wide double doors at the front of the house, decorated with matching holly wreaths, red bows and bells. A movement out of the corner of my eye caught my attention. I turned toward it. Raj was at the front window in the study staring out at me.

Something passed between us, a look of such steely resolve in his eyes, then stealing over me a confidence that this was not over, that he still loved me. Now, as we regarded each other silently, I couldn't stop trembling, wondering at the power of what I had committed myself to.

Chris came and stood next to him. I turned away, overcome with melancholy, with a sudden sense of utter loss as that link between us was severed. Then the painful realization that despite the anger and pain and explosive battles between them, love existed there too. Or was that kind of love so often a matter of putting a good face on things?

***

Manic as ever, I was awake again at five Sunday morning, unable to go back to sleep. A glance out the front window showed leaden skies, a blustery wind blowing through town, cold air seeped into the apartment around the poorly caulked edges of my window. Unusual weather for San Antonio. While the coffee brewed, I set a match to the cardboard and kindling I'd arranged the night before, then added a few smaller cedar logs. With a cup of coffee I settled back in bed to read more of Sylvia Nasar's "A Beautiful Mind" about John Nash, the Nobel-prize winning mathematician.

Nash's struggle with schizophrenia was grimly fascinating. What I found most riveting though was his explanation toward the end of the book of how he emerged from such a devastating mental illness: the "diminution," as he called it, of male hormones when he headed into his sixties. As those levels dropped, so too did the severity of his symptoms. With their waning he was able to work again.

I'd always heard that schizophrenia's onset occurred coincidental to puberty, the hormonal link seemed indisputable. I made a mental note to talk to Helmut about this the next time I saw him, he was sure to have a few fascinating insights.

Setting the book aside I daydreamed about being a geneticist, using trial and error to find a way to disable the genes responsible for turning on schizophrenia.

My cell phone rang; I grabbed it off the coffee table and flipped it open. Raj. "Hey there, aren't you up early?"

"Goddamnit, she's gone."

Too many brain cells had died with the champagne last night. Trying to think this new problem through gave me a headache, "Where'd she go?"

Patiently, as if spelling it out for a child, he said, "It's not like she left me a note Sophie, fucking A."

I laughed, feeling slightly better.

"I fell asleep as soon as we got home last night. When I woke up a little while ago to use the bathroom, I realized she was gone. She and Helmut disappeared for a while at the party last night, that's odd, huh? Is Owen with you? You two looked awfully cozy dancing."

"No." Right Raj, he's going to turn heterosexual just for me. "Why should he be?"

"Just checking. Hey, hold on."

I heard a door slam, a commotion, then he spoke again, "She's here, I gotta go, see ya'."

Freezing while I'd been sitting up talking on the cell phone, I closed it, setting it on the coffee table behind me, snuggling under the covers. Then lying on my stomach, elbows on the carpet, propping my head up, I stared at the fire, trying to figure Raj out. Too hung-over for even a simple analysis, I rested my head on the pillow, my long hair spilling across the side of the mattress.

It wasn't over. The ghost of Raj, his shadow, some incorporeal part of him that he'd left behind the last time we made love was still inside me. Intuitively I'd known that he would come back very soon looking for that lost part.

Asleep again, I dreamed about my time with Raj, going over each time we made love until every cell in my body was crying out for him. Then jerking awake, I heard someone knocking lightly on the door.

"Sophie, it's me, Raj."

I opened the door and he pushed his way in, untying my robe, warming his cold freezing hands on my midriff. "I've missed you so much."

He stepped away from me, throwing his sheepskin coat across the couch, then he sat down in the rocking chair to slip off his shoes and his clothes; we fell together down to the mattress, pulling the lavender satin comforter up over us, holding each other.

"God, I've missed you."

"Me too."

I cried when he had to leave later. On my way to pick up Liz back at the house I heard that song by Bryan Adams, "Everything I Do" and the tears fell again.

***

We'd both made arrangements for the holidays that didn't include each other. Couldn't include each other. Raj and his family were going to spend five days in Austin with Chris' mom, her two brothers and their families.

Nick's parents had cancelled their plans to visit us for Christmas, opting instead to leave Chicago and fly to Sanibel Island in Florida for the holidays. Unspoken was that Nick and I needed to get our lives in order before they'd be willing to visit.

When we first separated Nick and I agreed on a schedule for sharing custody of Liz. We were both reasonable enough and lucky enough to realize that the more amicably we worked out these sorts of arrangements—not having to get involved with lawyers—the better off Liz would be.

I'd made a promise to myself to use the time off from school to think long and hard about whether or not to drop out of medical school. Nick and I had countless conversations about it and it always came down to his willingness to see me through this, his hope that our marriage could survive. If we'd become bitter enemies, using Liz as a pawn in our battles, I wouldn't have been able to continue.

But he kept his promise to give me space and freedom. The time we spent together with Liz held much more meaning and pleasure than it had before.

Chapter Nine

I snapped the cell phone shut and leaned my head against the wall in the kitchen. Owen had called to tell me that Nadine Francke had died. I'd only known her for a few months but something about Nadine struck a responsive chord in me, more so than any other patient I'd worked with. The death sentence she'd received is one of the most devastating that can afflict a human being.

In a brisk, no nonsense tone Owen reported that she'd died two days ago after finishing off a nearly full bottle of Ativan and chasing it with a fifth of vodka.

Nadine Francke did not look fifty-two years old, more like thirty-five. Her auburn hair was thick and wavy; her unlined skin glowed as if lit from within by an incandescent light. An ageless beauty with luminous dark brown eyes, people were quick to notice her lively wit and keen intelligence.

In 1942 Nadine's parents escaped from Hungary, immigrating to America and settling in Perth Amboy, New Jersey. No one else in the extended Francke family survived World War II; they all died at the hands of the Nazis.

The first time I met her I was just finishing up with one patient when Dr. Jaworski handed me her chart. "You can handle getting a urine sample, right Trudeau? Lady in room 201 thinks she has a bladder infection."

Before going into the examining room I thumbed through her chart. With classic left-side upper and lower body motor neuron dysfunction she'd first been diagnosed with ALS, amyotrophic lateral sclerosis, shortly after her left foot gave way and she fractured her ankle. Genetic testing had shown a mutation on one gene in particular that was associated with a more lethal progression of the disease.

Diseases like Parkinson's, Multiple Sclerosis, and ALS are characterized by the destruction of the myelin sheath that protects nerves. With that kind of demyelinating nerve damage bowel and bladder problems are fairly common.

While we waited for the lab to quickly test her urine, I asked her about the ALS. She wore a short-sleeved blouse and I could see a faint twitching of muscles beneath her skin, textbook fasciculations.

She blinked several times trying to keep the tears at bay. "Oh Christ, finding out I had ALS was absolutely terrifying. The funny thing, well not so funny, but as an Ashkenazi Jew early on I had the genetic testing done for the BRCA1 and BRCA2 breast cancer mutations. Turned out I was at high risk for developing breast cancer. So for a lot of obvious reasons I chose not to get married, not to have children and short of having my breasts removed as a preventative measure, I played the waiting game, living life as fast and hard as I possibly could. My father was an investment banker, a brilliant man with his own hedge fund company. He made a lot of money and was very generous. When he and my mother were alive we travelled the globe together.

"Most of my adult life I thought I'd get breast cancer, but that it would be diagnosed early and I'd have the chemo, the radiation, the whole nine yards. I never saw this coming."

Now the tears fell. I reached out and took her hand in mine, shuddering at what a horrible death sentence ALS is.

***

I didn't see her again until a week ago when I happened to be in the rehabilitation wing of Texas Memorial. I saw her sitting in the waiting room; she'd lost a lot of weight and was now in a motorized wheel-chair but she had not lost that ethereal glow nor the sharpness of her gaze, though now you could see through to the pain she was enduring.

"Nadine, it's so good to see you. Are you here for physical therapy?"

She shook her head; her words were slightly slurred, "Paula Lambert is my therapist, she's so good and it did help in the beginning, but I'm just not up for it anymore." She showed me her cell phone clutched in her hand. "I just cancelled the appointment and called Faye to come back and pick me up. She's the home assistant who works with me." Her voice died away.

I sat down opposite her in one of the waiting room chairs. "When was the last time you saw Dr. Bennett?" Bennett was her neurologist, a brilliant guy with a charming collegiate manner, a devout Catholic. He and his wife Nola and their five children lived in a sprawling rancher on two acres where they'd also built a small house for his mother.

"Last week." Her eyes brimmed with tears. "After he examined me he asked if I'd made arrangements for my care. He said that my ALS was very aggressive and I would have to consider hospice within the next six months. I'm lucky I have enough money for the best home health care. I want to die at home."

Tears spilled out of my eyes, "I'm so sorry Nadine."

She gripped my hand with her bony, waxen hand; now it looked more like a claw. "What I hate most Sophie is that there isn't anyone around like Jack Kevorkian who has the balls to take on patients like me. To help me put an end to things before they get really bad. I'm so scared." The effort of speaking had taken the last of her energy and she ended on a ragged breath. Obviously her intercostal muscles were weakening, making it harder to breath. Probably very soon she'd have to be on a ventilator.

As if she'd read my mind, she said, "I won't let them put me on a ventilator and keep me alive."

***

With only slightly trembling hands, I poured more coffee into my mug, then stepped out onto the patio for a cigarette. It was Christmas Eve Day, Liz and I were staying with Nick at the house. Amidst much whispering and giggling they'd hurried away after breakfast to do last minute shopping.

Another storm was forecast for Christmas, the day was grey and cold. I sat down on the cushioned redwood chair opposite the six Thuja giant evergreens. Beautiful, stately trees, they topped out at over twenty-feet and protected the patio from the north wind. A deep jade green, they were lush and full, perfectly aligned like little maids all in a row. Nothing calmed me more quickly than to hear the wind rustling through them, that hypnotic soughing balm to the soul.

I said a silent prayer for Nadine, filled with relief that her suffering was over, hoping her death had been swift and painless.

A niggling sense of anger festered inside of me that she'd had to take matters into her own hands. A deep-seated malaise I felt at the totalitarian stricture which said that people had to keep on living, no matter what. There's no holding back the tide of humanity and the devastation caused by over-population. People should have the right to die. Kevorkian said it best, "We're all terminal."

In one of our gab fests Owen told me that Richard Rhodes, in his book "Deadly Feasts" predicted that the human variant of mad cow disease, Creutzfeldt-Jacob, would sweep through the over-populated planet with such devastating force that there would have to be euthanasia clinics to handle the onslaught.

"Just like that movie we saw years ago in Austin, "Soylent Green" where Edward G. Robinson goes to a clinic and watches blue sky, meadows, clouds and sunshine. Then he dies. I don't actually believe that a writer, even one as esteemed as Rhodes, can predict future plagues. But even Oprah worries about tainted beef. It's all about the dynamics of available resources and population. War, pestilence, famine, and death. End of story."

***

Early evening Christmas day, prime rib and Yorkshire pudding for dinner, a bottle of cabernet sauvignon so rich and loamy you could taste the soil of France's Loire Valley in every sip.

Santa really out did himself that year. He and the elves must have danced through Toys R'Us and just tossed everything that caught their eyes into the sleigh. Nick had also put up a stocking for Susie and stuffed it full of squeaky toys wrapped up in Christmas paper. She knew the drill and made short work of the wrapping. One of her toys was a large rubber rooster that crowed each time she bit down on it, making her squeal and moan in response as if it were a real baby of hers. Between she and Liz, not to mention the television and the stereo at full volume, the noise level in the house sounded like Grand Central.

Liz had crashed earlier, falling asleep on the carpet next to the Christmas tree; we tucked her into bed with the new Panda teddy she'd taken such a shine to. Irresistibly soft and cuddly it felt like the finest cashmere and silk.

In the bathroom off of the master bedroom, I lit candles and filled the Jacuzzi tub with hot water, adding scented bubble bath. Big mistake. Once Nick had eased himself into the steamy water, I turned the jets on. They whipped the bubble bath into mountainous peaks of frothy bubbles that overran the tub and spilled across the floor.

I threw towels on the tile in front of the tub, and brushed away more bubbles. Nick's head was framed with a sudsy halo.

"Want me to scrub you?"

Without opening his eyes he nodded, as if to say, *It's the least you could do for me after all you've done to me.* Admiring the lean, sinewy lines of his body, I used the washcloth to scrub his arms and chest, then his back, his legs, sudsing his feet, cleaning diligently between each little toe the way I do Liz.

"How about some more wine?"

"Do I have to get it?"

"Of course not."

The music of Nat King Cole and "Chestnuts Roasting on an Open Fire" drifted out from the stereo as I went to the kitchen. Refilling our wine glasses with Sauvignon Blanc I hurried back to the warmth of the bathroom, handing Nick his glass.

"There's room enough for two in here, I wouldn't mind the company."

"I'll be right there, just let me see what the weather's doing."

Then wiping condensation away from the window, I peered outside. A blistery cold wind whipped through the mimosa and weeping willow trees in the front yard, the keening noise it made sounded like something you'd hear in Antarctica, not Texas. The ornamental black lamp close to the sidewalk cast a circle of light over the trees which were encased in ice; they looked like delicate glass figurines. The luxuriant evergreens and the red-berried pyrocantha hugged the exterior of the house like a thermal blanket.

I sipped my wine and stared at the frigid world beyond, grateful that I'd had this break from school and Raj, enough to feel more grounded. That seeming calm in the eye of the storm of my life was like a retreat from battle, a Christmas truce. Peace on Earth. Raj would come back from Austin all too soon and derail my life again; this was known as irrefutably as if Moses had inscribed it on stone for me. That living thing, that hum, that vibrating, animating energy inside of me was muted now, crouched low like Raj's well-trained pet, commanded to "stay!" It seemed to lurk there silently, waiting, sure that the time would come when Raj would be back and it could uncoil and stretch and reach out for him again.

For now I relished the quiet of Christmas, doting on my husband and child.

***

A few days before New Year's I dropped Liz off at Nancy's and drove to the medical school at the crack of dawn thinking I would get a jump start on my next rotation which was OB-GYN. Surprisingly the east parking lot was jammed even though the holidays wouldn't be over for almost a week. I hurried to get in out of the cold and hit a patch of black ice and lay there on the ground for a few seconds before I realized what had happened. With my heavy wool jacket and backpack the fall didn't cause any damage, just made me feel like that guy who woke up to find he had been turned into a cockroach struggling on his back, arms and legs all akimbo: Kafka, "The Metamorphosis."

Clambering up in a most inelegant fashion, I heard my cell phone ring. It was Raj.

"Hi. Happy New Years'." At the sound of his voice something unfolded in my chest.

"Thanks. It's still a while away."

"Right, can't waste any time. Where are you?"

"On my way to the library to get a few books. I'll probably reread the 5th edition of "Obstetrics and Gynecology" for next term." I'd read it when I was pregnant with Liz

"Come have lunch with me and I'll show you some things to do with obstetrics and gynecology that will just blow you away. Pun fully intended."

There was a lilt to his voice, an innocence of all that was to come; beware of those who are quick studies, one step ahead of you, learning the rules of the game faster than you can change them. Men are astonishingly creative and intelligent, much more so than I had ever realized. And all too often with the morals of a Neanderthal.

"What have you been smoking, or did you forget about Chris?"

"Her mom's got something wrong with her sciatic nerve. She's on complete bed rest, I dropped her off at the Greyhound bus earlier and don't pick her up until after New Years'. But I've got the kids."

"Did you hear it might snow? It's been since I was in high school that it snowed here. This is the craziest winter; if they're right about global warming it is really freaky."

"Please come, I missed you." An irresistible pleading note.

"How come there isn't any noise in the background. Where are the twins?"

"Alma, our lady friend here in the complex, is watching them for me so I could get some housework done."

When I arrived, he was standing outside his front door dressed in shorts and his sheepskin coat, Nikes without the laces; his bare legs, covered with black hair, were riddled with goose-pumps. He opened the car door for me, helping me out.

His hair was very short, Chris always did his hair, he didn't trust barbers. I ran my hand over the bare sides, giving him a quizzical glance.

"She scalped me this morning before she left, retribution for you, glad it wasn't my balls. But I wanted it short, a friend told me it's less likely to fall out if I keep it short."

"You sure that's not just superstition?"

"No!" He was vehement, determined not to lose his hair, "If it's long it's heavier, the force of gravity makes it fall out faster."

"I hope you keep that bit of advice to yourself and don't share it with patients."

Time to change the subject. Having been a good girl and endured his week-long absence with his wife, I couldn't help asking, "Did she say anything about Helmut on the trip?"

He was open before, now that door inside of him closed. "No."

Can't I see the evidence before me? You don't give your husband a haircut one day and leave him the next. Scalped or not, it speaks of a certain harmony.

I watched him move around the kitchen making tuna fish, spreading it on bread. Those feminine talents, his ease with them, struck me as odd. The twin poles masculine/feminine so clearly delineated, who was the woman he had patterned himself after? There was a clue for me in his ability to relate meaningfully to housework, to bring to bear all of his passion even here. But I was not yet aware of the dangers of such hypersensitivity, such attention to detail. No doubts ever assailed the ferocious strength of my love.

His head seemed smaller, the body bigger with his long hair gone. His body fascinated me, was a weight on my eyes, he was dressed in baggy shorts and a red nylon tank top, my eyes wandered, noting the muscles in his arms, his broad chest, the pale, luminescent skin, beautiful, smoothly textured the way a woman's skin should be. Without his glasses he looked very young, exuding a potent masculinity. He noted my appraising glance, "I told you I've been doing housework all day, but mostly I'm clean." He grinned wickedly, helping me follow his thoughts out to their natural conclusion: sex.

Raj ate so fast there was no time to talk. As soon as he finished, he cleared his plate, rinsing it in the sink and then stacking it in the dishwasher.

Before I was even half-finished with my sandwich, he pulled me to my feet and then bent down, picking me up. There was still a wad of tuna fish and bread in my mouth, but he was not squeamish about such unromantic details. I grabbed for my glass of pink lemonade, swishing it around like mouthwash in my mouth. Able to talk again, I complained weakly, "Raj, no! I promised myself to get a head start on next semester; I've slacked off enough as it is."

Without a word, he passed down the hallway, into the bedroom and dropped me on their king-sized bed, moving over on top of me. He pulled up my sweater, unzipped my jeans, pulling them off then stopping just short of removing my underwear.

He reached up and brushed the hair away from my face. Again, that candor, yet intense mystery in his eyes. What was behind that look?

The shifting balance of relationships. When he went back to his wife in the beginning I'd felt so isolated and vulnerable, struggling to keep my distance. What had become of my sense of equality in this affair?

Had I capitulated too soon? Too late? Even if this was completely the wrong thing to do, was it really even worth worrying about? Hadn't I understood already that there were forces beyond my control at work here and I had no choice but to see them played out?

He hadn't said he loved me, was that an absurd concession to being with his wife? A hair you can't split. What had drawn me to him in the first place, the intensity of his emotions, the seeming unshakable allegiance to things he loved, had deluded me into feeling safe with him, when in reality there are never any guarantees to be had with those we love.

It was too pathetic to consider. We can't see into the future, pick and choose partners based on the refinements of abuse that might soon arise--all of it done unconsciously. My motives had not been that perverse, there had been hope in them.

Feeling foolish, used as only a woman can feel, I suddenly wanted to hide my face in shame. He reached for my panties. "Don't." I whispered fiercely.

With a cocky grin he sat back, watching me. "You look funny with your face all scrunched up and trying to be angry now." He mimicked my expression, "That's what you look like." Then he pushed himself toward me harder, pressing against the soft nylon of my underwear.

"Don't Raj, please."

I struggled against him, tried to push him off, angry, ready to fight. But that was what he wanted, an excuse to show his brute strength and power over me, to plunge ahead. Beneath his steady weight, my body felt fragile. His expression was unreadable, as I squirmed uncomfortably.

He thought: Why can't women be like men? She'd been on his mind on the return drive to San Antonio, drawing him on a string back to her. The rolling hills of the highway, music from the radio, it had all kept him mesmerized, focused on the thought of melting into her warmth.

He gently fingered the inch-wide lace edge of my panties, finally twisting it around tightly, roughly, his eyes sparkling, menacing, and daring me to protest. The fabric could stretch only so far, then it ripped in two. He slowly moved it out from under me, his eyes continually returning to mine as if trying to read my expression.

When he entered me, I jerked away, he fell back. "Bitch," he muttered laughing, then moved toward me again, using his legs over mine to keep me immobile. He gripped the sides of my head, his hands encasing my skull, cupping it tightly. My head felt small and vulnerable in his hands, everything inside of it reduced in importance, diminished by my desperate need to capture and keep this man. But how foolish of me to think I had dominated this relationship, I was merely a pawn. In the initial bloom of love and idealism, neither Raj nor I knew of the Machiavellian tendencies in his personality.

Stop trying to think like a man Sophie. Stop thinking that you can meet him on equal terms or that you have the same power he has, you're at his mercy. The thought sent something spiraling downward in my brain, like a bird shot out of the air.

Resistance was just a shabby masquerade. I loved him and didn't want to resist but it was clear now that this situation had degraded into the classic struggle between men and women. By resisting, I was asking him to make things right for me, if you're going to keep on seeing me don't do it within the context of staying with your wife, making me into that hated stereotype, the nagging mistress.

When he was through and I was again aware of my surroundings, I looked over his shoulder at the bedroom he shared with his wife, staring at the mess of bottles on the vanity table, tubes of lipstick, a bottle of hairspray without the cap on it. There was a bottle of Tommy Hilfiger cologne whose fragrance I suddenly recognized on the sheets around me. Raj shifted away from me, the mirror on the vanity came into view. A little note was taped on it. "DON'T FORGET TO TAKE YOUR BIRTH CONTROL PILLS!!!"

Could anything be more of an indictment against my behavior? This was worse than when Chris chased me out of their apartment. Bile rose in my throat. Raj's breathing was steady and shallow, he must have fallen asleep. I squeezed my eyes shut, swallowing several times to rid myself of the nausea. Gently I disengaged myself, "I have to go Raj." He moved over and let me up.

Standing at the doorway, he held me close, kissing me goodbye. As he moved away from me I noticed how much more prominent his ears were with his new haircut; along the outer rim of the right ear was a tiny scratch, a dot of blood where Chris must have nicked him with the electric shears. Next time Mrs. Kahn take the whole ear.

"It's just for the sex isn't it?" I hated the tremor in my voice, the tears that threatened to come.

His eyes were mocking. "Yeah, just for the sex."

***

Back at school, I shoved my backpack roughly into my locker, slamming the door shut. I hadn't noticed a sticky note toward the top.

It was from Owen asking me if I was back in time for lunch to meet him in the cafeteria.

As if it were a flashing neon sign, taunting me, I remembered the little note taped to Chris' vanity. In the cramped and narrow locker room, I leaned my head against the door and wept quietly saying a silent prayer that Owen was right and the Y2K bug would blow us all to kingdom come and end this misery.

Chapter Ten

I figured by now that I'd pretty much memorized Stedman's Medical Dictionary. As a medical illustrator I'd thumbed through it countless times and still kept it in my locker at school, dragging it out whenever I had new material to cover. That afternoon after leaving Raj I sat alone in the study lab, idly flipping through the pages, stopping often to read definitions and study the work of other medical illustrators.

I paused at the H's, rereading the description of "Harlequin Baby." Nothing had disturbed me more during my pregnancy than learning about that particular birth defect. Extremely rare, it is characterized by scaly patterns that cover the skin in diamond shapes. I trembled when I read the definition, horrified by the graphic medical illustration. How could such a thing exist? Could my baby be born with that defect? Of course she wasn't. But if you had any tendency toward being a hypochondriac, medical school was a minefield of diseases to choose from. I'd conjured so many symptoms over the years that by now I was probably immune to everything.

What I couldn't get out of my head that afternoon though was the idea of Chris Kahn pregnant. The image loomed so sharply in my mind that by the end of the day I pictured her already pregnant and choosing a name for the baby boy she and Raj had always wanted. Drained and depressed, aware that I'd not really done anything productive that afternoon, I gathered my things up and trudged out to the car.

Stopping at Nancy Metcalf's house to get Liz, I hurried up the sidewalk, anxious to get home.

"Stay for a beer?" Nancy was picking up the pieces to a puzzle of the United States, each piece a molded, wooden miniature of the state.

"No, but thanks. It's been a hell of a day, I'm pooped. Wish my apartment wasn't such a disaster. We were at Nick's off and on for the Christmas holidays.

She picked up the last three pieces, Arizona, California and Texas, holding them stacked in her hands, a look of concern on her face, "Things going okay?"

"Not really, it's hard to know the right thing to do." She waited expectantly for me to go on, but my emotions were in such disarray there was no way I could open up. The silence between us lengthened and guilt rose up inside of me realizing I might have hurt her feelings by shutting her out.

Liz finally ran into the room, grinning lopsidedly, conflicting emotions on her face, glad that I was there, mad at me for leaving her for so long. Her day must have gone like mine; normally I had to drag her away from Amanda and Nellie.

On the drive home she fell asleep and stayed asleep as I carried her into the apartment. Not wanting to let go of her, we sat together in the rocking chair, in the dark; she moved restlessly in her sleep, molding herself to me more comfortably.

Beyond the thin walls of my apartment I could hear others arriving home. A stereo suddenly came to life mingling with the noise of a car honking in the busy parking lot, two voices shouted friendly greetings. My emotions seemed to have strangely flat lined, leaving my feelings for Raj oddly blank and neutral.

Was I retarded, leaving my husband for a married man? No wonder there were still countries in the world where women were in "purdah," forced to wear cloth concealing them from head to toe with only a tiny piece of fabric lattice-work over the eyes to look out of. Maybe we're all dealing with genes that mediate our behavior based on the concept of women as chattel.

I wondered if Betty Friedan had been wrong after all. If I'd been a stay-at-home mom, little Miss Susie Homemaker, I never would have met Raj. Let loose upon the world you see options, you make choices, you evolve, often with unexpected, devastating economic and emotional consequences. I knew none of this was good for Liz, and what about that confused, lopsided grin? Mother, where were you when I needed you today? It's not necessary to know the dynamics of all the wrong I'm doing to her to still suffer enormous guilt.

Half an hour passed and she slept on. I put her to bed.

A cigarette burned in my red Lone Star ashtray, there was a Coors at my elbow as I listened to a cable music station playing an eclectic mix of tunes: country, rock, even a little rap. The music infected me with enough energy to tackle the stack of dirty dishes and cups and glasses and silverware balanced precariously high on the countertops. Two small Teflon pans, crusted over with a greasy film, littered the top of the stove. Left to my own devices I was a wretched housekeeper.

As I picked up my portable mixer and removed the mashed potato encrusted beaters, a winter cockroach slithered out from one hole. The bug hurried away, dropping a matching brown burden of incubating babies. We had been gone too long at Nick's; the indefatigable insects were taking over.

After making it through most of the dishes, I dried my hands with a towel and stared out the window for a moment at the cold clear night pushing gently at the pane of glass. The black nothingness of the sky reminded me of my freedom, reminded me that infinite possibilities existed again. Then unbidden, a prayer formed in my mind, the sudden fervent hope for a future with Raj, for more babies with him. The blueprint for this affair was somewhere inside my head, it kept whispering to me that to fight it was not a choice I had.

Chapter Eleven

New Years' Eve1999/2000

Nick and Liz had gone to Austin for New Years'. Nick's half-brother, John, and his family were there visiting and it would be Liz' first time meeting her two cousins, Beth and Andrew.

With nothing better to do I drove up to school in the morning. I'd gone to the medical library and checked out several books. After the OB-GYN rotation I'd be doing Psychiatry, a subject which fascinated me like no other. I checked out Charles Sherrington's "Integration of the Nervous System," Morton Prince's "The Unconscious," and Karen Horney's "Neuroses and Human Growth," all of which I knew to be excellent books, old but still very relevant. The case of Sally Beauchamp in Prince's book about the dissociation of personality drew me in with a haunting sense of familiarity.

With my feet propped up on a chair in the study lab I read straight through to one o'clock. Eating a Snickers and Coke for lunch, I tackled a stack of old *Journal of the American Medical Association* (JAMA) magazines in the bookcase at the back of the room. It was an interesting magazine if you overlooked every other page advertising antidepressants with pictures of women in the classic fainting pose, one hand to their forehead. I don't think so. Good thing women were now matching the enrollment numbers of men in medical schools.

At one-thirty I stuffed the books in my backpack and headed out, passing the dean's personal assistant in the hall. She was making the rounds of all the offices, bearing paper cups full of heavily spiked eggnog and wishes for a happy and safe New Year.

Just as I finished downing the fabulous concoction, ninety proof with maybe a whisper of eggnog, my cell phone rang. It was Raj.

"Whatcha doing?"

"At school, just hanging out, Nick took Liz to Austin to meet her cousins."

"Are you like some sort of nerd who does nothing but study?"

"Not at all, in fact only half of me is still here."

"Which half? My favorite half? The fun half? Come by, please. No tricks, I can't, the twins are with me."

I should know better than to talk to Raj after I've had alcohol.

***

When I arrived he was just sticking the twins into the tub, belting them into little plastic chairs and then running warm water mixed with bubble bath over them. Into this he dumped a bamboo carton full of rubber ducks, toy cars and rounded plastic dolls which fit into cute plastic houses and cars, and small rubber balls. The twins gurgled and screamed at each other, splashing water and throwing toys. Raj grinned happily at them.

"Watch them for me while I get us a rum and Coke, okay?"

He returned with the drinks and brought his yearbook from senior year in high school. We sat next to each other on the floor, our backs resting on the closed door behind us, sipping the rum and Coke. In the steamy bathroom, after the eggnog at work, now rum, all on an empty stomach, it went straight to my head.

We looked through his yearbook; there was a picture of him in his baseball uniform, back row, third in from the left, he looked the same then as now, that silent level gaze, so direct and unflinching; then next, a picture of girl he had liked. He turned the page quickly, adding, "It can't be like that with us though."

Enigmatic, no explanation of his words. Instead of pursuing it I sat wallowing in paranoia, my insecurities, inadequacies gnawing away at me, reminding me that I was unworthy of the love of such a younger man. He belonged more to the girl in the yearbook, than he did to me. He kept pushing his glasses up on the bridge of his nose, the moisture in the air made his skin slippery. Jane tipped over in her chair, the seatbelt held her awkwardly under her arm. Raj crawled on hands and knees over to her, readjusting her position more comfortably. There were too many faces of Raj in that room; the babies looked exactly like him.

He brought up Terry Martin's New Year's Eve party. "I want to be with you tonight. Why won't you go? It could be time to party like hell, after midnight tonight the world as we know it could end. Actually, I don't really think there's much to this Y2K shit, Chris is worried that all of the planes will fall out of the sky. Everyone from school's going to be there. We could meet up."

He lifted his eyebrows, then flexed them together several times in a cute, cajoling manner. His full lips parted slightly as he took a long sip from his drink, his teeth straight and white. Of all the contradictory, conflicting emotions he aroused in me, the need to mother him seemed the most odd.

"No, I've been working on a portrait of Liz, I promised Nick I'd finish it for him so he can get it framed."

The expression on his face turned ugly. "What kind of separation is it where you spend all your free time with him? I thought you said you were getting a divorce."

These arguments only confused me. How do you fight with someone who makes having returned to his wife seem like such a negligible thing in the overall scheme of your relationship?

"Come on. I want to be with you tonight."

He was so close. He'd taken his glasses off and in the steamy, sweaty bathroom his cheeks were bright red, his black eyes, velvet soft, sparkling seductively at me.

"Raj," God! I was so weak willed with too soft a heart. "Come by my apartment later, but I won't go to the party."

How many other people are out there in the world with black holes in their hearts and minds? Lost souls who wander from person to person looking for whatever it was they left behind. They see it in others and want to possess it, take it back, wrapping their well-being so tightly around that person that it becomes suffocating. I'd done this once too often. Faintly, it was beginning to dawn on me that there must be some imbalance at my core to feel so desperate about Raj. I felt as if I were a vampire, wanting to steal something from him. I wanted to steal his youth, his masculinity, his body, his energy, and his mind in as possessive a way as John Fowles' "The Collector" kidnaps the art student he becomes obsessed with.

Like the story of the little Dutch boy holding his finger in the dike, I had to hold on to Raj. He was that finger in the dike; without him I would drain away to nothing. But for the first time in my life, I'd stumbled onto someone with a bigger hole in the dike.

It didn't become clear until much later that no one would ever have the power to block the hole inside of me, and that really all I would be able to do was recognize it and work around it. Work around it like workmen in the street who skirt an open manhole leading to the subterranean bowels of the city, knowing that to fall in would mean certain death.

***

Less than a mile beyond the field adjacent to my apartment complex was the outer boundary of Norwood Hills, a tiny wooded enclave with homes on large lots built for the doctors from the medical center. At the far edge of the field was a greenbelt that wended through the development with a paved trail for joggers, bike-riders, and walkers.

It wasn't really safe to walk in San Antonio at night by yourself, but it was my contention that when the dark forces work at you from within, you are protected from them without. A natural law wherein two dark forces can't occupy the same space at the same time.

I had to get out. The night was cold enough for my blue parka, with a slight mist in the air that bestowed a halo on every street light. The walk along the trail was leisurely with houses visible beyond the thicket of brambles and bare trees. I stared unabashedly into windows like a peeping Tom, drawing off the warmth, vicariously living their settled lives. The discreet charm of the bourgeoisie. The wet smell of wood smoke from a cedar-log fire drifted to me through the misty air.

Back home I found that the mood to paint had passed. Susie was sound asleep in the middle of the mattress on the floor. I flopped down next to her. Sanguine as ever, she opened one eye, then closed it, simultaneously raising a leg, exposing her ventral region, without so much as lifting her head. Like Pavlov's dog. Petting her, I scanned my walls, reassured by my paintings that I too existed, that I was real, as if they were spikes in the ground around me, keeping me tethered, giving me substance.

When my cell phone rang my heart beat wildly; desire pulsed through me as my flesh strained against my clothes. *Please be Raj, please, please.*

It was Nick. Disappointment stung me and for a split second I stepped away from myself and wondered *who are you*? I was acting like a woman possessed, the calm, rational, downright bookish person I imagined myself to be had vanished.

"Hey, Soph, Liz wanted to say goodnight and I thought I'd check in on you, see how you're doing. Got time for a chat?"

I can't deal with this right now, no, no, no. "I'm sorry Nick. I really don't feel much like talking, my throat is raw and scratchy, it feels like I'm coming down with a cold, hopefully it's just that. What a bummer of a way to spend New Year's Eve."

His voice grew concerned, "Have you taken your temperature? Do you want us to come back first thing in the morning, just to make sure you're all right?"

Suddenly I had to bite my tongue to keep from lashing out at him. Why are you being so nice to me when I'm ruining your life? He was so eager, so anxious to please, such a wonderful husband. And such a harlot for a wife.

"No, please, I just want to go to bed and stay there, get a really good night's sleep."

"Honest, I don't mind. I think we have a lot to talk about, no time like the present. We could go out for lunch at Pancho's on the River Walk, drink margaritas. Liz loves that guacamole dip."

"No!" My voice rose, I struggled for control, "Don't come back early on my account. If I feel okay tomorrow afternoon, I'll come over then and we can talk."

"If you're sure you don't want us to come back early."

"I am."

***

By ten o'clock I was frantic, arms crossed defensively, pacing mindlessly back and forth like a junkie who needs a fix. Discovering that I was out of cigarettes I dialed Raj's cell phone to tell him I was running up to the Shell station and not to leave if I wasn't back when he got to my apartment. It went straight to voice mail. Who the hell was he talking to?

Nervous and oddly distraught—this must be the flu making me so crazy--I slipped into my parka and ran outside. The leather seats in my Volvo were punishing, the cold penetrating deep into my bones. The car wouldn't start. Five minutes of frantic efforts to start it, swearing like a stevedore, sure I had flooded it forever, the engine finally turned over. Shivering, my head full of incoherent, drifting patterns, I was still engaged enough to sobriety and sanity to shift into reverse, then first, then second, using the car the way men sometimes do, to express their anger and frustration.

The little pock-marked Cambodian behind the counter at the Seven-Eleven had a wary look about him, his eyes darting nervously to the back of the store where there were two long-haired guys, obviously nervous themselves. Apparently unable to find what they wanted, they radiated a certain existential angst. Maybe they were really only there to rob the place, a New Year's Eve heist. The bigger guy with all the tattoos, I could just imagine the wheels of his mind turning—Y2K is imminent, let's shoot the place up and grab the money, party until life as we know it is over.

Hurrying, terrified by the unaccustomed air of nervous tension, a tension that the drama of my night without Raj seemed to be adding to, I paid for two packs of Marlboros and a six pack of Budweiser and swiftly departed.

At home I finally had the sense to get angry.

"What a fool you are Sophie," I said aloud, pacing, Susie pacing beside me. Was it just lack of consideration on his part, which was ultimately more forgivable, or was it a conscious effort to keep me unbalanced? If the latter, it hinted at a certain cruelty, knowledge of the leverage value in deceit and manipulation, ploys I tried not to use myself, so didn't readily see them in others.

I called Raj again on his cell phone. When he answered, he sounded drunk, "Yeah, I'm still coming. I'll be there." It was nearly midnight.

How could he treat me like that? I smoked another cigarette, thinking of the domino theory of adultery, Nick, me, Raj, Chris, Helmut, who else—see, I'd even forgotten to include the children in that equation. By twelve-thirty, as each second that he didn't arrive kept tearing at me, I was ready to fly apart into a million pieces.

Sitting with my legs crossed Indian-style in front of the fireplace I crumpled the empty beer cans around me into a neat stack, then tossed them listlessly at the hearth. My lungs felt char-broiled but I smoked a cigarette down to the filter, then lit a new one off of the butt. The nicotine acted like knitting needles tightly weaving my thoughts together and endowing them with unexpected acuity and insight: If I ever intended to live a sane life again, it wasn't with Raj.

Susie used her strong snout to nudge my arm up, then settled with her head in my lap, wanting reassurance that I wasn't mad at her. Pulling her face up to mine I kissed her lavishly, pushing back her ears, holding her tight.

You have been brought so low, Sophie. My internal struggle would have been comical if it hadn't signaled the utter debasement of my character. It was like having multiple personalities, but without the convenience of amnesia. The warring factions continued unabated, dissembling with one another, one voice ascendant, then seconds later fading out while another claimed the spotlight. This wasn't about Raj anymore; that had only been the stimulus. Then what was it about?

From some remote core of sanity inside me, the voice of reason calmly told me to put my cigarette out, close the shutters to the fireplace and go to bed.

I crawled between the cool, clean sheets and closed my eyes hoping I'd be able to sleep. As one brain cell after another began to wink and nod off, I suddenly remembered that midnight had come and gone and the world still churned inexorably toward an unknown future.

Minutes later I fell asleep, with Susie's nose at my neck, her breath in my face, warm and reassuring.

Chapter Twelve

February 2000

Raj never explained or apologized about being MIA on New Years'. I suspect that he probably got too drunk to drive, passed out and crawled home later.

I kept a promise to myself all through January and the first of February to stay completely away from him and threw myself into my OB-GYN rotation.

***

The on-call OB-GYN resident, Dr. Kamod Gupta, was a horrid little Indian man with acne scars along his neck and lower jaw. He'd been to medical school in New Delhi and later was certified through the Educational Commission for Foreign Medical Graduates (ECFMG) to work at Texas Memorial and only recently had passed the US medical licensing exam. Swarthy, smug, with nervous, darting black eyes, he made my skin crawl with his constant boasting about his sexual prowess and being God's chosen OB-GYN for women.

I'd been on call the night the Jane Doe was literally dumped in the parking lot outside the Emergency Room naked except for her bra. When Dr. Gupta and I arrived in her room I was so appalled by the injuries to her face I thought she was dead.

Susie Jenkins, the ER nurse filled us in. "All of her vital signs are good. Pupils were equal and reactive to light, no signs of a concussion. There are severe vaginal and anal tears and bruising, a bite mark on her shoulder and a laceration on the inside of her right thigh just above the knee. AP and lateral chest X-rays were normal. She was extremely agitated at first so we added 0.5 cc's of valium to her IV. That's it, she's all yours."

With a dismissive nod of his head, Dr. Gupta turned to me. "We'll need to get the rape kit started, first..."

Before he could finish the young woman sat up. Crying and moaning, she tried to get off the bed, the white sheet dropped down to her waist. Gently, I pushed her back down, "It's okay, you're safe now, we're here to take care of you." I turned back to Gupta just in time to see him ogle the girl's red and white polka-dot bra; he was hardly able to tear his eyes away from the lush creamy breasts flowing beyond the restraints of the brassiere. When minutes later he was called away for an emergency Caesarian, I was extremely grateful.

"I'll be back shortly, but you'll be awhile, ever done one of these before?"

"Yes."

"Don't forget to collect the sheets."

"I won't."

The valium must have taken effect because my patient seemed to have dozed off, though a look of pain was still etched across her face. It was hard to tell exactly how old she was or even what she looked like. She had short curly brown hair, but her right eye was swollen shut, already black, blue and red. Her bottom lip was split and swollen to twice its normal size. My guess for age was early twenties.

Everything I needed for evidence collection was already in the room, slides, swabs, bags for her clothes and sheets, vials for blood. I'd only processed the rape kit once before so I had to occasionally refer to the instruction leaflet. There was a small digital camera on a shelf above the sink; I used that first thing to take pictures of her injuries.

A little while later a woman named Renee Johnson from Bexar County PD came in hoping to get a statement from the girl, but she was barely awake, and even less coherent.

I'd started at three fifteen a.m. and didn't finish until after five. Thankfully, Gupta never reappeared. Off duty now, I went to the cafeteria, bought a jumbo coffee and dumped cream and sugar in equal measure into it. The thought of eating anything sickened me.

Making my way through the parking garage, every sound made me jump; I was terrified that Jane Doe's rapist was right around the corner. Once in my car I locked all the doors and turned on the engine, waiting until I hit the street before I lit my first cigarette in over ten hours. I couldn't get the images of the damage done to the girl out of my mind.

Back at school a day later Dr. Gupta brought me up to speed on our Jane Doe. Her name was Carla Rennert, she was nineteen years old and a student at the University of Texas at San Antonio hoping to get a BBA in Information Systems. She'd been abducted after leaving campus and claimed she never really got a good look at her assailant.

I never have understood how surprised people can be when "bad things happen to good people." How can they not have some grasp of the randomness of events? That they are not wrapped in a Plexiglas bubble protecting them from harm.

F. David Peat said when man deserted life in the wild, moved indoors and wrote the Social Contract, like departing Eden, our thoughts turned in on us, spiraling, layering, intertwining, growing in complexity and paving the way for neurosis. Animals held captive in zoos often get depressed. We are all in some way pinned down by an insidious captivity.

My time with Charlie left me changed in many ways; I knew early on that the world was not a safe place, that there had never been such a thing as a "noble savage", only savages. Victims of any kind of abuse know this at the core of their being. Mother Nature never meant for us to let down our guard, to become so domesticated that we lose our hyper vigilance. Enlightened and civilized? Open your eyes; widen the banks of your consciousness: danger is everywhere, no one is exempt. People want to take your money, your heart and soul as well as your life; they might even want to torture you beforehand.

***

By mid-February when I'd hit my stride with the new term, adjusted once again to the constant stress and overwork, I forgot why I'd been mad at Raj. All we had time for were a few minutes snatched here and there. A couple of times we took short drives up to a hilly overlook in Helotes and sat next to each other in the car not talking, just content to be together. If I'd thought it was over between us, I was only fooling myself. He meant everything to me.

Would he ever be mine to have and to hold freely? I doubted it. It is a fact that when we cut ourselves electricity escapes from the wound until it heals over, it has to do with sodium channels and the release of ions. My love for Raj was like that, a wound drawing out my life force.

***

It had been a crazy day. Starting off I was at the red light waiting to cross the street, heading to the hospital, when this brawny black guy pulled up next to the curb in an old junker of a car. The passenger side window was open and he leaned over grinning at me. "Hey miss, lookie here, hey missy!" He was pointing to his lap and as my eyes travelled downward he whisked away a dirty red rag to reveal that his pants were undone and he had one of the more outsized erections I'd ever seen. The light turned green and I ran across the street, feeling slightly sick to my stomach.

What was it with the pervs that day? As our OB-GYN group headed by Dr. Gupta, was assembling outside the room of a patient, I overheard a couple of the nurses talking at the nurses' station.

"Yeah, the guy in 311, every time I walk in there he's masturbating; the guy belongs up on the psych ward except they won't take him because he's got to have dialysis."

Another nurse, Nicole, who had a sinfully curvaceous figure not the least bit concealed by her tight scrubs, laughed and lowering her voice said, "He told me that he had over five-hundred videos that he'd bought not to mention a few he'd downloaded from the web. If jerking off to porno movies were the equivalent of wind-based erosion his dick should have disappeared by now."

Those of us toward the back of the group nearly fell over laughing. Dr. Gupta turned and hissed at us to be quiet. He looked at his watch. "You all are dismissed."

Maybe it was a cultural thing, but Gupta had no sense of humor at all. Especially now that the rumor mill daily churned out tidbits about his failed attempts as a Lothario. Nicole had put him in his place and threatened sexual harassment; the man was as smarmy as they come, a total voyeur.

Actually I've always had issues with the use of that word. Voyeurism has a bad connotation as if it's something that only sexual deviants engage in. Although, I have a very distinct memory of my OB-GYN stepping back from the examining table when I was at my most pregnant and fulsome, staring fixedly at my naked breasts with more than just clinical interest. For lack of a better word, there is a certain amount of voyeurism involved in doctoring. It's especially exciting when you reach the point in medical school when you begin working with patients.

From Dictionary.com:

Voyeur: a person who obtains sexual pleasure or excitement from the observation of someone undressing, having sexual intercourse, etc. *Not me.*

French: literally one who sees from the French "voir" to see. *How I use the word myself, interchangeable with voyeur.*

Prurient: having, inclined to have, or characterized by lascivious or lustful thoughts, etc.

Having a restless desire or longing. *Tricky wording.*

I'd always thought that prurient meant someone who was intensely interested in the behavior, mostly sexual, but not solely confined to that, of others.

It's rather a jumble, what is normal behavior? We're all sexual beings, some to a greater degree than others. Is it prurient or voyeuristic to be avidly interested in all of the details of the latest crash of a jumbo jet? Where do we draw the line between a mournful sense of loss driving us to learn as much as we can about the crash, and an unhealthy curiosity?

It's believed that language arose to fulfill our intense need to talk about each other, to gossip, *to share.* Like what Christopher Wills describes in "The Runaway Brain" we've interbred so globally that everyone's brain has evolved to a point of no return. You can't go backwards on the evolutionary tree (unless of course that's just where the internet is headed.)

This doesn't mean that there aren't still people two standard deviations below the norm for intelligence on the Bell curve. As well as those who are two standard deviations above the norm. Still, the masses tend to cluster in the center.

So I struggle with my insatiable curiosity and the limits of decorum, everything is grist for my mill, but not so for the rest of the world and I need to remember that my patients deserve my discretion.

At the bank of elevators I jabbed the button several times, happy that we'd been dismissed so early and eager to head home.

The elevator doors opened a few minutes later and Raj got off as I was about to get on. He followed me back into the elevator as the doors closed on the two of us. "I was coming to look for you, can I see you tonight? I switched my hours with Steve in the lab so Chris won't expect me home until late."

I agreed without a moment's hesitation. "What time?"

"Six-thirty?"

"Perfect."

***

Standing on a chair to screw a light bulb into the overhead socket in the kitchen, I stopped for a moment to stare at the white opaque light fixture resting on the counter. It was filled with dead moths and flies that either had spontaneously generated inside or had contorted their bodies in such a manner as to slip through the tight seal the lip of the fixture made with the ceiling. Like the contortions I went through to be with Raj; the dead insects and I shared a fatal attraction to the light.

Right on time, Raj knocked on the door, I shouted for him to come in. He came in wheeling his mountain bike, parking it beyond the mattress which was still in its semi-permanent spot on the living room floor.

"Where's your helmet?"

"Don't need one, I'm careful. Wearing one would be like wearing a rubber during sex." He stared up at me, his face at the level of my crotch. Leaning into me, his hot breath on my jeans stirred lust inside me.

"Need any help?" he asked.

"Nope, I've got it. Thanks though."

Liz ran down the hall coming to a standstill in front of Raj, giving him a shy grin. He tousled her hair, then unzipped his jacket, bringing out a plastic bag. "Caught these before dawn this morning at Lake McQueeney and yes they've been in the refrigerator at the lab all day. Got any wine? You won't believe the fish I cook. We need wine for the sauce."

Finished with the light fixture, I stepped down from the chair and retrieved a half bottle of Sauvignon Blanc from the fridge.

"Why don't you pour us a glass and the saucier," he grinned, his French accent perfect, "moi, I will use zee rest for my sauce." His smile was electric, the air around him seemed to crackle and spark as if he were busy generating something beyond his normal electromagnetic field.

Liz noticed it too and wouldn't leave him alone, flirting with him like mad, teasing him, giggling and running away into her room. Then peeking around the corner, she screamed with laughter, brown eyes dancing, as he pounced on her, tickling her.

Dinner was a semi-formal affair with candles and more wine, steamed carrots and wild rice. The sauce was perfect, creamy with a delicate wine-flavor and tangy from the half-bottle of capers he'd thrown in. After Liz went to bed we watched the original "The Fly" on the Science Fiction channel.

On our stomachs on the mattress, legs entwined, toes

touching, Raj and I were intrigued by how good such an old black and white film could be. We both jumped when a branch from a tree just outside the living room window tapped rhythmically on the pane of glass. It was like surreal symbolism, "Wake up inside, the specter of death is nigh!"

For a moment I was stuck back in my teen years after seeing "Nightmare on Elm Street" on a summer visit to my grandparents' small ranch in east Texas, near Woodville. My brothers and sisters and I had all slept outside in tents and hammocks in a stand of trees not far from the house. Despite being covered in "Off" mosquito repellent, (an odor which to this day conjures up the face of Freddy Krueger) the mosquitoes were dive-bombing Kamikazes. My terror was great then, lost so high up in the trees, enveloped in our hammocks like incubating pod people, monsters lurking behind every rustling branch.

***

Later, after the movie, we made love, coming together with an almost desperate intensity. For once I was on top with my legs stretched taut between Raj's legs, pressing my hips into his. Then from such a tiny start inside, from some unknown region of my anatomy, as if I'd discovered a new country long obscured by the South Pole, a swelling sensation slowly gained momentum.

Curious, fascinated, I worked it harder, my feet pressing hard against the mattress, gaining traction. Then Raj moved with me, caught in the grip of passion, his hands moving roughly over my flesh. He thrust deep inside me, the warmth continued to build and build and build inside the walls of my vagina. It was a new feeling for me, a tension poised on the brink of orgasm, thought it was a myth, thought women only had clitoral orgasms. Raj groaned as he came, the spot inside me began to break up, radiated outward. The magic that always happened with him, we traded places back and forth, assumed a different mass. We could not get close enough to each other. I cried out over and over again, then suffused through and through with hot, breathless warmth, we fell back, our hearts beating wildly.

Moments passed and gradually, as if making room for refugees returning to their homeland, my mind once again became a place for thoughts. All the years I spent looking for Raj came back to me and it seemed clear now that each decision made along the way was just another step leading me to him.

It was such a delicately balanced game we played, shifting back and forth between each other, dominant, dominated. Within those movements toward him, like the moths to the light, was the essence of myself, how surprising to find that this was also the essence of Raj. Were we doomed to this repetitive dance step, attracted then repelled?

With my fingers I traced a line along Raj's arm where there were several moles. Like a blind person reading Braille, I gently pressed the tips of my fingers to them, wondering if I might read my destiny in them.

***

I sat in the lounge opposite the medical library, next to the vending machines, drinking a Coke and trying to summon the energy to go outside for a smoke. I had to quit, but it was pointless to even attempt right now, maybe when things calmed down. A bunch of other med students from the surgery rotation were seated on the couches across the room. Talking animatedly, they practiced intricate loops and knots with silvery thread that caught the fluorescent lighting, shadows dancing in the afternoon sunshine.

Then suddenly, like someone putting on 3-D glasses, my fellow students were transformed as I remembered the opening scene from "2001: A Space Odyssey." I saw an open vista on a virtually empty planet, definitely the "land before time." The camera focused on a bunch of cavemen who looked very much like chimps. They used bones as tools and as one bone flew off into space, you knew that mastery over their environment was less than an eye blink away.

My friend T.J. Thomas, a year ahead of me, appeared beside me, flashing tickets to the "Journey" and "Foreigner" concert at the Summit Convention Center.

"A patient who was just admitted today gave them to me. It's for tonight. You free to go?"

T.J. was one of my most favorite people. A black guy from Tustin, California he had a wry sense of humor and an ingrained sense of the noblesse oblige that would come his way once he could put the letters "M.D." after his name. He'd told me not long ago that sometimes cruising around town at night, once he made sure it was safe he just breezed on through all the red lights that came his way. His time was too important to waste.

"Sure. What time?"

"Around seven, draw me a map to your place. About time you agreed to go out with me, you've been moping around here for weeks. And hey, I'm not married."

The concert would be a welcome distraction, escaping for the first time in a long time from the intricacies of surgical loops and knots on my psyche.

The Summit was packed that night, stretching the limits of its seating capacity. T.J. and I had to walk up into the ozone to reach our seats, braving the swaying balcony, its trembling beneath the weight of so many people. I grew dizzy at the sight of thousands of bobbing heads below us, dizzier still when the swirling, pungent, sweet aroma of reefer hit me, drawing me into its field.

Once seated, shyness descended, leaving me unsure in this new setting how to act around T.J. To cover the awkward moment, I used his Zeiss binoculars to scan the rows, people watching.

If T.J. was affected in a similar way, he gave no hint, keeping up a constant stream of entertaining chatter, easy in his role of the quintessential Don Juan. Though it was muted now, out in public, away from his turf, he continued in little ways to prod and poke, undermining my resistance, seducing me with his intellect and energy. When I brought the binoculars down and gave him my full attention, he reached for my hand and grinned wickedly at me, whispering in my ear, "I want to suck each one of your little toes, especially in-between the toes, down the length of your foot, up to that tender, tender soft spot that everyone has on the inside of their ankle. Then I'll move my tongue up the slender curve of your calf to that soft place on the inside of your thigh, then up to your...."

"T.J. enough." His mouth was moist and glistening, he ran his pink tongue languidly over his full lips, my body grew warm and damp at his touch, that hair-trigger desire.

"Don't look so shocked." Still grinning at me in the poorly lit auditorium, his eyes bright with unrequited lust, he brought my hand to his crotch, "You know your way around one of these," he rubbed my hand along the bulge of his erection.

I sought refuge again in the binoculars, pretending to need both of my hands. A warm-up band played awful, atonal, metallic rock, their instruments screeching, the treble unbearable.

Chris. Was that really her? Oh my God, yes, that was her. She'd lost so much weight. Her hair was cut to below her chin, dyed light blonde in a sort of Afro that fanned out around her face, making it appear much tinier, delicate. With black mascara and eye-liner, bright red lipstick, she looked very pretty. Fine-tuning the focus, I scanned closer until Raj's face filled my field of vision.

The ache in my chest threatened to overpower me. It was an ache of captivity, of bondage, of knowing you weren't free, nor likely to be soon. Lowering the binoculars, I saw Raj look in my direction. Our eyes met across the vast distance separating us, he gave me a slight wave.

I was an outsider peering in through clear glass windows, peering at a world beyond my reach. It made me feel like a tragic Siamese twin who after years of trying to keep her other twin alive found that she was dying, withering on the vine beside her. But the doctors refused to surgically remove her. Her punishment for being bad was to carry her around as a constant reminder. But it was Raj I carried with me, the only thing that was going to exorcise his spirit from me was time or death.

Chapter Thirteen

March 2000

My ability to feel empathy sometimes bordered on the distortions of schizophrenia. It was easy to desert a fixed image of myself, to become something else, the characters in a book, the actors in a movie.

Did that explain why I felt so trapped, not myself, as if I were a wild animal in the woods caught in a cruel steel trap. There were frequent tales about animals who escaped their traps by chewing off their leg. But this was different; there was nothing tangible to chew my way out of, to effect my release.

Obviously I had some complicity in my situation, even if at times I felt like I was under the spell of a zealot, madman, genius: Svengali. Caught in this trap was what was most essential about me, a psychic incarceration, a mental Siberia from which I had to suffer not even knowing if I wanted to be released.

But it was such sweet imprisonment, the key in the lock, Raj the key master.

After seeing him with Chris at the concert, Raj and I had argued bitterly on the phone, finally agreeing to end our relationship. Within minutes of hanging up the telephone though, I could feel some unknown, invisible part of me slip out of my body. It moved down the sunny suburban streets, past the bare winter branches, the evergreens and stately magnolias, moving ever closer to the busier thoroughfares. It uncoiled inside of me, extending through space and time to link me inextricably back with Raj.

***

My OB-GYN rotation was followed by Psychiatry and Neurology. The pace of this rotation seemed way more humane than previous ones. We spent a lot time in the lab and at lectures, interpreting the results of brain imaging: CT scans, X-Rays and MRIs. The rest of the time was taken up with rounds and seeing patients in the clinic.

Our troupe followed the Grand Rounds doctor du jour like little duckies who'd imprinted on a human, hanging on his every word, desperately hoping we'd know the right answer when called on. The second patient of the day had presented with a history of increasing dementia, complaints of blurred vision and loss of physical coordination. Owen jumped right in offering a diagnosis of Creutzfeldt-Jakob disease, a rare but always fatal disease.

Dr. Singer raised his eyebrows, deeply creasing his forehead. "You're told not to look for zebras in medicine; horses are way more likely to be part of the answer. But in this case, there might be compelling reason to do so. We'll wait for the results of the CT scan, but you may be right."

As Dr. Singer moved on to the next patient, Owen whispered to me, "It's just like I told you, remember? "Deadly Feasts," euthanasia clinics on every corner, Richard Rhodes most recent book? Prion diseases. Extremely spooky stuff, there's no way to kill a prion. Transmissible spongiform encephalopathy or the bovine variant, mad cow disease, like CJD. It rolls off the tongue and echoes through the brain 'transmissible spongiform encephalopathy." And he literally rolled his tongue at me.

Before I could think of a suitable response, Raj joined the group hanging around on the edges, and then moved over to stand in front of me. He could be such a strutting rooster at times. I smiled in spite of myself, yearning to reach out and caress his broad shoulders, to slip my arms under his white coat and around his waist.

Sensing my eyes drilling a hole in his back, he turned and gave me an impenetrable look. What went through his head? He kept his expression impassive, we both did, fooling ourselves that our latest resolve to leave each other alone would work, that we wouldn't scheme to introduce yet another permutation in our relationship.

A few days later I was taking a history from a thirty-three year old woman, Francis Hardy, who had two small children. She'd had bronchitis and sore throats off and on for six months and now she felt like her joints were on fire. My cell phone rang. I reached in my pocket and turned it off.

After writing up her chart, I left a request for the lab to do three blood tests: the C-Reactive Protein (CRP), Erythrocyte Sedimentation Rate (ESR), as well as an Anti-Nuclear Antibody (ANA). All three would give me a pretty good indication of the level of inflammation in her body, the hallmark of auto-immune disorders. With the dusky mask across her nose and cheeks I was betting it was SLE, systemic lupus erythematosus.

The resident would review my work, just my luck that it was Dr. Ratner again. He'd sent me a scathing email in response to my musings on why drawing a few vials of blood might make a person feel really good. I knew how to draw blood, why hadn't I thought of testing myself first? That was the cornerstone of the scientific method: develop a theory, try it out in the lab, then if you can replicate it, you might be on to something.

Heading downstairs, I remembered that someone had called me earlier on my cell phone. It wasn't a number I recognized but I pressed the "send" button anyway.

When Chris Khan answered I was momentarily speechless and stumbled spastically toward the ladies restroom looking for some privacy.

"Sophie, is that you?" She laughed, not an ugly short laugh, but genuine, almost friendly, "Look, I'm sorry to call you while you're at the hospital but I had something I wanted to say to you. I've got a job at night now, and when I've saved up a little money, I'm leaving. Our marriage is over; I thought you'd like to know what my plans are. You can have him now."

"But what about the kids?"

This time her voice hardened. "I wasn't the one who destroyed our marriage, he's just going to have to get used to the consequences."

Then slowly, worming its way into the denseness of my brain was the almost inconceivable notion that Raj knew she wanted to leave, they no longer had grounds for a marriage, but now it was Raj refusing to let her go, to grant her a divorce and let her take the children. Was he hiding from me behind the excuse of his wife and children? Or was it as he had so often hinted, that he did not trust Chris' commitment to the twins beyond using them as leverage for what she wanted?

A jumble of emotions assailed me, rising and falling as the hopeful thoughts were shoved out by the realistic ones. This was just more of the same old shit. I said a heartfelt prayer that the end was in sight.

***

At the stove on a Saturday a week later, I used a fork to break up the bigger pieces of Italian sausage frying in the pan. Nick restlessly paced the kitchen floor behind me, like a lawyer summing things up for a jury. We had been at this all afternoon. With my new resolve not to see Raj anymore, he was pushing for reconciliation.

"You still don't see what's wrong in what you did?" He sipped from a glass of cabernet sauvignon.

"Yes, yes, yes, and no. Nick, aren't you ever attracted to other women?" Why couldn't it have been the reverse, with me the one wrong had been done to?

"Yes. But I never even consider acting on it."

"What's the answer then? I'm not at a point in which I can see my way through to getting back together again. It was traumatic enough for me to hurt you the first time." It was pointless to make promises. I felt like I was in a little dinghy floating down the river Styx with a wild ass current filled with deep eddies all around.

I couldn't guarantee that if I returned to our marriage, tried swimming against the perilous current of whatever blueprint had been celestially mandated for me, that I wouldn't end up hurting him again.

Liz sat at the round oaken table, a red-checked plastic picnic tablecloth covering it. From a big wad of dough she took chunks and was making original cookie designs, her face and hands covered with flour, as were the rolling pin and cookie cutters next to her.

Sounding priggish, he said, "That doesn't offer much hope for our marriage, I thought you said he was out of your life now."

He poured more wine into the glass I held out to him; if I stayed mildly drunk through the rest of my life, the pain would be less sharp. Pain like what I'd felt in my cell phone conversation with Raj earlier that day.

He'd called just before I left to meet Nick. "Sophie? I know I promised not to bother you anymore but something's happened. I really need to talk to you about it." His voice was low, he sounded worried.

Oh God, what had happened now? For an instant I imagined him revealing this sort of Ted Bundy side to his character. You think you know a person, but do you ever really?

"What?" After my conversation with Chris, knowing he'd kept so much back from me, I couldn't help but sound belligerent.

"Chris got home around five-thirty this morning. She'd spent the night with Helmut, she's feeling more assertive now because she has a job, and she's lost all that weight. She wants me to move out."

"That's not exactly news to me, she called me already, didn't she tell you? Sounded like she means to get sole custody of the kids too. Wasn't that always your reason for staying?"

"We'll work the kids out later."

Can't I see how he's using me? Think this through Sophie, he loves you, but not enough to fight for you, then she kicks him out and when it's easy for him again, he wants you back.

"For now I'm moving in with Rob, he offered to let me live with him until I can get settled."

What did Rob have to offer that I couldn't?

"Can I see you tonight?

"No! We both wanted this over, let's stick to it."

"Sophie no, look I've missed you so much."

I hung up before he could talk me into anything.

Nick brought me back to the present. "You're going to burn that Sophie." I moved the pan off of the burner.

"Sorry. Listen Nick, it's too soon for any promises, will you quit picking at it and accept things the way they are for a while?" We kissed each other lightly. "Let's just have a quiet family night, okay?"

"Sure."

***

Neither of us could get used to the new satin sheets on the bed. They felt delicious against my naked skin, both Nick and I slipping and sliding on the unaccustomed slickness, it added a whole new kick to our love-making. Afterwards, I rolled away from Nick, calling out cheerfully, "Goodnight Raj."

Both Nick and I had had a lot to drink, wine with dinner, then cognac, my brain was fuzzy but not too fuzzy to realize my mistake, to hope he hadn't heard. Nick did the only thing he could do and rolled back toward me. In the dark, with an unerring sense of direction, he placed both hands around my neck and squeezed tight. It felt entirely appropriate, exactly the kind of behavioral response you'd expect to elicit from any normal male in the same situation. He squeezed tighter but I wasn't afraid, there were no dark, murderous undercurrents in Nick's personality--yet. Nothing like the kind of guilt and fear Charlie could inspire in me just being alone in bed with him, unable to picture the dark labyrinth of his mind because it was so spooky and foreign and empty.

Finally, Nick let go, muttering, "Fuck you, bitch," and rolled over and went to sleep.

Sober as a judge by then, I lay there pondering my life.

Hadn't I always been polite and civilized to people, stiff upper lip from my English forebears? Definitely not the kind of person people casually said, "Fuck you, bitch," to. People had always liked me.

Like one of the less startling insights Charles Darwin had, this time about dogs, "they can show no greater love for you than to lick you." When you all but lick people, obviously, it was going to be very painful to undergo a metamorphosis into the kind of person who was often told, "Fuck you, bitch."

Susie looked at me with an expression of both sorrow and disapproval as I got up and dressed. Wrapping Liz in a blanket and hurrying out to the car, I drove home.

Chapter Fourteen

The medical school library had a complete set of the *Archiv für Pathologische Anatomie und Physiologie und für klinische Medizin*, the world-famous "Virchow's Archives." Rudolph Virchow was famous for his seminal work on cellular pathology and comparative pathology. Once upon a time when the best medical schools were to be found in Europe, all important medical books, research, articles, etc. had been written in German. Always keen about science, as an undergrad needing to fulfill my language requirements, I had chosen German.

On impulse I pulled down one of the Virchow volumes and flipped through the pages, lamenting that I understood very little of what I read.

Then passing the biography section I plucked the book "Robert Koch: A Life in Medicine and Bacteriology" by Thomas Brock from the shelf. It was in English and I was desperate for some diversion from my obsessive thoughts about Raj.

Driving home I wondered about Chris and Helmut. Were they really serious? How could you be serious about a man who still carried around a picture of his maid? Besides, what do a highly educated, sophisticated man in his thirties and a twenty-two-year-old have to talk about? But no, if Helmut could love his maid ardently, he could love Chris.

Raj moved in with Rob the following weekend.

His freedom lasted for one week, freedom being a relative term. When Chris called Saturday and asked him to baby-sit while she and Helmut went out to the movies, he agreed, reluctantly. I listened politely to his bitter complaints on the cell phone, "My first night free and it's spent baby-sitting, fucking A this is no different from being married. She said she'd give me a divorce, but only if she gets to take the kids. I'm not losing them and we're not splitting them up. Speaking of which, where's Liz?"

"With Nick and his mom. They'll be back Monday." Monday was a holiday.

"Do you mind if I come over tomorrow at ten?"

"Fine, I'll see you then." But the prospect of seeing him didn't make me happy the way it usually did. I'd ended the call with a deep sense of foreboding, convinced that his having left his wife again was merely a charade.

I'd sat in the dark smoking and worrying, and ended up polishing off a bottle and then some of Sauvignon Blanc.

With a killer hangover the next morning, I stumbled into the bathroom. The bright light felt like someone slicing my eyes open. They were swollen and puffy and a nervous tic under my right eye pulsed to the rapid beat of my heart. Definitely a wild-eyed beast with a continually unraveling interior. What happened when I got to the end of the roll? With a sigh of frustration, I shook my head, tired of trying to be something that I wasn't--Raj's age.

Exhausted from my excesses of the night before, after breakfast I went back to bed. My sleep was fitful, as if another part of me did not want this enforced indolence and was beating with little fists against my skull for me to get up.

Then I was dreaming about being with Charlie, having sex with him, clinging to him. The feel of his body on mine had set off a mournful sense of grief in me, of loss and confusion from the passion he had once aroused. Raj was nearby, I could feel a deep sense of restlessness and anger in him. So I forcefully wrested myself awake to keep Raj from also appearing in my dream, like a demon Freddie

Krueger, where even our dreams intersected and he might discover my unfaithful thoughts.

Then someone was pounding on one of the doors, the sound reverberating through my brain. I woke up more fully, groggy and disoriented.

Raj pushed his way in, moving me forward, then closing and locking the door behind him. "Who were you talking to when I tried to call? Nick, Dr. Nick fucking Nuisance? His cell phone was busy." He pressed me against the wall, leaning against me. I could smell coffee on his breath.

"No, it wasn't me. I've been asleep."

"Liar." He could so easily change the truth around, manipulate me into thinking I was the one at fault. I'd never seen him so edgy and manic before.

He was calmer after we made love and on the spur of the moment we drove to Austin and spent the day touring the capitol, the University, wandering through the Chinese gardens. We drank Lone Star in a run-down bar on Lake Austin, watching the sunset across the vast expanse of green woods that lined both sides of the lake. From there we went for Mexican food at a restaurant on Red River.

Raj was subdued. By then it was easy to read his moods, his mind, to know just exactly what was in his heart. The sad truth was that he and Chris would never be able to resolve the custody issue; Raj would have to go back to her again.

It was after nine before we started down Interstate-35, heading toward San Antonio, both exhausted, sluggish from the beer and too much food, depressed.

Between San Marcos and New Braunfels Raj saw a sign advertising Wimberley, a resort community to the west of the highway, deep in the hill country. He exited from the highway, then turned a short distance down the feeder road onto another dark two lane highway. After a mile or so he turned left and drove on a dirt road until it petered out. Live oaks towered overhead, the noise of the cicadas blended with the sound of the engine.

We approached what at one time must have been an unpaved gravel driveway, now overgrown with weeds. Raj stopped the car and got out, then came around to my side, opening the door and grabbing my hand. "Come on."

We walked along slowly, relishing the fragrance of loamy earth, the cool, moist air. The wind picked up, rustling through the leaves as the clouds disappeared and a nearly full moon shone overhead. We spotted a small pond in a clearing, moonlight dappling its surface. Then several yards beyond the west rim of the pond was a cement foundation with crumbling bricks from the fireplace settled in a heap at the base.

After exploring the area, we sat on an overturned tree trunk watching the moon rise higher in the sky, leaving a smooth sheen of light on the pond, like silvery frosting on a cake. A dragonfly plowed slowly across the surface, its tiny wake rippling behind him.

"Nice, isn't it?"

I nodded, holding his hand, leaning on his shoulder; a churning pain gripped me, this time it was really over, he was serious about making his marriage work. There would be no more futile attempts to escape his responsibilities.

We lay down on the ground together, stretching out, enveloped by the night. The sky was black as pitchblende and looked like a velvet canvas stretched taut with tiny pin pricks through which you could see the light of billions of stars. In the lower right quadrant of the sky one of those lights pulsed its way across the inky blackness, a satellite perhaps?

An errant dervish of wind blew dead leaves and debris across us. I shivered, pulling my sweater more tightly around me, closing my eyes, breathing deeply of the dankness of the pond, the damp weeds underneath us, the leaves decomposing into humus.

Then suddenly the air around Raj and I seemed charged with more than just our thoughts flowing back and forth. The physical fabric of matter seemed to inexplicably, almost magically, wrench open, allowing us to stand together on the brink. It was like stumbling onto a two way conduit between our minds, a strange kind of deja vu that hit both of us at the same time. As if at the subatomic level the vast distances between us, what irrevocably separates one human being from another had been crossed and somehow meshed.

Had some weird neural gate been left open? Had we made love once too often, the act somehow lending itself to teletransportation between two souls? Like the mad scientist in "The Fly" whose machine goofed and made him part man, part fly, the act of making love had made me part Raj, part Sophie.

Don't think I'm crazy; I could make a distinction between Raj and myself. The final scene in that movie "The Fly" came quickly to mind, the one where the poor half man/half fly is caught in the spider's web, crying "Help me! Help me!" The detective picks up the rock and brings it down on the tiny monstrous thing. Were Raj and I so trapped, so doomed?

Raj sat up, squeezing my hand in his. "What the hell was that?"

"I don't know." I was shaking, edging closer to Raj for protection, trembling as if ghosts had been swirling and dancing around us, but when we turned to catch them, they were gone.

It passed in a flash, we lay back down.

Rolling over on top of me Raj said, "Kind of what you imagine it would feel like living the Bermuda Triangle all the time." He rested his head in the curve of my neck for a few minutes, then kissed me.

Abruptly he got up and walked back toward the car. I couldn't move, every cell in my body straining toward him. The sound of his shoes crunching on the gravel receded then stopped, he opened the car door, the ignition turned, there was music from a mixed CD he had, K.C. and the Sunshine Boys, "Please Don't Go."

He could be such a tease; he knew how much I wanted him. I closed my eyes, tears squeezed out of the corners, after that night I probably wouldn't see him again for a long time, if even that. Please, just this one more time...

"Okay, just this one more time."

***

We stood together at the door to the door to my apartment. "Are you coming in, can you stay the night?"

"No." He leaned his forehead against mine. "Goodnight Sophie." He turned and walked quickly away from me.

Wishing to be asleep perchance to dream of Raj, I tossed and turned sifting through the memories of the day with the intensity of someone panning for gold. The day had had a dreamy quality to it and unrolled in my mind like a hallucination. I wondered what made our dreams such epic metaphorical sagas with a cast of thousands. Fireflies dancing in the quantum interstices of our minds; dream states where you were hooked to the mother ship in some alien port. And how effortlessly the lights twinkle out again and you are awake.

But now, reliving the "déjà vu" moment with Raj, I was able to snag a tiny bit of that transcendental moment and ride it, naturally, to a dreamless sleep.

Getting dressed for school the next morning my mind churned with thoughts of Raj, Nick, and Charlie. An inimical void to have developed at fifteen: the allure of captivity, reinforced by Charlie to be driven to surrender. Worse still to find that void filled by the one man you can't have.

Still my time with Raj had pushed me beyond the emotional quagmire left behind by Charlie. The defensive ramparts in my brain had been built up like a distant castle atop an impossibly remote peak in the Alps, into whose dungeons I'd hidden my entire, utterly fragile emotional core. Now, like the collapse of the Berlin Wall in 1989, it all came tumbling down in an hypnotic almost hallucinogenic way it was so keenly tangible an experience.

Chapter Fifteen

April 2000

I was on-call at the hospital, hanging out in the doctor's lounge on the second floor. I'd just finished making my rounds, checking on two recent post-op patients. One, an eighty-seven year old man who'd fallen and broken his hip, amazed me. Shortly after surgery, when he emerged from the cloud of anesthesia, he was already talking coherently to his wife and son. The wife looked a little the worse for wear, hair standing on end like she'd stuck her finger in the socket. When she asked why they were in the hospital for the second time, I realized she was suffering from dementia.

My other patient was a woman with uterine cancer who'd had all of her reproductive organs removed, a hysterectomy and bilateral Salpingo-oophorectomy, another mouthful that Owen said just rippled off his tongue. Helen Griffin was sixty-two and a lifelong smoker which typically makes it more difficult for the anesthesiologists, but she was resting peacefully and all of her vital signs were good.

That time of night the lounge was almost always empty. Not long ago one particularly snotty doctor had lectured me about being in there, "Go back with your fellow students where you belong."

Raj had called me on my cell three times that night, trying to convince me to see him my next free day.

Neither of us had kept our word about not contacting each other. There were times like tonight when he'd call. But it was too painful for me; I couldn't bear the existential hell we were trapped in. One of us had to do the right thing.

"Raj, we agreed, we're not doing this again." I flipped my cell phone shut and turned it off then checked my pager to make sure it was working properly.

The pot of coffee I'd made was almost through coming down the chute, day old donuts were in a box next to the coffee pot. I grabbed one, stuffed it down, got my coffee and ate another donut with pink frosting and colored sprinkles. Ambrosia. Seated on the buttery soft leather couch I channel surfed for a while. With each pass through the channels I kept seeing this interesting looking man talking and decided to see what he had to say. It was the BBC channel.

The man had intelligent eyes and well-sculpted features. He was intense and articulate, gesturing a lot with his hands. The scene changed to a laboratory and the narrator mentioned several occurrences in nature which lent credence to Dr. Richard Dawkins theories.

Of course, I knew who he was, I'd read his books, who knew he was so handsome?

Dr. Dawkins' s, an Oxford evolutionary biologist, was best known for the "The Blind Watchmaker" and "The Selfish Gene." Beautifully written, with brilliantly reasoned insights into nature's secrets, they are the kind of books which have inspired people to write fan letters, thanking Dawkins for at last explaining aspects of human nature that have baffled us for so long.

According to theories he put forth in "The Selfish Gene," the problems women have with male dominance began back before any of us had evolved very far, eons before we'd grown to the point of attempting to transcend the biological basis of our behavior. In fact, it happened so long ago that there was no such thing as sexual differentiation.

As the theory goes, back in the primordial soup there were only simple one-celled life forms learning the rudimentary art of replication. Selection pressure was exerted on one exceptionally fleet-of-foot variety of these life forms. There was an advantage to being small and fast, as in the motility of sperm. So they proliferated. We, the larger, plumper cells--the future homemakers of America--did not have the advantage of size and numbers. Still we survived.

As we both became more complex, multi-celled individuals, the female reproductive side of the coin remained a large, ponderous cell, outnumbered by the male gametes. It wasn't enough, once it was fertilized, to incubate inside us for nine months. No, then our progeny were subject to further nurturing on the outside for give or take eighteen more years.

Men, on the other hand, are never so encumbered. Never out of commission sexually, they can spread their seed with the speed of a Roto-tiller Seed Spreader, passing on their particular package of genes in as profligate a manner as they care to.

Assuming they are not sterile, they can afford complacency. Male members of the species have millions upon millions of sperm cells to dispense like candy. Cultural values subtly follow biological values. Male babies are more highly valued. With fewer opportunities for self-replication, women are in a more vulnerable position relative to our genes hidden agenda: immortality.

Dawkins books resonated deeply with me; his explanations had the ring of truth. Helping me understand why Raj Kahn so obviously had more personal cachet than I could ever hope to have short of a sex change operation. Then I would just be a freak.

***

Liz, Amanda, and Nellie were outside at the playground just beyond the entrance to our apartment. Hardly noon yet and the humidity had to be close to the ninety-five percent range, my body covered in sweat as I swept the kitchen floor.

A knock on the back door, Raj opened the door a few inches, calling out my name as he walked down the hall. Paler than usual, the fine skin on his face was stretched taut from tension, the lack of sleep, the pitched battles with his wife. Under one arm he carried a six-pack of Heineken beer. As he seated himself at the dinette table in the kitchen, he asked me to put the beer in the refrigerator.

"No. I don't want you to stay. I told you that already, on the phone." There was a tremor of nervousness in my voice.

"What's wrong?" A slight ironic grin, the one that seemed to say, so what that I'm doing this to get back at my wife, so what that you know it, you've always succumbed before, why not now?

Lost sleep while I was on-call, anger, too much coffee, winds whipping up a toxic blend of pollutants, an overdose of ambient electricity, you name it, combustion was imminent. Raj got up, making a move toward the refrigerator, his smug self-confidence the final straw.

Then screaming like some horrible harridan, my screechy voice rising with each word, I chased after him, "What's wrong? What's wrong you jerk? You are what is wrong. Get out."

Still turned upside down on the dinette table, out of the way while I swept, was the embroidered foot stool with the dingy picture of the palace at Versailles in petit-point, the one I used in the kitchen to reach the high cupboards. Grasping it by one leg, I threw it behind my head, ready to take aim at him. Instantly, he threw his hands up to protect his head and face,

"Get out, just get out. I hate you. I never want to see you again." Screaming hysterically, my voice broke hoarsely.

He grabbed the six-pack and ran out the door.

I looked out the back window and saw him driving away in the Toyota. Feeling a little calmer I ran downstairs across to the playground. Sitting on the bench opposite the sandpit, with my face turned up to the sun, I listened to the happy sounds of innocent children, screaming and laughing. Just beyond the complex two young boys ran across the field, one of them holding a kite. The wind caught it and snapped it up into the sky. The kite was shaped like a Chinese dragon with a long, narrow tail, the splash of red, yellow and black against the blue sky a beautiful thing to watch.

"Who wants Kool-Aid and fig newtons?"

With screams of "We do!" the three girls ran ahead of me into the apartment.

Later, still in a somewhat black mood, I poured scouring powder into the toilet, swishing it all around until the bowl fairly boiled over with cleansing bubbles, my nerves all prickly and on end like a cat's fur. *When I graduate from med school (God willing) I will never clean another fucking toilet.*

The prospect of a life ahead of me in which I never had to clean toilets made me smile. Yes, my little scene with Raj was unpleasant, a reminder of how easily you can lose control. Nevertheless, my mood was elevated, now he knows what a bitch I can be; it seemed an important piece of information. You often don't have time to let on how human you really are in the kind of God-like aura that rests like a mantle on the shoulders of doctors. Truth in advertising demands full disclosure.

***

In the break room Raj stood next to the table where I was studying.

"Sophie?"

I turned around and gave him a slight smile, wondering if my shrewish behavior had had any effect on him. "What?"

"I'm sorry about yesterday, for taking you so much for granted."

"Forget it." I turned back to my studies as he wandered over to the coffee machine. A rapprochement of sorts, we were on speaking terms again.

But then my rational mind shot a poisoned dart into my brain, inquiring minds want to know, doesn't this always degenerate into something ugly? At three a.m., that long dark tea-time of the soul, it often comes to me that we must all be giant mutant iguanas driving Mack trucks through the idiocy of life; we have about as much control over our behavior. I deserved to be more than this man's mistress.

***

At home later that night my younger brother called. We were not a close family growing up and had made little effort to stay in touch. I was the only one still living in Texas.

Nick told me Ted had called a few months back. "Yeah, I said that you'd left me for another man. A married man."

As if I'd call my brother back after that revelation.

Ted lived in Salt Lake City. Years ago he became a born-again Mormon after a ski trip to Park City, Utah where he met and soon married this darling big-bosomed blonde telemarketer. It made me sad to see my brother change so drastically. He'd always seemed to happily embrace the world exactly the way it was. Ted now had five adorable Mormon munchkins and was as reactionary as they come. Love conquers all.

With impeccable timing, finding me at my lowest of lows, utterly depressed and dejected and caught in this spiral of self-destruction that I couldn't seem to extricate myself from, he called to give me a piece of his mind.

After preliminary greetings appropriate for a not-close brother-sister relationship, he asked, "Did Nick tell you I'd called a few months back, I thought you might have called me back. You're seeing another man?"

My voice was hoarse, the words strained, this imposed intimacy unbearable. "Yes, Nick told me you called."

"Don't you know any better than to behave like that Sophie? Didn't our parents raise you up any better than that? What if everyone in the world changed his mind after committing themselves to marriage? There'd be nothing but chaos. So you're not with this other guy right now are you?"

"No."

"Had to leave you too? See that's what happens. You're what? Thirty-five years old, who's going to want a thirty-five year old woman with one kid? I tell you who, no one. No one, Sophie. That's right. What do you think is out there? Nothing. What you had is all there is. You need to just grow up and quit misbehaving, go back to your husband, that's where God intended you to be. If it's too late for that, I'll come out there to get you, bring you back here."

Never. Utah was a scary place, talk about invasion of the body snatchers.

After Ted hung up I dissolved in a heap of tears, sobbing at how old and haggard and ugly and used up I must be.

Ted's voice reasserted Charlie's sinister grip on my self-perception, the credo of low self-esteem, never say yes to yourself, deny yourself that which you most want. Then, on top of everything else, an apocalyptic voice I hadn't heard in years and thought had disappeared, whispered again, reminding me that med school was a precarious choice for me to have made if my life was going to be in such constant turmoil.

Get a grip Sophie, a normal person would have hung up on your holier-than-thou brother with a crisp "Fuck you asshole."

Chapter Sixteen

May 2000

Grease was flying and snapping at me as I gingerly turned each piece of chicken. A sharp sting above my eyelid made me wince and cry out with pain. Any sense at all and I'd put the cover over the frying pan instead of standing there taking so much abuse. The story of my life. Which came first, a high tolerance for pain, or so much pain that you develop a high tolerance?

Seating myself at the dinette table again, Nick watched my face expectantly. Originally, I had invited him to dinner to talk about divorce. In spite of Ted's lecture, my marriage to Nick now seemed like a wounded soldier on a battlefield, half his guts hanging out for the entire world to see. For Nick to watch as I grappled so ungraciously in this tormenting relationship with Raj was awkward. Without divorce papers signed and filed, his obvious hopes for saving our marriage tore at me.

Measuring my words carefully, sipping from my wine, I began, "Nick, we need to think about divorce, our separation has gone on for months now, can't you see that I'm not any good for you? I don't exactly bring out what is best in you."

"That's not true."

My eyebrows shot up in disbelief, remembering the feel of his hands wrapped tightly around my neck, the warm fuzzies of "Fuck you, bitch." How quickly he had been willing to forget that little episode.

"Denial is not an option tonight. We've got to be honest." But could I ever be really honest? Could he ever perceive that I was no longer a cool and rational being, overwhelmed as I was by the passion of my life? Back at the stove I removed the chicken, then drained the potatoes, my thoughts floating off like soap bubbles.

Not long ago I read about these experimental mice who'd had electrodes implanted in the pleasure centers of their brains. They were trained to press a bar that would stimulate their brain via the electrodes. Just idle scientific curiosity, right?

But the mice liked it so much they couldn't stop, pressing the bar until their hair stood on end from sheer exhaustion. That was sort of my view of Raj, like having electrodes implanted in my brain. All I wanted to do was stimulate that pleasure center with his name on it.

"Our marriage would be great if you could just get that fuck-up out of your life."

I wondered just exactly how to do that. You're the physiologist, Nick, scan my brain and you'll see which area is most frequently lit up and in use, or abuse, that pleasure center going full tilt. Just because my hair isn't standing on end, you have to think of it as figuratively standing on end. "Your ego's getting in the way Nick, it's become a matter of winning now, hasn't it?" Did I only figure in there nominally in this clash of masculine egos?

It wasn't a matter of winning Raj anymore so much as it was achieving the maintenance dose of my addiction. Once again, his going back to Chris hadn't changed anything. He would insist on seeing me, claiming his marriage was lousy, only to back off when I began making demands. Just how lousy, I often wondered?

In a rush, as if someone off-stage were whispering my lines to me, I kept hearing his constant excuse, "Chris will never relinquish custody of the twins. I'm not losing them."

With one of those typically feminine turnarounds, from one-minute thinking divorce, then to Raj's words, "never relinquish custody of her" rebounding through my brain, my mind pictured a whole scenario of loss, loss of Raj, loss of Nick, Liz and I the big-time losers.

Ted's flat, uncompromising words came back to me, who will want you? You're too old! No wonder I had collapsed in tears, just try to fuck around with Mother Nature. Raj, viewed from that perspective, almost nine younger, terrified me; he was not someone I could trust.

The summer break was only ten days away; I'd signed on to work with Ginger on the breast cancer research project. Locked away in a lab all day I'd never see Raj. He'd decided on a residency in Emergency Medicine and had signed on to work in the ER.

It was a vulnerable moment for me, the alcohol, Nick's earnest face, the urge to put behind me the debacle that my life had become. And why hadn't it ever occurred to me that Nick's heart had to be pried open the way a diver robs an oyster of its pearl?

"All right. I'll have over a week and a half off before I start working with Ginger. I'll move back in and we'll give it a go, see if we can make our marriage work."

"You won't regret it Sophie, I promise you."

Liz and I moved back home that weekend.

***

Easy to see how multiple personalities might develop from unbearable psychological stress; forks in the road, obstructed from the main highway by amnesia; bifurcations from the normal linear path of most personalities.

I stayed in bed late Saturday morning trying to unravel my own gothic personality structure. Not unlike the tangled mass in my jewelry box of bracelets, slender gold chains and tiny pierced earrings, held together in knots with bits of red thread from an unraveling spool.

Brown silk oriental pajamas from China, "borrowed" years ago from my father after his visit there. They have stood the test of time, only a few threadbare seams. My body felt soft, melting and ripe inside the sensuous material, caressed by the cool, silky fabric. Hair trigger desire. The scent of Marcel Rochas "Femme" perfume drifted to me, mingling with the blue smoke from my cigarette.

It had been two weeks since I'd seen Raj. Like an alcoholic facing rehabilitation the bottom line question was, can I go the rest of my life without him? The part of him taking up residence in my soul whispered that all my foolish plans were worth nothing, I ached for him.

My cell phone rang, I knew it was Raj, knew before even answering it--that sixth sense we share. The pajamas were about five sizes too big for me; I tripped on them as I leaped out of bed. Nick was at the medical school preparing a Power Point presentation for his upcoming lecture on brain physiology at the National Institutes of Health (NIH) in Washington, D.C. Liz had spent last night at her first birthday slumber party for her friend Michelle Jennings. She wasn't due home until mid-afternoon.

I upended my purse on the kitchen floor, tossing junk aside until I found my cell phone, flipping it open.

Raj spoke quickly, "Don't hang up Sophie."

Catching my breath, it amazed me how swiftly I could go from lust to resentment. "What? Are you pregnant and don't know who the mother is? What could you possibly have to talk to me about Raj?" Last I'd heard he and Chris were going to counseling. His high-profile, obviously healing marriage was a bright, hot light of pain in my mind. "I'm free of you now. You've made your choices, you can't have both. You must be retarded if you think I want more of your abuse."

"This is different. I have to talk to you."

Don't fall for this Sophie. "It's always different with you Raj, the same song, but a different verse. Look, I'm going grocery shopping in a little while. If you just happen to show up, well, that's not my affair." I hung up before he could laugh at my poor choice of words. My cell phone immediately began to ring again and I switched it off.

You had to give it to him. Intuitive, resourceful, he was also the most persistent person I'd ever met, a quality that could be enormously seductive when you were the focus of that persistence. There were three different grocery stores in my neighborhood. I used all three on occasion. Having forgotten about him for the moment, just finishing up grocery shopping, it took a moment for mental images to shift when I looked up and saw him racing down the aisle at HEB toward me.

A new dance step in the warped and strange minuet between Raj and I; this mad pursuit of me, ignoring the constraints that commonly bind people, made minions of them to weak ideals. With his charm, his recognition of all my secret weaknesses, the easy buttons to push, in the end I did things only a desperate woman would do. He was like a vampire who sucked all of your blood out and instead of leaving you to die in peace, left you to wander eternity as another undead.

***

Flanked on one side of the aisle by cereal boxes, coffee and tea items on the other side, Raj gripped the top of my grocery cart, breathing fast, grinning proudly at me. I couldn't help but smile, he looked so triumphant, so pleased with himself for having found me.

After I went through the line and paid for my groceries he steered my cart over to the automatic double doors, "Come on, I'll help you out with these."

His car was parked next to mine. The groceries were dealt with swiftly, his nervous energy infecting me as he led me over to his

Toyota, holding my arm in a manner that brooked no arguments. "Get in."

"No."

We regarded each other silently. His dark eyes signaled something--need, lust, pain--I wasn't sure. Or something far less complicated, merely availing himself of opportunity.

"Please."

Only so strong, I got in.

We drove for a while in silence, then he began, "I think I finally have you figured out."

"Shouldn't be that hard to analyze." I was smug, confident of being beyond such a simple analysis; proprietor of a jewelry box filled with knotted, hidden, inaccessible treasures.

"Oh, don't belittle yourself, it's complicated." Right, you make it that way.

It wasn't enough to have left my husband for him. To him, that was a silly game I played at, the way children play house. At heart the problem was that neither of us believed in each other enough, or believed in ourselves enough. Neither of us believed enough to feel secure that we wouldn't end up empty-handed.

We turned in to a crowded parking lot, the tacky bulk of a Wal-Mart Supercenter sat in the distance. Raj killed the engine, then stretched his legs, bending one at the knee, propping it against the handbrake. The inside of the car was a mess. Dog-eared medical tomes, Burger-King boxes, toys, a baby's pacifier, newspapers, torn and dirty from being stepped on. A life so busy.

Eyes dark as ebony behind silver frames probed mine silently. Black hair, trim mustache, full mouth, lips rose-colored, slightly parted, his teeth glistened as he moistened them with his tongue, oddly nervous, about to speak. He does not know how to surmount the obstacle of my building resentment. He never lied to me, never built false hope in me, but we destroyed each other's confidence with our games, using Nick and Chris as shields to deflect the intensity, to run from our fear of each other.

He never finished his thought, pursuing it silently, while I stared out the window, close to tears, realizing once again what I had lost by going home. Raj restarted the engine, moved on to the feeder road to the north Loop, heading east. The sun was directly in front of us, blinding me, hiding the fact that gradually we were drawing nearer to his apartment. He exited the freeway, taking the first right, then another right, turning in to the complex parking lot, parking in front of his apartment. "Come on, you can get out, she's not here, she's in New Braunfels with no way back until I pick her up early this evening."

Reluctantly, I got out of the car.

Once inside and seated on the couch, he brought me a Budweiser, foam rising gently up the neck of the bottle. I drank from it then lit a cigarette. "So talk." Silence, his eyes darted about, withholding from me all that was on his mind. While still a nifty hormone, testosterone was secretly the greatest inhibitor of verbal communication going. Raj only knew one way to communicate. Or was he so silent because he was left-handed and the speech side of his brain never developed? Did his silence conceal mental disorder on a level to match my own? Walk softly and carry a big stick, but also don't open your mouth and give anything away. That was partly true; suddenly I knew intuitively that half of my passion for him was in recognizing the wild disorder of his own heart.

After a few minutes he took my cigarette from me and tossed it in the toilet. When he came back he picked me up in his arms, groaning under my weight, while I complained self-consciously that he was going to hurt himself; I'm not fat but certainly not as thin as Chris these days. "Raj no, you can't. Not this time, not again. I don't even have any condoms, please, it's too foolish."

He refused to listen. In the bedroom he placed me gently on the bed and then sat back, watching me. Still and small as a rock, I wanted him, but was terrified. Without Nick I had nowhere else to go, no means of support. I had seven years of scientific schooling, I could get a job somewhere, but it wouldn't be on my terms. Even now, it was often difficult for women to forge economic independence, for every aspiring young female with an MBA, a law degree, working to become a doctor, there are ten others living on subsistence wages.

No good at imagining intervening stages, I immediately leaped from being with Nick to standing in line at the soup kitchen, lice and vermin crawling all over me. Too weak to face that, so I made a mess of everything else. My life seemed to defy attempts to settle into a comfortable niche, not affluent, not poor; not young, not old; clearly bright about some things, abysmally stupid about others; not really married, not a lover. I would stand out like a sore thumb as homeless woman. Where do I fit in?

After undressing both of us, Raj moved across the bed toward me, I felt strangely embarrassed with him, awkward in my nudity. He stopped for a moment, leaning back, staring at me, an inscrutable light in his eyes. Then I almost did a double-take, remembering this bizarre dream.

Ingmar Bergman made a movie called "Cries and Whispers." In one scene a woman sitting at a vanity table breaks a glass bottle. Someone, her husband or her lover, stands to the side watching her. There are shards of glass that she toys with for a moment. With one of the shards in her hand, she moves to the bed and sits with her knees drawn up, legs apart and inserts the piece of glass into her vagina. It is a scene both stunning and repellent, memorable. At that time I was incapable of understanding Bergman's subtleties.

The scene reappeared in my dream, only it was Raj sitting at the end of my bed watching me insert this glass. As now, he had an unreadable look on his face. Then swiftly, the way dreams work, his face changed, one minute it was Charlie and the next minute Raj again. Is the measure of our passion that we find our dark past in the hearts of those we love? Is that what we all seek so desperately in our relationships? Or does that happen only when those early relationships were perverted?

Now, back in real life, Bergman's convoluted message came to me clearly as Raj and I stared silently at each other. There are men who might as well be shards of glass to the women they make love to.

He moved slowly toward me, stroking me, kissing me, his eyes moving over my body with a look that was so tender, a gentleness that was almost out of place. His face next to mine, we stared at each other. I could taste cigarettes and beer on my tongue so I averted my face. Chris smoked, I knew he was used to it, but I still felt self-conscious. He turned my face back to him, moved his mouth stiffly over mine; we never kissed with abandon, only fucked that way.

Everything inside of me was soft, compliant, yielding, melting, suddenly reordered--order out of chaos--as our bodies merged together, the lowest energy level, a contradiction, a conundrum, what death must be like. Raj gripped me to him fiercely, his face buried in the curve of my neck, his breath becoming ragged, then he spit my hair out of his mouth, brushed it away. He rose up on one arm, bent his head to look down the length of us toward the triangle of my light pubic hair, his thick penis moving slowly in and out, disappearing, reappearing. He grinned, primitive, proud; more triangles reflecting light in his eyes, made them incandescent and mesmerizing. Then he pressed back against me, we made love urgently, as if it might be the last time. He came inside of me; in that unguarded moment, he cried out my name, then more controlled, his voice a whisper, full of emotion, "I love you so much, Sophie."

The pain I felt pierced me like a dagger a thousand times, hearing what I'd so longed to hear again, knowing it was impossible.

Chapter Seventeen

June/July 2000

"The newly fertilized egg, a corpuscle one-two-hundredth of an inch in diameter is not a human being. It is a set of instructions sent floating into the cavity of the womb." *Chapter 3: Development, from On Human Nature by E.O. Wilson*

In the bright light of the bathroom I looked closely at my breasts in the mirror. It wasn't my imagination, they were larger than normal. The veins, abnormally close to the surface, were a rich, deep blue-green color. They criss-crossed the flesh in dense, nourishing tangles, already with an eye to the future. If I let my eyes fall out of focus the delicate skin just beyond the aureoles appeared altogether blue, as if they were encased in a lacy blue brassiere.

There ensued an inch by inch inspection of my body as I hoped to read an encrypted code in the cells. Placing the lid down, I sat on the toilet with a depressed thud, then using my fingers counted back, relief spilling through me, it wasn't even time for my period, a day or two away.

But what to make of those brightly colored veins, didn't my face also appear fuller, softer, the eyes brighter? Decoded the message read "pregnant." It had been two weeks exactly since Raj had whisked me away from the grocery store. Too soon to tell. No it wasn't, the body knows, the mind must be forced to believe.

Then wandering into the bedroom, I checked the clock. Liz wouldn't be home from Michelle's for at least an hour. I laid down on the bed, pulling the covers up over me, placing Nick's pillow over my face with an eye to suffocating, then giving that up quickly, instead burrowing down into a dark, little hole.

Raj's baby.

It couldn't have been Nick's, we hadn't had sex in weeks. Both of us had been working like demons, by the time we fell into bed at night, usually accompanied by Susie and Liz, we fell instantly asleep.

Maudlin tears of self-pity stained the pillow over my face as I remembered one of the few times Raj had tried to be responsible about our relationship. Months ago. We'd been making love. Right at that point where you know you're on the brink of orgasm, in absolute total communion with your lover, with all the forces of nature at your command, he had suddenly pulled out. The abruptness of it was horrible, like being in an iron lung, happily breathing along and someone suddenly pulls the plug. I was devastated and burst into tears. "Why'd you do that?"

The light streaming in from the hall left a halo around his figure as he sat back, kneeling between my legs, his heels supporting him. The expression on his face was hard to fathom, "For us."

The window across from us was open behind drawn curtains, I heard the steady clicking hum of bicycle wheels turning as someone walked their bike past the window; in the enclosed courtyard beyond was a row of cottonwood trees, the wind soughing uniformly through their leaves. I rolled away from Raj and buried my face in the pillow. His hand was on my naked shoulder, he tried to pull me back, "The definitive word here is `us', we don't need more babies to complicate things."

That age old ploy, trap a man by getting pregnant, I wasn't above doing such things, every fertile cell in my body conspiring to wrap around his seed and make a new life. Quite beyond a rational approach. But he led, I followed, my heart a ball and chain I dragged behind me.

Goddamn Raj, why couldn't he have been responsible like that two weeks ago? But hadn't I let it happen too?

I was grateful to have finished the work on Ginger's breast cancer project. There'd been over three thousand patient's charts to review. I'd summarized my findings, complete with statistical analyses of the results, and produced a twenty-five page paper. But it had been a very sad task, so many of the women were young, only in their forties. A few had infants and one had still been nursing a baby when she discovered a lump.

While Ginger never even bothered to thank me for all of my hard work, one of the post-docs told me it was a publishable paper and I should be very proud of it. The soup kitchen began to recede a little bit.

***

"What are you going to do?" Nick's face was strained and pale, beneath his tan he had the gray look of someone just diagnosed with cancer.

There was a bottle of Chivas handy on my grandfather's round oak table, two glasses, sticky with fingerprints and filled with a light amber liquid, melting ice; a black plastic industrial size ashtray full of camel-colored butts heaped high and a pack of Marlboros. Susie was sound asleep on the rough red corduroy fabric of the window seat cushions. We'd been at this for hours as I counted back again and explained that I must have been pregnant when I moved home.

"The obvious thing is to have an abortion. I'm committed to making our marriage work Nick and that can't be done carrying another man's baby."

"No shit. It would leave you tied to him for life. But Christ, I can't ask you to do that for me knowing how much you loved that shithead. You couldn't really have an abortion could you? You're sure you're pregnant?" Only the tenth time he'd asked me that.

I nodded, breathless suddenly, afraid of hyperventilating; I drank more Scotch. Just drinking alcohol while pregnant told me that at a very basic level I was committed to having an abortion. With Liz I never drank at all.

How many times can you go over a scene in your mind, like that last time with Raj, until it falls apart, loses meaning, like so much trash in a trash compacter. A tight little rectangular package you sift through, analyzing, searching for something to give you hope; as useful as reading tea leaves. Instead, resentment toward Raj gained momentum.

No quarreling or equivocating with myself, only inner resilience, total conviction. And quite possibly, I'm drunk, "Yes, I could--I will--have an abortion." With very little emotion involved, the feminine pragmatist, I'd arrived at this all alone, based on hopes for my marriage, a show of commitment to Nick. Still, my marriage was only half a sanctuary, what I could siphon off from Nick until I was strong enough to say no to Raj.

The next day Nick called me from work to tell me about Planned Parenthood. "I made an appointment for you to see a counselor Friday, but you have to either have the test done there or take the results of your test--a laboratory test, not the home kind--showing you're really pregnant."

The phlebotomists at Quest were all so efficient. It took less than fifteen minutes to get the results. As I wrote the check to pay for the test my nausea was almost incapacitating, spilling through my body like toxic waste. With the pink 'patient's copy' stuffed in my purse, I hurried back to my car, throwing up in an empty HEB plastic bag. Tears streaming down my face I drove home, stripping down to my panties as soon as the front door closed behind me.

Only by lying perfectly still in bed could I fool my body that there was no nausea. Nick had kindly agreed to pick Liz up from preschool. When Susie jumped up on the bed, standing on the quilt beside me, sniffing the pillow, trying to shove it aside with her snout to get to my face, it was like a veritable tempest in a teapot. I had to race to the bathroom where I threw up again.

Lying on the tile next to the toilet, I thought about Raj's baby, more tears in my eyes as I fell asleep, my face pressed to the cool porcelain, only waking up when Liz put her sweet hand on my forehead.

"Were you sick Mommy? Are you okay? Poor thing."

***

My days and nights are measured by degrees of nausea; it is so awful I can't even smoke. I can barely manage going from the bed to the couch then to the kitchen to eat something and back again. If there had been doubts about the abortion before, my intense physical discomfort swept them away. For company in my misery, late in the evening when Liz and Nick were asleep, I read, for the second time, "Too Late the Phalarope," by Alan Paton, another book from Charlie's collection. My memory of it was appropriately keen, the story of Piet, an Afrikaaner, many years before the end of apartheid, whose life was destroyed when it was discovered he had slept with a black woman. He lost his family, his job, his high standing in the community, all because he was a man of passion married to a cold, unresponsive woman.

We lived in such an era of moral freedom now. The microcosm of America: belief that justice could be benign or at least offer you the hope for a court of appeal to see things your way. Pregnant by one man, married to another, a benevolent husband my court of appeal. But my confidence wavered, should I get off so easy? What a mess to have made of things. In the past, I must always have mistaken mental disease--disorder--for intellectual, emotional depth and resonance, flexibility. Flexibility on the one hand freed me to arrive at this point, but it hid from me the driving force behind life: competition, with its intrinsic potential for cruelty.

My gaze kept returning to the painting behind the couch, on the wall above the Bose speakers. One of my only attempts at impressionistic painting, a still life set in a heavy dark wood frame, with beige raw silk matting. A kitchen in a villa in the south of France; a table and two chairs beneath a window opened to reveal a vineyard beyond. A plate of apples rests on the table. Such a tranquil setting, I imagined Raj and I escaping through that open window to a non-punitive world.

For a moment I fantasized about keeping the baby. But my practical nature (really? maybe sometimes.) would not brook even this tiny softening, insistent on throwing out the facts to me. It would be pure folly to think I could save my marriage and finish medical school with this baby.

I hadn't been to church in forever and the next day I drove downtown to St. Mary's for the early mass. As a kid I'd always loved the peace and quiet of the cathedral and would piously kneel and get right with Jesus for whatever sins I'd committed. I'd long ago lost my faith, but I needed to be there that day, to talk quietly to myself about my impending abortion.

While the priest went through his arcane ceremony, his cell phone went off. He fumbled in his vestments to silence it. Surely the father, son and the Holy Ghost did not look favorably on cell phone use during transubstantiation, turning the wine and wafer into the blood and body of Christ. Moreover, what could they possibly think about the scandal of pedophilia among priests?

My hopes for humanity plummeted.

***

The Wednesday before my appointment with the Planned Parenthood counselor, Raj called. Undecided what to tell him, I wavered, knowing the abortion was inevitable, not even harboring a strong hope that his knowing could change things.

"I haven't seen you around for a few days. What've you been up too?"

I swore I wasn't going to tell him but the words just fell out of my mouth. "I'm pregnant and it's not Nick's."

The finality of his and Chris' current commitment to their marriage filled me with despair. The iron-grip of responsibility was choking the life force out of Raj. But wasn't that the core of my moral bankruptcy, that I always excused the executioner? Convoluted reasoning, I was so well-programmed in the art of servility, too painful to let people disappoint themselves, must seek out battered egos to prop up; you can't escape giving totally, asking for nothing in return, not even this tiny life growing inside.

Seconds ticked by in heavy silence. "You don't have to worry, Raj, I'm getting an abortion."

"Why can't you keep it?" Naive question, a child who doesn't understand the realities that constrain other people's lives. Actually he knows them too well, his words meant more to defuse potential fireworks, it would not do to say `are you sure it's mine'?

At noon the door-bell rang. I went to answer it, not surprised that it was Raj, but terrified Nick would come home. Liz was still at pre-school. His face was drawn, appropriately serious for the occasion, but his eyes were bright and warm.

From the air-conditioned Toyota to my air-conditioned home, the short distance left him damp with moisture. Clouds blocked the sun outside but did nothing to assuage the heat, the blast of hot air when he came inside. Susie joined us, sniffing delicately at his jeans. I felt a transitory, fleeting hope--did he have a new slant on how to deal with this problem?

We stood together in the foyer; he pulled me into his arms, my cool body drawing heat and moisture from him. He leaned against the slender rectangular opaque window adjacent to the door, while I rested my head on his shoulder plucking at the curtained panel behind him, at the sheer green material stretched top to bottom. The house felt like an oppressive, heavy encumbrance, an over-sized snail's shell for so flimsy a life. I longed for the narrow confines of my apartment, the freedom to be with Raj openly.

Pulling away finally I went into the kitchen to get a beer for him. Raj sat on the velour couch in the den, while I paced, nervous having him there. Opening the glass door to the stereo cabinet, I turned on the CD player, chosing a CD at random, punched buttons, then adjusted the volume to Faith Hill's "This Kiss."

A fat haus-frau in my billowing house-dress, snaps firmly in place all the way up to my neck, totally unsexy, I sat stiffly across the room from Raj in one of the soft, leather wingback chairs.

"You like country and western?"

"It's okay, this is a good song."

Just idle conversation as he peeled the label off of his beer bottle, depositing the pieces in the mouth of the purple and red Murano ashtray. A slender glass vase, with a scalloped rim, held red roses from my back yard; their fragrance was cloying, the old petals littering the coffee table.

Cocking his head to one side, squinting his eyes at me, probing, Raj asked, "What is it exactly about this song that appeals to you?"

"Dunno. I guess because you know that she knows it's way more than just any old kiss she's ever had, she's trying to keep her distance maybe. Nick says C & W is vulgar, guess I'm just hopelessly drawn to the vulgarities in life." My eyes shot a look to him, *Like you.*

He grinned cynically then leaned back on the couch, silent. There was an odd tension in the air, combativeness, a pivotal moment in our relationship but one he had no control over. He hated maneuvering in a weakened position. How will she use this to manipulate me? How far will I have to fight for what I want her to do?

Your lucky day Raj, this tense, servile woman arrogates all responsibility to herself. So what that it was your abduction, your sperm. She'll pay and let you slink off, safe again.

For a moment, a rent of greater insight appeared in the everyday illusion of reality; a parallel tape that showed the sea of calm in a life not held captive by this man. To be whole, to be free, let me lasso it, drag it back into real time, put it to use. The gap closed and I could see that an objective assessment was impossible. Too many contradictions. Not just Raj, but all the ones my father had passed on to me intact most notable the Catholic demand for perfection which can lead to paralysis, how perfect does it have to be? Emotional detritus ripe for bursting out of me like that alien being who burst forth out of John Hurt's chest in "Alien."

"Got anymore beer?" I nodded.

"Yeah, come on."

In the kitchen we stood together in front of the refrigerator, peering in. He grabbed another Budweiser, my eyes were riveted on a leftover pork roast, not from hunger; nausea welled up in me, I turned quickly to throw up in the sink. A neat, circumspect pile, thankfully issued forth without any harrowing dry heaves. The dainty act of vomiting in front of one's lover. When I recovered, rinsing my mouth out, Raj relaxed. "You okay?"

At my nod, he twisted the cap on his beer off, fiddling with it on the counter, tapping out a rhythm to some song.

Just a young kid to have so much dumped on him. Maybe he was right, maybe I should take heed of what he'd said about being a fuck-up. He wore a red and black T-shirt tucked neatly into Lee jeans, wide leather belt with a burnished metal buckle cinched tightly around his waist, he'd lost weight. Pregnant, I'd gained, large breasts, round face, pale skin, soft and pink, a ripe avocado around a growing seed.

Drinking half the beer down in one sip, he leaned tiredly against the almond refrigerator, sighing deeply. "I'm beat. I went into school really early to do some catch up work. Jennifer was up all night with croup. Spent part of the night in a steamy bathroom." He wiped more sweat from his forehead with the back of his hand.

"Where was Chris?"

"At work. Shit, I don't know, sometimes I think she skips out of work to see Helmut."

He set the beer down and put his arms around me. We stood unmoving for several minutes, then he pulled away from me, staring at my face, "You do look pregnant, your face is fuller, your eyes have this certain look...Jeez, I love pregnant women." His breath came faster against my hair, his hands moved restlessly across my body.

Later, lying in his arms, Raj asked me, "When did you get pregnant, after you moved back home?"

"Yes, when you kidnapped me from the grocery store. If I have to do my own DNA test to prove to you it's yours I will. That was the only time I've had sex in weeks and weeks."

His face was earnest, his sense of responsibility a knot around his heart, almost insecurely, almost a question, "I love you, Sophie."

***

The day arrived for my appointment with the social worker at Planned Parenthood. After a brief wait in the reception area, a tall, imposing black woman emerged from an office down the hall. She shook my hand and introduced herself as Trudi, guiding me back to her office, inviting me to sit down in the chair next to her desk. Her burnished skin glowed with good health; her hair was brushed in marcelled waves up and away from her face and neck, emphasizing the slender curve of her neck. Adopting an impartial, non-judgmental air, she began by explaining the alternatives to abortion that I was free to choose from.

"There are many, many people who would gladly take your baby."

"I know, the problem is, if I have it, I'll keep it, I could never give it away."

"I see."

After explaining the risks involved in abortion, what the procedure entailed, she ended the brief consultation and stood up, moving toward her closed office door, "You'll be required to undergo birth control counseling once you've recovered. We'll provide you with whatever inexpensive birth control devices you want. Any questions?" "Nope. Thanks." As we shook hands again, I felt the slender bones in her hand compress slightly. "See you next Friday then."

In the car I sat doubled over the wheel caught in an agonizing spasm of nausea, not wanting to drive, crying, tears of frustration falling into my lap because I have to wait so long. Next Friday? That was an eternity when measured against my nausea.

Then driving away from the clinic, the humor of a long-forgotten memory brightened my mood somewhat. A once-upon-a-time visit made to the County Health Department clinic. Senior year at UT I had unprotected sex with a gorgeous male model I'd met at Dante's, a bar on Sixth Street. Your basic one-night stand except that Trevor Chase (could he have had a more made up name?) came back two weeks later to say he'd found out he had gonorrhea. "You have to get tested."

The global eradication of small-pox after 1977 was thought to usher in a new era; infectious diseases could be a thing of the past. But the emergence of AIDS in the early eighties, the fact that it was incurable, a death sentence, was a horrific blow to the medical community. In a terrifyingly short period of time casual sex would become a possible death threat.

I'd been terribly foolish and agonized over what to do, finally opting for a clandestine visit to the County Health Department where I could pay in cash and didn't have to give my real name.

At the clinic I was given a block of wood with a number on it. "Take a seat in there. We'll call you by that number."

Trembling, positive that Trevor was bisexual and had probably had multiple homosexual liaisons and that I would turn out to be HIV positive, I thought about sitting on the floor and bursting into tears.

Just take one more step Sophie; you can at least do that, then another. I went into the tiny alcove the receptionist had pointed to. Segregated from the other visitors in the waiting room, it was obvious that we mongrels of society guilty of having a sexually transmitted disease could not sit with the general population. I was the only female seated amidst a group of Hispanic men who grinned as I timidly joined them. Why hadn't I just sucked it up and gone to my family doctor?

Gripping the block of wood in my sweaty palm I looked down to see that someone had used a wood burning tool to burn the number "SIXTY-NINE" into it. An hour later a woman stood outside the door and bellowed, "Number sixty-nine."

Crimson-faced, stunned with embarrassment I hurried past the men laughing loudly at me, the number sixty-nine, being part of that international lingua franca, a word easier on the tongue, pardon the pun, than the stiff formality of cunnilingus or fellatio. Far worse, though, was the doctor I eventually saw. He wore tortoise shell glasses that kept sliding down his greasy nose; he must have forgotten to shave for a couple of days. It was not a look that did much for him, was totally unsexy and gave him the air of a homeless man.

He thrust a form at me. "Habla Ingles?"

"Yes."

"Then fill that out with the names of all the people you've had sex with since you were first infected."

I managed to mumble through my juddering jaw that I hadn't had sex at all since then.

He sniffed as if he didn't believe me.

"Very well."

Accustomed to people with minimal education who spoke little English, he immediately began to draw for me, with the proficiency a first-grader might possess, pictures of penises and vaginas--what you see on sleazy bathroom walls--to graphically illustrate how venereal diseases are transmitted.

Without ever making eye contact with me he ended our visit by giving me another form to take to the lab. "Down the hall to your right. And remember, the vagina is normally like a self-cleaning oven, it will work hard for you if you use rubbers, protection and so forth. Let's hope you don't have an STD."

Walking on a bed of hot coals would have been preferable to the indignities of the county clinic, but when the blood tests came back and everything was normal I wept with joy.

***

The Thursday before my appointment at Planned Parenthood I finished loading the dishwasher then turned on the disposal. It made a grinding noise as if a rock was stuck in it. Reaching beneath the black rubber cover over the drain, I rooted around dragging up a lump of pale flesh: a speckled membrane of raw chicken. Nick had grilled chicken breasts the night before and probably just tossed the residue in the disposal.

I couldn't help comparing the wretched lump in my hand to what I'd be going through the next day, what diabolical symbolism. Instantly my stomach lurched, bile rose in my throat. I threw up violently followed by heaving spasms that racked my body over and over until it felt like I'd turned myself inside out.

In bed later my stomach had settled somewhat but I was anxious about what the next day might bring. I knew what to expect, had been at Dr. Gupta's side for any number of procedures, amniocentesis, endometrial biopsies, and therapeutic abortions. I'd been surprised at how quickly you could terminate a pregnancy, seconds to conceive--surely it must take hours to abort. Then once in Labor and Delivery, I'd watched in astonishment as Gupta reached in almost savagely to pull a baby from the birth canal, causing the perineum to tear. While he tended to the baby, he snapped at me, "Stitch her up Trudeau."

Why hadn't Charlie ever made me pregnant? Maybe he was sterile. Thank God for small favors.

Once, years earlier, I'd driven by his house. Two men sat just inside the garage on white plastic chairs drinking beer in the middle of the day. The house was shabby, sagging on its foundation. The strip mall where his bar and grill had been seemed equally decayed, windows boarded up. Everything was spray painted with fat runic-like symbols in gaudy colors.

Had his life really been as hollow and empty as I imagined it to be? There seemed no trace left of him anywhere. It made me think of Macbeth's soliloquy. "That struts and frets his hour upon the stage, and then is heard no more."

And with those happy thoughts the warm cocoon of sleep that envelops the pregnant female descended upon me and I slept the night through.

***

I sat in the waiting room at Planned Parenthood for two hours before my name was called. Nick stood up with me, closing the "Field and Stream" magazine he had been glancing at. An odd choice for an abortion clinic, where was "Zero Population Growth Quarterly?" Our eyes met for a moment, his were warm, full of a reassuring concern.

"Good luck, and think of the beach," he hugged me.

"Thanks."

"Sophie, nice to meet you. I'm Ellen Banks." She was willowy and exotic looking with high cheekbones. The smooth black sheen of her skin struck me as impossibly dark. Had all of us really evolved from the same Mitochondrial Eve? Her eyes met mine as she guided me into a small room, her gaze level, straightforward and kind.

Neon bright light with sun streaming in through clerestory windows made me blink several times. A mirror on the dingy green wall reflected the stark pallor of my face.

"Honey, you need to take off everything from the waist down and get settled on this table."

Damp with perspiration, my palms slippery with sweat, I stripped out of my clothes, and then lay stiffly down on the exam table.

Ellen draped me with a blue paper sheet. "Now scoot down till your fanny hits the very edge of the table and put your feet in the stirrups. That's right."

The doctor entered the room, closing the door behind her. "I'm Dr. Stephens."

She shook my hand limply then turned to the sink and washed up. She was young with long blonde hair, sensitive brown eyes; pretty in a serious way. I was so nervous my lips were numb and my brain felt like a block of cement. Which was just as well because I really didn't want to blurt out that I was a medical student, as if I didn't know the first thing about birth control.

Glancing at my chart she plucked latex gloves from a wall-mounted box, pulled them on and turned back to me. "We're going to start now."

Ellen held my hands, instructing me to breathe evenly in and out. "You have kids Sophie?"

"Yeah, just the one, her name is Liz." I couldn't keep the tremor out of my voice.

"That's a pretty name."

The walls of my vagina were retracted with a speculum; there was a gentle push on the womb, a not unbearable cramp as the cervix was dilated. Why had I refused the Valium drip? Masochistic fool.

"You're okay sugar. Just breathe slowly." Ellen's mellifluous voice, her gentle demeanor and wide mouth curving into a reassuring smile, it was all so soothing.

My ribs hurt from the spasms of vomiting the night before. I'd never been sick like that with Liz, never even threw up. What was so different now?

Another cramp, this one slightly more painful, lanced through my uterus; graphic scenes of women dying from abortions, from coat hangers stuck up their vaginas assailed me. My anxiety ratcheted up to an almost unbearable level, spreading like fire, dissolving my tenuous courage the way mercury dissolves gold.

Ellen sensed my panic. Holding my hands tightly she said, "Hold on, it won't be long now."

With my eyes squeezed shut I tried to ignore the noises around me: a whirring sound, the clatter of instruments on a steel tray, the steady drip of the faucet the doctor hadn't turned off completely.

My eyes flew open as Dr. Stephens stood up and moved to the sink behind her. "You can sit up now."

The relief from my severe nausea was so instantaneous I couldn't believe it. What had transpired in that split second hardly seemed possible. The incredible speed with which biochemical information sped through the body amazed me.

Tossing her latex gloves in the trashcan and adjusting her lab coat, the doctor turned back to me. "Part of the procedure includes sending the tissue I removed to the lab to make sure that it was all there. I doubt there'll be any problems." There was an odd, paradoxical solemnity about her, almost an accusation; the weight of so many tiny potential lives working against her belief in this right for women. Or maybe I was just projecting again.

Dispatched to a comfortable waiting room, they gave me orange juice and cookies. After half an hour of post-op convalescence, a skinny, poker-faced vocational nurse, with mousy brown hair, gave me a prescription for medication I would need and instructed me not to bathe, "Take showers instead, and no sex for a few weeks. You'll want to avoid any possibility of infection."

And that was that.

Chapter Eighteen

August 2000

Owen wrote the first draft of his serial killer novel, "Ready to Depart," during the two week break before school started. He'd flown to Las Vegas and checked in to the MGM Grand, writing all day and playing Blackjack at night.

I ran into him at my locker a week after the abortion. He seemed a little nervous; perspiration had lightly pearled across the bridge of his nose. He handed me a rectangular box. "I finally did it, wrote the monster, pounded out nearly four-hundred pages over the break. Will you read it for me? I trust your judgment more than just about anyone. Besides, you're the only other person I know who makes time to read. Rebecca told me she hasn't read for pleasure since her junior year in college. Not a single book that wasn't about medicine or surgery."

"Her mother's Chinese, that's probably why." I shook the box with his manuscript. "Has a significant heft to it Owen, this is awesome. I'd love to read it. When do you need it back?"

"When you finish it. I want total honesty too, if it sucks, you have to tell me. The whole nine yards: grammar, syntax, vocabulary, tone, pacing, is it a page turner?" He flashed a smile at me, his brown eyes lighting up warmly. "Any and all suggestions will be appreciated."

"Ready to Depart" delves into the mind of a predator, a fiendishly clever psychopath without a soul. He abducts women from what seem like impossible situations, a sort of latter-day Houdini who thrusts his cape open and makes you disappear. The first to vanish is the trophy wife of lawyer, Ryan Thomas. One minute she's in the kitchen making dinner, he goes upstairs to change and when he comes back down she's disappeared into the cold night air, leaving her purse, her cell phone, everything. She didn't even have time to turn the burner off under the pan of rice.

The book was genuinely creepy and sucked me in from the first sentence, so vivid and gripping I read until the wee hours of the morning. There were a few choppy parts where a simple rewrite would be needed but nothing else.

I saw Owen first thing the next day, both of us heading for a quick breakfast in the cafeteria. "I am so impressed with your book; you are absolutely the next Michael Crichton." Crichton wrote "The Andromeda Strain" when he was still a medical student.

"Ah, that man died way too young, he had so many more books in him, what a tragedy. It was like he was able to pluck the next big thing people would be hooked by, before they even knew. Totally had his finger on the pulse of the times. So you liked it, really?"

"It was great. Can't you see the bags under my eyes from staying up all night?"

"Yeah, actually I can."

"Thanks."

***

Even though sleep had begun to elude me once more, I wasn't wracked with guilt about the abortion. My body, my decision, and it was the right one. What I hadn't anticipated was how desperately I wanted to see Raj, to talk through what had happened between us.

We'd tried twice to get together but our schedules made it impossible. Then as luck would have it, Nick got all excited about a famous Noble Prize winning physics professor who'd been invited to speak at UT in Austin. Nick and Dave McIntosh planned to attend the lecture Wednesday evening, then drive back the next day.

Coming off of an on-call shift, I'd have Wednesday off and Raj was also free that night.

Instead, Nick woke up Wednesday with fever and chills, all the symptoms of the flu and had to cancel his trip. Resting under the afghan on the couch, he watched CNN with the volume turned so loud you'd think the fever had robbed him of his hearing.

Liz rode her three-wheeler in circles from the living room to the den to the kitchen, singing her current most favorite song. "Three little monkeys jumping on the bed, one fell down and cracked his head, doctor, doctor, fix him please." Susie chased after her barking, nails sliding on the kitchen linoleum.

The sliding glass door was open and a tiny Siamese kitten, a stranger to these parts, tentatively walked across the metal runners into the den. On her return trip through the den, Susie spotted the kitten, fur went flying, the kitten freaked out, streaked away across the backyard, Susie right behind her. A large black bumble bee flew in, then sensing the high level of tension, realizing his mistake, he flew out again. Nature was too much with me.

The screen, cheap and falling off of the runners, became stuck as I tried to slide it closed, infuriating me. I angrily forced it along, dislodging it entirely, it fell outward on to the cement ground, coming to rest against a whiskey barrel filled with dirt, red geraniums and petunias, several of which it crushed.

Then I stomped back inside the den and stood in front of the television, yelling, "Jesus Christ, Nick, can't you hear with the volume a little lower?"

He looked wounded as he reached for the remote control, inching the sound back down to where it was barely audible. Irritated by the look, crazy with frustration that my careful planning to be with

Raj had come to nothing, I complained nastily, "Why'd you have to get sick anyway, can't you take better care of yourself?"

His face crumpled in pain as a spasm of coughing swept over him; I could tell he was really sick. When the coughing subsided he asked weakly, "Don't you think you're being a little selfish?"

Liz came barreling through the room on her three-wheeler, barely missing my toes. "Sorry Mommy!"

"Oh, goddamnit, who can stand this fucking chaos." Grabbing my purse, I hurried through the kitchen, out to the garage then into my Volvo, driving away angrily. At the Seven Eleven near the loop I pulled into the parking lot and brought out my cell phone, dialing Raj's number; he answered on the first ring, his voice guarded, "Sophie?"

"Can you talk?" My voice was still shaky with emotion. Cars pulled into the parking lot, their heat and exhaust fumes mingled in the humid air hovering over me; sweat beaded my forehead, collected under my arms then dripped down, my brassiere absorbing it.

"Yeah, what's up?"

"You can't come tonight, Nick is home sick."

"Shit. I really need to see you Sophie." His voice was low, he sounded depressed. "Things are so bad with Chris. When I got home last night the kids were a mess, no food in the house, the dishes were still dirty, piled all over the place. She quit her job and now she just lies around reading all day, chain smoking." I'd never heard him so down before, never heard him criticize his life.

"You wouldn't believe how much more weight she's lost, she looks sick. She must think this all happened because she was overweight. Shit, I didn't mind that. When can you meet me?" A man who didn't mind fat women, what more could you ask for? A single man who didn't mind fat women.

"I don't know, probably not anytime soon." Flies buzzed around a half-eaten hot dog on the macadam parking lot, heat shimmered above it reacting with decades of oil dripping from cars. "Then when?" His words tore at me. Eyes closed, gripping the cell phone, I imagined his touch, his strong hands, the tiny black hairs curling on the knuckles, the way his darks eyes moved with mine, searching, reassuring. When I seemed lost to him, he wanted me the most.

"I don't know, God, I'm sorry things are so bad."

"Yeah, me too. Hang on, I've got another call." Raj clicked over to the new call. My face crumpled, I forced myself not to break down and start sobbing.

A car pulled into the slot next to me. The guy killed the engine then turned to stare at me. His eyes were freaky, as if they were lit by some internal flame blazing away in his soul. His hair had receded all the way to the back of his head and there were only a few greasy strands to comb over. Everything in his face sagged: the pouches under his eyes, deep crevices marked his cheeks on either side of a long fleshy nose, his mouth was a wide slit in the skin, sagging at both ends. He wore a high necked white shirt, buttoned tight and a wide tie. Those eyes were so demonic, like if you looked long enough into them you'd end up stuffed in a garbage bag in the dumpster missing your head. Suddenly I felt paranoid and extremely vulnerable, remembering Owen's book and poor Carla Rennert, not to mention almost getting abducted in Brackenridge Park.

"Sophie, you there? Sorry, it was mom; you know how she loves to talk."

"That's okay." I locked the doors and tucked the phone between my left ear and shoulder, then started the car. "At least I'll see you at school tomorrow."

We hung up. His marriage was slowly dying, like mine. How stupid to stay married when so in love with someone else. Find the strength to admit your mistake; it had to be better than living this double life again.

***

I thought long and hard about making the decision to leave. Nick recuperated quickly but still I waited. Then finally the next Sunday afternoon the words just spilled out of me in a rush.

"It's not going to work Nick, I can't stand myself. I can't stand the way I've been treating you. One minute clinging to the hope that our marriage can still work and the next sucked right back into the very thick of things with Raj."

Nick sat stiffly in one of the wingback chairs with his eyes closed. He could be repeating a silent mantra, meditating, except for the pain etched across his face. I kneeled beside him, he opened his eyes, there were tears in them.

Liz came in from outside, the Siamese kitten in her hand, "Can we keep her, Mommie? She's so lonesome living out there in the woodpile."

I nodded, hoping to distract her from her father's sorrow, "Why don't you get a plastic bowl and give her some milk. What will you name her?"

"Michelle, because she's so cute like Michelle."

"Hey, cute is right, we'll call her Mickey for short. We'll make an appointment to get her to Dr. Dorritt, Susie's vet."

Later, Liz and Mickey fell asleep together, the kitten curled snugly against Liz's chest. Curious Susie sat by the side of the bed watching them, eyes alert.

I stood forlornly in front of the refrigerator, staring at the contents, looking for junk food to dull my pain; a champagne bottle, hidden behind the gallon jug of milk and a Tupperware pitcher of cranberry juice, caught my eye. I reached for it.

On the floor in the den, I plopped down in front of Nick who was listening to the stereo with his headphones, Eric Dolphy blaring out the sides.

"Want some?" I asked, holding up the champagne and two glasses.

He nodded, setting the headphones down; lucent eyes like bright metallic orbs watching me solemnly as I popped the cork. Champagne frothed up the neck but didn't spill; I quickly filled the two glasses.

Touching his glass to mine, Nick said, "To divorce."

"I don't want to toast to that." A fact of life now, but not something to celebrate.

"All right. To being single." He leaned across the floor and kissed my cheek.

***

September 2000 and beyond

I rented another apartment on a month by month basis and worked out a financial aid package that would see me through this final year in medical school.

Nick was cooly distant now. Remaining friends had been too painful. Now we only saw each other briefly to exchange Liz. We agreed completely on all the issues concerning custody and child support and division of property. He put the house up for sale, adamant when I pleaded with him not to. "Too many memories."

The divorce papers were drawn up by Nick's lawyer, signed and filed within the first month we separated. After a nominal waiting period, we'd meet in court to finalize the divorce.

Our fourth year in medical school was a breeze by comparison to the third year. The doctors were nicer, the schedule was less hectic and each of us knew that barring unforeseen and/or tragic events, come May we'd graduate from medical school and go on to our residencies. By then most of us had planned the next several years of our lives with such attention to the tiniest detail that our trajectory should be flawless. Or not.

Chapter Nineteen

March 2001

You can tell yourself that it's over, but once you've been to hell and back with a person there's a relationship there as solid and concrete as any you've ever hoped to have in your life.

The trouble now was figuring out if I was talking about Raj or Nick.

The housing market had tanked and we decided to lease the house for a while. Once we leased it, Nick rented an apartment in the same complex where I lived. Inevitably we began to spend more time together. Nothing changed, we were still separated but decided to keep it that way for the time being, canceling the actual divorce. Raj and I still saw each other occasionally. He couldn't quite work up to separating from his family.

***

That Sunday dawned clear and bright. Months of playing the waiting game with Raj once again and my first thought of the day was: *Raj Khan, I'm done with you. Somehow, I'm done with you.*

I took Susie for a long walk and thought about how I would spend the rest of my day. Saturday night Nick had taken Liz to Wimberley with a young woman he'd started dating, Sarah something. They wouldn't be back until that evening.

This was troubling to me. While I wanted Nick to be happy, to get on with his life whether I was with Raj or not, I had not expected to feel so possessive when he showed interest in another woman. A little late, I realized that no other man would ever love Liz the way her real father did. Could I let him slip away to another woman?

Around noon I went to the Barnes & Noble Starbuck's at the mall and sipped on frothy sugar-laced Cappuccinos, stuffing myself with two almond croissants and reading Robert Sapolsky's "A Primate's Memoir." Sapolsky is a neuroendocrinologist at Stanford University who like Hans Selye focused on the impact stress hormones have on the body. He's also an awesome writer. The hours slipped away as I sat enthralled with his memoir about summers spent in Kenya with Masai warriors. Some of it was so funny I laughed out loud.

Raj found me. The tiny hairs on my neck stood on end, a shiver ran down my spine, I felt someone watching me and looked up to see him standing a short distance away. He looked so serious, almost sad, clearly wondering why I was avoiding him. But in the next instant he looked triumphant. You cannot escape from me Sophie.

What did this man want from me? He had already sucked me dry, left me numb; yet without even objecting, I followed him docilely back to my apartment where we made love.

Not making the slightest attempt to wait a decent interval afterwards, he moved away from me and began dressing.

I felt used and dirty and jumped out of bed, slapping him hard on the back. When he turned toward me I tried to slap his face. He grabbed my arms.

"Goddammit, let go of me!" Tears blurred my vision. "I don't know why I put up with all of your bullshit. You're poisoning my life." I wrenched away from him, screaming. "I hate you. I hate the fact that you are so cheap, that you always try to get what you can out of people without giving anything back, that you have no better morals than an alley cat. You are greedy and selfish and what I ever saw in you to begin with is beyond me. You have no character. Get out of my life."

Not to put too fine a point on things.

***

Dr. Jameson had come back from Sweden near the end of my fourth year. Over six feet tall with ramrod straight posture, his hair hadn't so much greyed as it had burnished like brushed nickel. Not yet seventy, his face was heavily lined and leathery from years of exposure to the sun, but still a gritty, handsome face with piercing blue eyes. Never married, there was something about him of the father confessor, a wise patriarch who offered good counsel.

I asked him if he thought I should even bother with a residency, wondering if my emotions were too volatile, too mercurial to be a good doctor. I never expected to make it all the way through medical school. All bets were off when I first fell in love with Raj and still had a year and a half of school to finish. Somehow both of us managed to remain in good standing at school, even if sometimes it was by the slimmest margin.

"I've known you since your first year here. You're quite the quick study with an amazing breadth of information you effortlessly retrieve. So my advice is no, don't quit, give yourself a little more time before making such a final decision. You'd be amazed at the number of emotionally unstable doctors and nurses I've known over my career. Some make it, some don't."

That was an eye opener.

Chapter Twenty

April 2001

Mickey, the Siamese stray who had adopted us, draped herself across my shoulders, purred and fell asleep, her beige-white fur shedding on my blouse. Liz sat in a pint-sized yellow rocking chair drawn up to the coffee table working on a jigsaw puzzle.

We were watching an episode of "Law and Order" but I could tell that Nick wasn't really interested in it. Detectives Briscoe and Green were interviewing a homeless person with a Jesus complex. Out of the blue Nick says, "That guy on TV is as much of a fuck-up as Raj, you thought he walked on water too." He only mouthed the profanity, protecting innocent ears.

Where did that come from, how long has that been simmering just beneath the surface?

"You're right, I admit it, I probably had no idea what Raj was really like." How often people impute to another person the characteristics they're looking for.

The set to Nick's jaw was tight, his mouth a grim line, Liz looked up at him, "Smile daddy!" She grinned wide to show him how.

A quick, reflexive upward tilt, not quite a smile, "Okay sweetheart." Then back toward me, "Let me seek to inform you, no class, no breeding..."

What exactly went into the possession of class and breeding? Was it really something you could quantify? "What do you mean?"

"I can't believe you have to ask; in fact I'm sure you know better." He ticked a few items off, "Integrity, honor, nobility, aristocratic bearing, no rough edges, awareness of all the social niceties and an impeccable knowledge of when not to make transgressions thereof."

Phew, that didn't even describe Nick.

And it certainly didn't describe Raj. So what? It didn't describe half the people in this dog-eat-dog, competitive world, maybe a long-dead King of England? Doubtful. Survival of the fittest in modern times often made for strange bedfellows.

We'd been living together again for less than a month, it was a trial, Nick hadn't even given up his apartment yet. Neither of us really wanted to start over with someone new, but after what we'd been through with Raj, was it really wise to stay together? Take yesterday for example. The Volvo was in the shop for diagnostics, I rode to school with Nick.

After we dropped Liz off, just as I was climbing back into the car, my hose snagged on Nick's briefcase. "Goddammit."

"What's wrong?"

"These hose, they're brand new! I've got my interview with Dr. Prendergast this afternoon, shit. All I did was climb into the car and they ran." I'd applied to the Forensic Pathology department for a residency and had my final interview with Prendergast, the head of the department that afternoon.

Nick stared sullenly at me, his voice was a whine. "Can't you twist them around or something?" He started the engine and we drove away from Nancy's house.

The run in my hose was an imperfection I suddenly couldn't abide and it was all Nick's fault, that damn briefcase. "We're going to have to stop at Walgreen's, get a new pair."

With a heavy sigh, he lit a cigarette and let it sit in the ashtray, the smoke billowing up into my eyes, burning them. "Jesus, Nick, do you have to smoke in the car?" Ever since the abortion, cigarettes in the morning nauseated me. Meekly, he stubbed it out then turned off the feeder road heading toward the Walgreen's parking lot. Over the eastern sky the sun's rays were faintly visible bringing the world into focus.

Why did he always give in so easily? I reached over and pinched his arm. "Why don't you ever stand up for yourself? Is it just easier being a martyr, always making me out to be the bad guy?"

The hurt, forbearing look on his face killed me, I didn't want the power to hurt anyone. But medical school had made me a little thicker skinned, and while the power to hurt was an unwieldy weapon for me, I wouldn't survive if I didn't learn how to use it.

"That's not true, quit pinching me."

"No." I pinched him again, harder.

He shouted at me, angrier still. "Stop it."

Savagely angry now, I reached up to slap him; he gripped my hand before it connected, then jerked the car in to Walgreen's parking lot and killed the engine. His face paled, turned gray, his lips bloodless, there was a murderous rage reflected back and forth in both of our faces.

"Let go of me you sonofabitch," I hissed at him. His fingers dug into my wrist, twisting my arm away from him. "Forget the fucking hose."

A heavy, bitter silence descended on us as Nick started the engine again and maneuvered back into traffic.

Suddenly, I was crying uncontrollably, random images fusing in my mind, the abortion, a favorite dog that had been run over, a friend who'd been paralyzed from the waist down after a car accident. I cried all the harder.

Jesus, I'd lost so much, made such a mess of things, perverting even Nick.

At school I locked myself in a stall in the restroom and did repair work on my eyes with the help of a little Visine. For my interview I'd worn a white silk blouse and a black Donna Karan suit with steep Manolo Blahnik pumps but by then I felt like I'd slept in the outfit. Staring at my reflection in the compact mirror I added a bit more lipstick and tried a shaky smile; then snapped the compact shut.

Midmorning I called Nick on the cell phone. He answered immediately. Neither of his spoke until finally I offered a feisty growl. He laughed and soon we were tripping over ourselves to apologize.

It was a start, clearing the air and putting things back together again.

***

I'd said no to seeing Raj twenty times, on the twenty-first, sure that I was completely over him, I said, why not?

He opened the door as soon as I knocked, quickly leading me into his friend's apartment; his face was taut and white, music from the stereo was bone-rattlingly raucous. At my look of displeasure he turned it off.

"I brought wine, do you want some?"

I sat down on a green Naugahyde couch, pock-marked with cigarette burns. His overly solicitous manner irritated me. There was no relationship here, right?

"No. I can't stay long." Why had I even come? We hadn't been together in so long.

Ignoring my wish he poured two glasses of Sauvignon Blanc, passing one to me. A few sips, then suddenly full of nervous energy, I set it down, pacing, wondering how to convince him that it was over between us.

Raj came up to me and pulled me into his arms. If he could not hold me to him with his wit or charm or the breadth of his intellect, he wielded a not insubstantial physical presence. My resistance ebbed away in his arms at the push, the force his personality had always exerted over me.

Then in bed with him, my eyes stared at the light fixture on the ceiling, a dull upside down looking cake with white rippled frosting. Extending away from it was a crack in the ceiling that traveled from the fixture to the molding over the bathroom door. It reminded me of Roman Polanski's weird movie "Repulsion." Cracked walls caught in an implausible earthquake and putty hands emerging from the walls in dark, narrow hallways. A smear of red lipstick across Catherine Deneuve's face; she is held in the grip of those hallucinatory hands caressing her breasts. Her sexual terrors made her terrifyingly homicidal.

From the ceiling, I shortened my gaze, watching the bare length of Raj as he pumped away on top of me. I thought: my other husband. I was a bigamist, as bound to him as I was to Nick. Would I ever escape him?

Certainly he had given substance back to my emotions; they were no longer inaccessible to me. Yet I couldn't help feeling a prickly animosity toward him. He sensed that he had been the force I used to work out that thorny, distorted adaptation, the need to work through the devastation of my relationship with Charlie.

As those internal stresses were removed, so was the basis for our relationship. Autonomy had returned, yet oddly, with it came certain tender feelings for Raj, this man who had enslaved me. Autonomy this side of enslavement had a much sharper focus, an infinitely more dear character. Perhaps what I felt was genuine love.

Regardless of that, I couldn't and wouldn't continue in a pointless relationship with a man who would never leave his family.

The room was in shadows, my eyes opened sleepily, it was so very quiet. Raj was asleep, my fingers rested lightly on his flesh, checking his pulse, listening closely to the sound of the blood coursing through his body. His mouth was parted slightly; there was a gleam of saliva on his teeth, so young and vulnerable.

It had started to rain, the sun blocked by swelling black and gray clouds. A slight mist passed through the screen on the window in back of the bed. I turned on my stomach and peered out, the soft, moist breeze felt deliciously sensual against my face. In the distance a line of trees formed a scalloped edge along the upper horizon, dense and dark. I had nothing to be afraid of, yet a shiver of fright passed through me, a quick surge of electricity like touching a frayed wire.

It seemed as if there was a substrate of melancholy rippling undetected through physical matter. I had been halfway convinced it was merely heightened perception; that it worked on me from without, instead, like the black hole, from within.

Raj stirred beside me, stretching, drawing me closer, his slack penis resting against my leg, the black hair and pink soft flesh, damp and fused against mine. One tiny glistening drop of semen on the tip, more babies, just add water and watch them grow from micro-Lilliputians, amazing that scientists once believed in that Homunculus.

"Who's place is this?"

He mumbled against my neck, "Steve Shepherd from the ER, he rents it from a woman who lives across the street. He's up in Austin every weekend to see his girlfriend at the university. Said I could use it whenever I wanted."

Feeling sticky and warm, I disengaged myself from him. "I have to go."

"Meet me here next weekend?"

"No, I can't. We have plans."

For once he didn't argue or come back with a tart comment.

***

The streets were slick and shimmering with moisture as I drove home, the headlights blasting through the dark.

Once at home I home I showered and slipped into old flannel pajamas then headed for the kitchen to start making dinner.

Nick and Liz got home from the movie around seven; they'd gone to see "Crocodile Dundee in Los Angeles".

Slicing avocado for a salad Nick and I chatted about the movie. Liz had already run off to find Mickey.

"How was it?"

"Liz got a kick out of it, I guess it was okay. What have you been up do?"

With a guiltless lilt to my voice that implied happiness with my life--all that Nick wanted from me--I said, "Shopping, I bought new toss pillows for the couch, do you like them?" A visible sense of relief as he turned to inspect the brightly colored pillows.

"Yeah, they're nice."

"Want me to fix you a drink?"

"What did you have in mind?"

"Something exotic, a pina colada?"

"You're on."

The slight increase in self-esteem from having surmounted, for the most part, the obstacle of Raj had given me a new generosity of spirit. Since our last epic battle Nick and I had gotten along much better. Like a blind person granted vision in a tiny sector of their retina, I'd become much more attuned to Nick's feelings, his obvious sensitivity and humanity. Cruelty and deception had no place in marriage and if we were going to work things out together, I had to understand the consequences of my behavior. Why had it taken so long for me to understand these things?

Floodlights illuminated the backyard and from the kitchen window I watched as the dog, cat, husband and Little Mermaid gamboled in the backyard. A few months back one of our neighbors had been bitten by a rattlesnake in her backyard and lost her little toe. I'd thought about walling off the entrance to our backyard but that was impractical, so little rubber boots for Liz were now *de rigueur*.

***

Raj and I drifted further apart. He cornered me in the underground parking lot one afternoon as I was leaving to meet Nick. It was the end of May and we'd be graduating soon.

We talked nervously for a few minutes

He stepped away from me, giving me an appraising glance, "Jeez, you look great, what have you done? I really like your hair short and curled away from your face like that."

In turn, he did not look so good. He had gained weight though if you hadn't known him well, it wouldn't be obvious. He looked tired.

Paranoid, afraid of being caught, I said goodbye and started to hurry away. Raj caught me as I was about to rush past, pulling me tightly against his solid chest, kissing the top of my head. "I've missed you," he whispered.

I felt only coldness toward him. He seemed manic, possessive, clutching for something no longer there. I pulled away, eager to leave the dark underground lot, the hot smell of exhaust fumes, thick in the back of my throat, the dirt and oil on the ground, part of a cloying miasma I had to escape.

The necessity for an outward equilibrium in my life was enormous, growing, a façade I could work at with Nick, who stayed with me for convenience and called it love. I fought the impulse to see his day-to-day approach to love as the more normal, correct, psychologically healthy one. Life was hell for him too, in its own way; to face every day your loss and betrayal. My guilt made me work to minimize his pain. I didn't always succeed; shared domesticity was enough for now.

Aware of my eyes wandering over his face appraisingly, Raj touched his head self-consciously, "Yeah, I've lost a lot more hair. Shit, I hate it, every time I shower now the tub is filled with them. *C'est la vie.* Did you hear that Eastern Medical in Charleston accepted me for my residency?"

"Yeah, that's great."

"Yeah, I heard you'd been accepted into the Forensic Pathology residency, congratulations."

"Thanks."

If anything could ever give truth to the theory that there is more to us than that which comprises our personality, knowing Raj convinced me of it. There are other levels at which we behave in day to day life, perhaps a lower, or even higher, order of mentality that we are generally unaware of, but which still exerts enormous influence over us. Why else did I always have so much trouble saying no to him. There must be something then about cellular knowledge, when the body knows its home, but the brain is obstructive?

"Can you meet me for lunch tomorrow? Please."

Something in his voice penetrated through my fragile armor, my resolve weakened. "All right, I'll meet you, but nothing else, there won't be time for anything else."

His voice was husky as he held up two fingers, "Scout's honor."

"In a pig's eye, honor means nothing to you." He turned to go, the cockiness of his grin was gone, the urgency of his pleas made him somehow slightly pathetic, less appealing. It had been such a long fight, but even fighting as hard as we had for each other we still lost.

***

We drove north into the hill country, then out to Lake McQueeney to wander along the edge of the lake. We sat down on a gnarled wet tree stump, facing the western sky, not talking.

Not far from us, around the curve of the lake, a huge blue heron landed on the edge of the sandy beach. It was as unexpected and out of place as if it had been a pterodactyl suddenly descending from the profusion of branches overhead. The resonant hum of hordes of insects died down momentarily as if they too were surprised. Gracefully, sure that she was alone, the heron drank water from the lake, the slender curve of her neck arching backwards as if she were gargling mouthwash. A noise in the bushes, then suddenly, the cicadas resumed their incessant drone. The heron turned and held our gaze with an almost human stare. Gathering wind beneath her, she spread her incredible wings then loped forward, so big and ungainly I was sure she couldn't fly.

"Obviously on sabbatical from the zoo." Raj said.

Back in the car we drove around, not talking, easy with each other, my anger gone. It was the first of May, late afternoon, hot and humid. We parked under a canopy of live oaks, the air a few degrees cooler, a soft breeze came in through the windows, ruffling my hair and bringing with it that odd, long-forgotten sense of mystery, the magic carpet ride had taken me far.

Raj sat unsmiling across from me, face impassive, though I knew him well enough now to read his unhappiness. He talked about a concert he'd been to in Austin with Chris, then silence.

He moved toward me, brushing my hair gently away from my face. "You remember the first time we ever met at the Texas Star Inn? You drove into the woods probably down this same empty road." I nodded, wondering where he was going with these memories. "You had to use the bathroom and you parked the car and just hopped out. I could see you faintly outlined by the lights of the car, squatting there so uninhibitedly." He looked away from me, holding my hand. Did he sense that numbness surrounding my heart, blocking off my feelings for him.

"I fell in love with you then, right at that moment."

He was a magician, pulling rabbits out of a hat, how was it that he knew to remember the tiniest, stupidest detail, the only one that might soften my resolve? Too much contact with him and I could fall back into the same old rut. Like people addicted to cocaine, once you get over it, you should never expose yourself to it again. Just sitting next to him was dangerous.

"What is it Raj? You said you wanted to tell me something." My voice was low and sad.

"Chris and the kids and I are leaving right after finals. Just enough time to get settled in an apartment and ready to start my residency."

Images wheeled through my mind like a kaleidoscope. The moments of intense pain loving him had caused me, shifting, changing color, bits of broken glass piercing me. Don't leave me Raj. Still, almost two years later, moments stolen with him were the most real in my life. Tears blurred my eyes, the volume of noise inside my head, always amplified, rose to a higher pitch.

A few feet away from the car an old oak tree towered above us, acorns littering the ground beneath it. Above a massive trunk the limbs spread far outward, curving sinuously, wide enough to lie on. Two birds sat perched on a hollowed out niche where the branches forked. Squawking bitterly, their wings fluttering wildly, they argued over some treasure, breaking off to descend quickly to the ground where they had more room to squabble.

A niche like my own black hole, something that had left me vulnerable and open to Raj, incapable of resisting when feather by feather, with bits of bramble and brush, he built a nest inside of me.

But birds aren't torn by human conflict; they don't build more than one nest at a time.

I leaned against Raj, this man whose presence always seemed so solid, the gravity of his expression so compelling, real, candid, so much expressed to me without words, a secret world we wrapped ourselves in, like twins who early on devise a language known only to them.

Half an hour passed in silence. Finally he said, "I'd like to see you one last time before I leave, to be with you. Would that be possible?"

I turned my face into his chest and nodded, not trusting myself to speak.

***

Match day came and went, most everyone satisfied with the results, eagerly looking forward to their residencies. I saw a few tight-lipped frowns in the crowd but at the Lancaster Club party that evening the champagne flowed and judging from the way my class-mates cutloose most were thrilled at having reached such an important milestone in their lives. A few of the new M.D.s, those who'd always been back stabbers with outsized egos and overweening pride, couldn't stop cutting deals and jockeying for position, opportunists to the death. Some would go far, some wouldn't.

The dean said that we were the most optimistic class he'd seen in years. I bet he said that every year.

Owen signed with a literary agency in New York City who immediately found a publisher for "Ready to Depart." Mike Goldberg, the head of the agency, offered Owen a sizable advance when he signed a contract agreeing to write five more books. He and his new partner, Reggie Miller, were moving to Brooklyn where Reg had family.

Rebecca won a place in the highly selective General Surgery Training program at Johns Hopkins. Dennis and his family were off to Los Angeles, he would be doing a plastic surgery residency at the UCLA Medical Center. No doubt he'd get lots of practice on his incredibly vain wife.

There had been times when I thought I would never make it through the four years of medical school. Two huge chapters were closing in my life, Raj and practicing medicine. I'd decided that I couldn't handle dealing with human suffering, that's what prompted my decision to intern in Forensic Pathology. I'd found myself too often leaving a patient and hurrying to the ladies room to lock myself in a stall and cry, miserable over the pain so many people had to endure. Dr. Hitchens said I probably had residual childhood post-traumatic stress syndrome. Whatever. At least I could handle the dead, their suffering was over.

***

Time passed and without Raj around, wearing down my resistance, I was able to put him out of my mind, to get on with my marriage and my internship.

Six months passed, it was November 2001. Seated at a table in the basement of the medical library I thumbed through the Table of Contents Volume II of the "Journal of Epidemiology." A Japanese doctor working at the CDC in Atlanta, Dr. Brad Tanaka, had written a fascinating article about the influenza "cytokine storm" in "Morbidity and Mortality." Intrigued by the body's immune system wreaking so much havoc that it caused multiple organ failure then death, I'd been doing more research on the cytokine inflammatory response.

Statistics in the journal I was reading calculated that, world-wide, approximately fifty million people died from the "Spanish" flu in 1918, the deaths caused by the "cytokine storm." It's generally thought that the flu initially broke out at a Kansas troop installation. Later President Woodrow Wilson gave the go ahead for those troops to be shipped over to Europe to fight in World War I. Tragically, so many of them could have been saved by the simple use of cotton face masks over the nose and mouth.

You know how you get that spooky feeling when everything is too quiet? You wonder if you're *really* alone. And I wasn't. With my scalp tingling, I stared past the rows of books, down the dark aisles until I caught sight of a lone figure moving toward me. It was Raj.

We watched each other silently for a moment. Last time I talked to him he hadn't said anything about coming to San Antonio. He often called me from South Carolina, keeping me up to date on how his life was going. Not well. His step-father died of lung cancer that had metastasized to his adrenals, a particularly painful form of cancer.

Chris had abandoned the children, filed for divorce, then flew off to Argentina to marry Helmut. Raj had full custody of the twins. Jennifer was diagnosed with epilepsy, but so far Jane was symptom free. Did he deserve all that? Even I couldn't have envisioned such retribution that went beyond the measure of his sins.

One of the tubes of fluorescent lighting, visible past a missing panel of the ceiling blinked like a strobe light then went out. His dark eyes glistened, his gaze intent and probing.

'Having fun?" God, how I remembered that low, intimate tone of voice he used, such a seductive weapon.

I stood up and pushed the chair back. The scent of his cologne drifted to me, mixed in with the fainter smell of sweat, of breathless urgency. Tucking my shirt in and smoothing my jeans, I tried to contain my astonishment at his sudden appearance, at his mad, persistent, romantic behavior.

"Did you get my flowers?"

"Yes, thank you, they were lovely." What better place than a hospital to receive unwanted flowers? They went a long way toward making a lonely patient's day brighter.

Raj reached for me, drawing me closer, he was trembling.

"Meet me tonight, I need to talk to you. I came all the way from Charleston just to see you."

The basement door opened and closed with a slam; one of the doctors from Cardiology moved through the aisles two stacks over, light bouncing off the glistening dome of his bald head. His sharp, bright eyes watched us for a minute, enough to invoke my paranoia.

I jumped away from Raj. When he reached for me again, I backed down the aisle. "Raj," I whispered urgently, "this is my life now, the hospital, my family. You've got to go."

He came toward me, a wild look in his eyes. "Not until you agree to meet me." I'd heard that implacable tone in his voice before. He was not to be deterred. The cardiologist came toward us giving me a stern look.

"Fine, where? What time?" Nick and Liz and I were going out for dinner, I didn't even bother trying to remember what Raj said.

In his absence I'd begun the slow process of healing; the deeply entrenched roots squeezed tightly around my heart, eased their grip, became desiccated then finally disappeared. Capricious fate and her never-ending cruelty: his freedom was meaningless now.

***

Eventually it would become apparent to me that people are not totally locked into anything, they can change, and relationships can shift. Life is chaotic, turns on a dime spitting out magical miracles alongside of heart-breaking sorrow and loss. But watching Raj move nervously around the stacks, all I could see was his past tyranny over me. The fire, the dance in ever-widening circles of despair had been defined, explored to its limits.

Stability and being treated with respect were too important to me now. I couldn't take a chance on losing it.

Months passed before Raj made contact again. He called me on his cell phone and came right to the point.

"Sophie why won't you come out here with me? You could finish your internship here. I'll fly down and get you over the long weekend."

Anger surged through me, Christ it made me so angry, why now, why couldn't this have happened years ago? His motives seemed blatantly obvious. "Who keeps the girls for you?"

"My mom and my sister have been helping out."

Pacing up and down in the lab, cell phone pressed to my ear, I sipped from a can of Coke.

"Raj, I can't." An angry block of resentment sat squarely in front of my emotions, there was no compassion, no equivocating, only a mild sense of superiority at having won this round.

"Why not?" His voice was petulant.

"Why not? Because for the first time in my life I'm doing something for myself. You wore my love out. Besides, I'd never know if you just needed someone to look after your twins."

"That's bullshit."

"Really? I don't think so. You had a chance, several in fact. I would have married you in a second. You broke my heart, here do you want me to tear it out of my chest and let you do it again?" My voice rose as the anger mounted, I fought off tears at how perverse life could be.

"If you had really loved me then, you would have stayed with me. Now when you're free, when the time is right for you, you want me to desert everything and everyone who stood by me when I lost you? You can walk away from a marriage only so many times before you don't get asked back.

Tears stung my eyes, no chance to gloat here really, it was just too hollow a victory that all that love could end up in such unhappiness. But he wasn't really so much like me after all, he was way more pragmatic. With two children to care for, who wouldn't want a convenient ready-made relationship, like a TV dinner? I hadn't been his whole life the way he had been mine. The pain of losing me now, wouldn't be as searing for him as it had been for me.

"Okay. That's it then."

"Goodbye Raj."

***

I'd been peering at pathology specimens under the microscope all morning and was nearly cross-eyed. I sat in the lab eating a ham sandwich and downing it with a Coke when Dr. Artie Black, an associate professor in Forensic Pathology, walked past the doorway, then backed up and came in. We chatted for a few minutes; he had a stack of mail in his hand and was tossing the junk mail in the trash can, glancing at a magazine.

"Gets awful lonesome down here doesn't it?"

"Not really."

Then slapping the pages to his magazine shut, he turned to me, the light in big blue eyes cunning, almost feral. "Yeah, mine was the deciding vote that approved your internship here, a few of the team were concerned about the gossip surrounding your personal life. I convinced Prendergast to hire you anyway, in spite of the gossip. Ginger especially had severe misgivings, voted against you."

Surprised, unwilling to open my mouth and give anything away, I gave him a tight smile. What a flaming bloody bitch Ginger was, always had been. She'd written a glowing letter of recommendation for Raj when he applied to at Eastern Medical.

Then point-blank, Black asked me about my affair with Raj. Slack-jawed with disbelief, I nevertheless plunged ahead, informing him that Raj and I had been very much in love, the kind of thing that happens once in a lifetime. Even to my tone-deaf ears it sounded like bullshit.

"It's been over for quite a while."

"Yeah." grinning lecherously at me he said, "I know what you mean about once in a lifetime. I'm in the midst of one just like that now." His eyes held mine for a beat, as if to say there's plenty of room for anyone else who's ready, willing and able. Thus began a vomitous account of poor, poor pitiful Dr. Black's love life. Inwardly recoiling, I pitied his long-suffering wife.

When he added the final, inevitable excuse for being a philandering dickhead, "I can't leave because of my kids," I wanted to take my scalpel and cut off his penis. If another man used that flimsy excuse on me for wanting to have his cake and eat it too, I'd slice and dice their prick and feed it to the lab rats.

***

Even when Raj found someone else and remarried, he did not lose touch with me. In those infrequent telephone calls, he rarely mentioned his marriage.

He called late one Friday afternoon, we talked for a while, then he said, "You remember that song "Please Don't Go"? I heard it on my way to the hospital this morning," he stopped talking for a minute, then went on, "it reminded me of you Sophie, of how things used to be." His voice was low and quiet, with an almost longing quality to it.

As close, perhaps, as he would ever come to saying that he hadn't done things right, that he wished he had grabbed at the chance for us to be together when he had the opportunity.

"Why don't you come out here? I could show you around, you could stay for a few days. How about it?"

My pulse raced with a split-second of excitement at the prospect of seeing him again. Time and distance had softened my resentment of him. Then with a longing sadness that matched his, knew that I couldn't.

Opportunities elude you so swiftly if you don't take them. All week-end long he was on my mind, I wrote him an email but didn't save the draft properly and lost the whole thing. Just as well that he not learn what my thoughts were.

Chapter Twenty-one

2007

As a pathologist I had a renewed respect for Rudolph Virchow's *Archiv für Pathologische Anatomie und Physiologie und für klinische Medizin.* Having written him off years ago as old school, sure that "Virchow's Archives" were no longer relevant, I was surprised how many times I now perused his journal collection comparing cellular specimens.

His journals were in the basement of the medical library, gathering dust in a dark corner, a place of old ghosts where few of the living ventured. I'd been down there for hours one day, leafing through several of the journals when I couldn't put off going to the bathroom any longer. An "OUT OF ORDER" sign was taped to the door of the women's restroom.

Without hesitating, I walked into the men's bathroom and locked the door behind me. After I finished using the toilet, I pulled my jeans back up and zipped them. Humming to myself, lost in a mindless reverie, I noticed writing on the wall to my left. In the poorly lit stall I squinted at the words, trying to read them. Unbelievably, since only doctors or medical students would know about this bathroom--unless it was the janitor--it was a quote from Kahlil Gibran, one I had never read before.

"It was but yesterday we met in a dream, you have sung to me in my aloneness...if in the twilight of my memory we should meet once more, we shall speak again together and you shall sing to me a deeper song."

Scrawled in red Magic Marker on a bathroom wall was the essence of what Raj had meant in my life. Overcome with a sense of yearning for him, tears stung my eyes, would not be held back. Sitting back down on the commode, I wept bitterly. All of the fortifications I'd built around my love for him had crumbled, where was my earlier conviction that I had made the right choices? My lost love, my lost children, I wanted to go back to the beginning, and step out of this black joke called life.

***

The moon was very bright and high in the sky, just visible at the top of the French doors opposite me. Panels of blue-white light were cast across my bed, one panel framing Susie's sweet, sleeping face, showing the erratic growth of white fur along her chin. Quick to awaken, she joined me as I slipped from bed, moving with stealth through the doors to sit on the patio. The lush fragrance of wisteria and lilac drifted to me from the clusters draped across the back fence. The cement birdbath appeared starkly white in the moonlight, branches from the Chinese umbrella tree, bent gracefully over it, gave the scene the funereal solemnity of a graveyard.

The aftermath of my afternoon spent crying in the bathroom: can't sleep, can't get Raj out of my mind, a pain of longing in my chest. Then more tears.

In the kitchen I prepared hot chocolate. Liz's parakeet, Louise, chirped in response to the tiny note played on the microwave as I pushed numbers on the digital panel. It was a melancholy, almost questioning note, *Who's out there in the cosmos, someone to love?* What sad note is that you play? Louise, and the two gerbils in the cage next to her, tore at my heart, as if I were a Nazi presiding over a concentration camp of tiny animals. That they were unaware of their captivity and too dim to care, I couldn't accept.

Settled on the couch, I thought about my own gilded cage. How it had closed tightly around me again, only this time with my compliance. That long ago decision to stay with Nick had always had the right feel to it. Why question it now? Nick and I had merged more and more toward the center of the continuum, a smoothly running, unconscious engine. Lately I could even see a new light in his eyes, his face reflected more awareness, more cunning and craft than ever before, his lips pursed in concentration.

To have lost that guileless expression, how much was I responsible for corrupting his innocence? Never had patience with innocence, least of all my own, and saw it as something to eradicate.

Betrayal more than corruption. Like the mirrors in a funhouse, reality becomes distorted. When reflecting Raj's face, I could only see his betrayal of me, my loss. I turned to another mirror reflecting Nick and saw my betrayal of him, got sucked into a swampy mire of guilt. The guilt I swiftly put into place, I chose not to be with Raj, Nick chose to remain with me. The path of least resistance equates to the lowest energy level of physical matter. Confusing for me that Nick should be the former, Raj the latter.

At dawn on a summer visit to the Grand Canyon, Nick and I stood alone on the precipice, death only inches away, the panorama awe-inspiring. Two minds, the same thought, one push, how easy it would be. As one, we turned and quickly backed away from the thought and the danger, the dizzying prospect of what lies in the north rim of our mind. It's human to want revenge for betrayal.

I had no idea how long the need for revenge could fester in someone.

I stretched and yawned deeply, finally beginning to feel sleepy. Susie opened drowsy eyes, then quickly resettled, we fell asleep together, images of Raj still filling my mind.

Too late for second chances.

***

Another year passed, days unfolding one into another like interchangeable eggs in a carton. An equilibrium unknown in my previous life, the black hole knit over, at last on that safe trajectory from cradle to grave.

Raj came back to see me last week. Even before I looked around and saw him in the hall, even before I heard the low murmur of his soft voice asking for directions to my office, my body strained toward him as if there had been a split-second of foreknowledge. Then across the short distance, closing the gap of so many lost years, I saw him standing just beyond the door to the office, my eyes riveted on his, the world seemed to recede, details blur in the mind. I rose up effortlessly out of my chair, drawn irresistibly to him.

From my confusion, from the narrowing of all my senses to a fixed point with Raj at the center of it, my brain slowly began to work again. We had walked to the end of the dim corridor, standing beneath the one round inset light, now focused on Raj's face. The young man I had known was gone; in his place was this well-dressed stranger with the checked tweed cap and a beige raincoat.

Tense, stilted, sure that Nick would suddenly appear, there welled up inside of me the instinct to flee from this man who had been such a disruptive, pivotal force in my life. His ease, the obvious confidence he had to appear like a *revenant*, a ghost from my past, in these halls always sadly redolent of his memory, seemed an affront. As if the person he was now bore little relation to that troubled youth; that the misery and deception of our relationship was no longer a source of pain to anyone. He'd always been unwilling to heed the rules of propriety.

My eyes fell on the bags filled with the sacrificed experimental mice set out each night in the hall next to the entrances to the labs, ready to be picked up by the custodial people. The tiny, motionless bodies, visible through the clear plastic, pulled at me, an undercurrent of guilt as I finally spoke, "Raj, what are you doing here?"

"I'm here for the Emergency Medicine Symposium; one of the guys from Eastern Medical is delivering the keynote address. I thought it would be a nice chance to visit San Antonio again. Could we have dinner tonight?"

Our eyes locked; his were so black, as appealing as ever, unblinking, fixed on me with an intensity that was dizzying. From the twenty-five year old I would abduct and hold captive, drawing life from his warmth and vitality, to this gentle stranger. The years had not taken anything from him, only added other connections to further define him, a vindicating success, marriage and more children, surmounting so many obstacles.

"I don't think that's such a good idea." I frowned, not wanting to have to make awkward excuses to my family.

"Please, it's been so long. I brought pictures..." He started to reach into his pocket as if to offer the pictures as an inducement. There was a pleading quality in his voice, a vulnerable light in his eyes. My eyes moved across his face, taking stock, his new glasses were a brown molded plastic, lighter weight than his old silver frames; his black hair was longer again, curlier than I remembered. After all of his complaining, he still had lots of hair.

"Why didn't you call first? I could have arranged something." Lord, how old and grouchy I sounded, as if I were nagging at Liz. A lab tech with a long, thin pipette hanging out of his mouth came out of one of the labs down the hall, walking toward us. Sensing the almost palpable air of tension coming from me, he stopped and held my gaze for a second, a question in his eyes, then hurried by, his brace of test-tubes rattling.

"Because I knew if you had any advance warning you'd figure out a way to slip by me."

Why did it matter so much to him to see me? Tension mounted inside of me, all these years as a relatively happy, plodding ant had taken away that ease in juggling different levels of duplicity. Few dark obsessive strains to cloud the routine cheer of everyday life. Escape from him suddenly became uppermost in my mind, deal with details later. Thinking fast, settling on La Scala, I agreed to meet him there at seven.

"It's been what? Over six years, I've forgotten where that is." What else had he forgotten?

"Oh God, let me see," how best to guide him?

He took a piece of paper from the pocket of his raincoat and wrote quickly on it as I spoke, "On Bandera, two blocks north of Fredricksburg Road, at the second light turn right and it's in that alley, you can't miss the huge red neon sign."

I'd quit smoking years ago, but as nervous as I was, a cigarette sounded great. What did I have to be so nervous about? I wanted nothing from him, could meet him with a clear conscience, there was no harm in that. Two strangers with a shared past, I could afford generosity because he had come so far.

When I arrived at the restaurant, he was already seated, sipping from a wineglass filled with the rich lemony hue of Chardonnay. He stood up, holding the chair out for me, "You look good, you haven't changed much at all."

As my own worst critic, I did not press him to clarify, feeling suddenly rumpled in the same dress I'd worn at work, a pale turquoise rayon shirtwaist, one tiny spot of Bolognaise spaghetti sauce below the belt gained while racing around to feed Liz and Nick before leaving. There had only been a minute to freshen my lipstick, to brush my hair, back to the same shoulder-length style I'd always worn, blonde still, no gray yet. No time to daub on a little perfume, romantic thoughts so far out of my mind I didn't even take time to brush my teeth. Now when I looked in the mirror, I was shocked by the serious, solemn set to my features, gravity's gift that hinted at my age.

"You look great." He wore an expensive wool hound's-tooth suit, the beige London Fog raincoat he'd worn earlier hung on a brass coat-rack nearby. Beneath the suit jacket he wore a crisply starched white shirt with a subdued silk tie secured with a gold tie-pin. A memory lodged in my mind of him in the kitchen years earlier, wearing a ragged red nylon tank top while scrubbing his apartment, how sexy and cute he had been.

The waiter appeared with menus, hovering, making a show of filling the water glasses from a silver pitcher beaded with condensation. Raj asked for a bottle of Sancerre and another wineglass, then he perused the menu while I peered around the room, suddenly paranoid. It was early, there were only two other couples in the restaurant. Across from us was a raised fireplace filled with brightly burning cedar logs. Set into a red brick wall, short outcroppings of brick formed a mini-hearth.

Raj was nervously solicitous while we ordered from the menu, which struck me as odd, jarring. Alone again, we both started to speak at the same time. "You first." I said.

"No, ladies first." Said the spider to the fly. Which of us had the more diabolical motives? Never one to reflect long on his behavior, I suspected his true intentions for this evening were unconscious, concealed even from him. But they exerted no small amount of pressure, judging from his stiffness, that almost overbearing concern for my comfort. Resentment that this woman who had opened her life to him had withdrawn it in the end. His worst nightmare: to lose out on both relationships, his wife and his lover. To have to plead and still lose. Was it only then that his love for me had taken on such substance? The purpose of his visit was to show me how he had transformed himself. See what you lost? I want you to love me again.

"You're quite the prodigal son, aren't you? How does it feel to have undergone such a stunning meteoric rise?"

"Meteoric rise? That doesn't include double payments for my student loans. Finished that off a few months back in a blur of constant work." The same cocky grin of old as he reached into his breast pocket to bring out pictures. Then he stopped in a slightly tense, almost contrived way, as though something had just occurred to him. "You don't really want to see these do you?"

"Yes, of course I do."

Trying to follow his silent train of thought--You didn't want to come, you don't want to be here with me now, I had to plead. His confidence faltered. Was I reading too much between the lines? Or was it more a sudden consideration that pictures of his family might be painful for me?

He thumbed through the pictures. "This is my wife and our daughter, I met Sam--Samantha--at Eastern, she's a nurse anesthetist."

I looked at the snapshots, happy for him, still feeling safely distant from the turbulent past we had shared. His youngest daughter,

Rachel, looked more like Sam, pretty and blonde. Curious, I wondered what kind of marriage they had.

"God, look at how Jennifer and Jane have grown, they're beautiful little girls! With your same dark black eyes."

"Yeah, they're great, Jane's epilepsy is still sometimes a problem. I plan on surgery for her when she's older. I just keep my fingers crossed." The concern on his face, the love, was really quite touching.

"Is that a very scientific approach for a doctor?"

He grinned easily as I handed his pictures back, then suddenly we were once again totally at ease, the stiffness gone.

"One of the nurses that Sam works with just found out she's HIV positive, from her ex-husband. It amazes me how cavalier we were when we were together. And we were well-informed and knew the consequences."

His face had an odd, closed set to it, "And being in the medical profession we were a fairly high-risk group. Did you ever worry that I played around on you?" I'd forgotten how he could so easily draw you into the intimacy of his thoughts. Key words, spoken with reticence, his inflection, his hesitation, were all seized upon by my mind, caught again by the seductive quality of our shared thoughts. Too late to see the danger of this man's charm, unaware of how it could work away at me. So confident of my distance, I erected no defenses.

"Certainly one lover was enough, right?"

He grinned and was about to say something but the waiter arrived with our dinner.

"The plates are very hot so be careful. Bon appetit!" After refilling our wine glasses he disappeared, his black trainers squeaking slightly as he crossed the tiled floor.

I watched Raj while he ate. This man of quiet determination, with his fiery sense of competitiveness, his personality volatile, possessive, yet he turns bad karma around and succeeds. Still, the complexity of his mind leaves him with too many conflicting motives.

"Are you ever going to eat?" He pointed at my plate with his fork in his left hand, as if I were one of his kids he was coaxing into eating. Something else about him long forgotten, that he was left-handed, as if that in itself explained his eccentricities.

"Yes." We ate in a companionable silence, then Raj wiped his mouth with the linen napkin, placed it back in his lap. Without preamble he spoke in a low voice, his features pinched with a certain tension as if the words were difficult to release. "It was always because of the twins, you know? Why I stayed with Chris. And because I was nothing back then, I had nothing..."

Nothing? He had meant everything to me. So what could I say? None of this was particularly a revelation. Was he a man of conscience and wanted to put things right, make an apology?

"I know." My appetite wavered, his careful scrutiny of my face made me self-conscious.

"Look, don't be so resigned Sophie."

Would we ever communicate on the same level? A time warp separated us. Ted had been right all along, there was nothing else out there. Freud knew best: there is only work and love. You must abide in your heart and keep hope alive because no one else on the planet can or will do it for you.

"I'm not resigned Raj, I've done everything I wanted to do, but after forty, things begin to slow down, ambition, energy, sexuality."

Still totally unsuspecting of what was to come later, I thought, who cares? A man of conscience indeed, he meant nothing to me. He could have good manners and be polite to the waiter and order the perfect wine to go with dinner, and not be gauche with the cutlery, remember to wipe his mouth before speaking, pay the bill without once haggling with me or complaining about how much it cost. None of it would impress me. Leopards don't change their spots, the only difference between Raj then and Raj now, was that he had more credit cards.

Then as we were leaving the restaurant he suddenly remembered his raincoat left hanging on the brass coat-rack. His long, tapering fingers with their pristine nails, doctors always seemed to have such obsessively clean nails, wrapped around my arm.

"Hang on a sec, I forgot my coat." His touch sent a sexual thrill through me, no man other than Nick had touched me in so many years. With his touch it all came back to me, my defenses fell away and my desire for him reawakened, surging through me. How absolutely unbelievable that this could happen to me again.

It was cold and damp outside though the rain had finally stopped. The moist, icy air was invigorating after the warmth of the restaurant. Bruised masses of clouds hung low in the sky, threatening more rain; light from the city reflected off of their billowing gray structure, illuminating the gravel parking lot. Raj asked me to sit with him in his rental car, a Nissan SUV.

"Just for a few minutes? Would you mind?"

"No. That's fine." I joined him in the car, drawing my coat tightly around me, feeling skittish, afraid that he would be up to his old tricks, spiriting me away.

"Afraid I wouldn't let you go?" He had not lost his ability to read my thoughts.

"Well, yeah, a little afraid. Don't want to be late." Don't look at him Sophie. The sudden return of desire left me too vulnerable, left me feeling old in a way I hadn't felt earlier, fearful and cringing at the thought of exposing myself to what I sensed was a newly critical eye. Deep-seated insecurities flared up, a tear in the black hole from the only person I remain vulnerable to. Could I work any harder to build up barriers between us? He would not let me read his mind, to learn what motivated him; nothing would yield to my silent probing for hidden meaning.

The air felt so heavy with what "might have been," you could choke on it. Raj, why did you come see me, did you come to show me how well you're doing? Was it to put the idealized version of me to rest? Or was it to show me how much I missed by not going with you? Did your hesitation with the pictures mean for a moment you had insight into your motives? Look deeper, tear the defenses down, will the moment come for you too when your world will topple if you don't face it? I hated being the bug under the microscope of his keen eye as he worked something through that he would not, or could not share with me.

Finally, he spoke, "I'll be back, we can see each other again." Again? All I wanted was to be away from him, from the sudden knowledge that I did care after all. I offered to shake his hand, he ignored it. Tension began to mount inside of me. The longer I was away, the more cause Nick would have to become suspicious.

"Do you think you could kiss me goodbye?" He stared straight ahead, not daring to look at me. The danger of people who blunder into the lives of others without forethought, without vision, without the sensitivity to know how appealing their long-lasting confusion and need can be. Trade places with me Sophie, let me hang this albatross around your neck now, set me free from the past. I deserve that much after how hard I've worked. Unsuspecting, I fell into his trap.

I kissed him the way a nun might, pressing dry lips to a young student's forehead, in complete innocence. Frightened by even that small measure of intimacy, I told him goodnight and hurried over to my car, climbing in. Staring at him through the window, it struck me that the difference in our ages was insurmountable, as if a geographical barrier had risen up between two formerly related species. At too far a remove to reach across that barrier, they evolve along different lines and lose their ability to mate.

Raj got out of his car and climbed into mine, shifting the passenger seat back to give him more leg room. "Please come back to the motel with me."

***

Not that long ago people didn't realize the significance of fossils, perhaps thinking that a particular dinosaur jaw was evidence of some grand feast by our forebears. The forces of nature pummeling the earth make for a constantly shifting topography. Seismic convulsions, wind, torrential rain, even fires from lightning all worked their magic, pushing long-ago buried fossils to the surface. And then a few very clever people in England and Europe began to posit other theories.

The topography of my mind shifted in much the same way, fossils of emotions surfacing. Lying in bed in Raj's motel room, an aching sense of grief held me in its grip: he will be gone from me again soon. There was the sudden sure knowledge that I never lost the need for him, never had enough of the warmth of his heart and body, merely repressed it, the way I'd repressed memories of the baby I carried; of the abortion. Through the panes of glass in the window opposite the bed, I could see that it had begun to rain heavily, the gloomy dark world matching my mood. Did I know then that I would cry for a full year after seeing him?

What had always been at stake for me was learning to be emotionally related while retaining my sense of self. Do we never end the quest for love? It must remain a fire in us, an existential urge, like Jean Paul Sartre's "No Exit" where people try time and again to escape from hell, with no success.

I'd been taken unaware, had obviously ached somewhere deep inside to be with him again. This complex man who had defined me, who had pulled the best, most secret parts of my soul, of my sexuality, up and out of me as easily as a virtuoso plucks the strings of his violin. And when he was filled with the secret music of my inner soul—that lyrical refrain which matched his own--I thought we would always be together.

What I had to face now seemed so hard, readjusting again to the decision to stay with Nick. Raj's visit would inevitably throw our marriage off balance; it had always been so delicately balanced before. Throw it into a relief which showed it to be as deceptively three dimensional as the Princess Leia hologram in "Star Wars;" the unbreachable distances in relationships. Yet it had worked well all these years.

But readjust I would. Raj would go; I would heal, and never allow this to happen again.

I had finally learned to understand, and accept, the essential aloneness of my life.

The End

29931429R00169

Made in the USA
Lexington, KY
13 February 2014